SAVIOR

NEW YORK TIMES & USA TODAY BESTSELLING AUTHOR

NICOLE BLANCHARD

Savior

Copyright © 2016 by Nicole Blanchard

All rights reserved. No part of this publication may be reproduced, distributed or transmitted in any form or by any means, including photocopying, recording, or other electronic or mechanical methods, without the prior written permission of the publisher, except in the case of brief quotations embodied in critical reviews and certain other noncommercial uses permitted by copyright law.

Publisher's Note: This is a work of fiction. Names, characters, places, and incidents are a product of the author's imagination. Locales and public names are sometimes used for atmospheric purposes. Any resemblance to actual people, living or dead, or to businesses, companies, events, institutions, or locales is completely coincidental.

DEDICATION

To Pierre, a good man and a great friend.

CONTENTS

Prologue	1
Chapter One	9
Chapter Two	19
Chapter Three	29
Chapter Four	37
Chapter Five	51
Chapter Six	67
Chapter Seven	79
Chapter Eight	93
Chapter Nine	103
Chapter Ten	113
Chapter Eleven	125
Chapter Twelve	133
Chapter Thirteen	143
Chapter Fourteen	157
Chapter Fifteen	173
Chapter Sixteen	181
Chapter Seventeen	191
Chapter Eighteen	207
Chapter Nineteen	221
Chapter Twenty	235
Chapter Twenty One	247
Chapter Twenty Two	259
Chapter Twenty Three	267
Chapter Twenty Four	277
Chapter Twenty Five	285
Epilogue	293

Acknowledgments	301
About the Author	303
Also by Nicole Blanchard	305

PROLOGUE

HE WOULD START OVER. A kind of rebirth, he figured. A new place, a new life, a new name.

He'd do it right this time. Be more careful.

The Sunshine State was the perfect place. It was far enough away from his mistakes that no one would know him, and close enough to bright landscapes that were full of opportunities. Miami itself was awash with activity and color—vibrant. Life begging to be taken, possessed.

He followed the crowd out of the airport and slipped into the back of the first cab he reached. He was already sticky with sweat from the heat, and the cabbie had his air conditioning blasting, which didn't do much to cut the humidity.

"Afternoon." The cabbie looked back over his shoulder with a weary, but friendly, smile. "Where to?"

"Southern University. Thanks."

He had no concrete plans other than to get as far away as he could. No place could be farther than the southernmost state in the country.

Traffic was hell. Normally, it would test his patience, but

nothing could shake his good mood. It took more than an hour to get close to the campus, and by then the fare was well over fifty dollars, but he was too elated to care. It was better than he imagined, so fuck the money. He'd figure something out.

Didn't he always?

"Anywhere specific?"

He was silent, his voice lost beneath the pressure squeezing at his chest, exhilaration caused his hands to grip the leather seats until his knuckles ached. The cabbie repeated his question, and he had to grit his teeth to keep from shouting back in impatience.

"First motel you see."

"All right," the cabbie replied in a lazy drawl.

The sprawling campus boasted an excellent and very sought after curriculum. Students from all over the country flocked to Miami in droves come the start of term, which made his choice even more appropriate. July was just shaking off its last few days, and with August, the swarm of new co-eds would arrive. He'd be able to lose himself in the crowd.

After another half hour of fighting with traffic, the cabbie pulled into a near-vacant lot in front of a dilapidated motel, a far cry from the posh hotels lining Collins Avenue.

He paid the fair with a slight wince, stepped out into the soup-like air, and let his bag dangle from one hand. The cab took off, and a barrage of beeps sounded from the fifteen or so other cars he cut off in his rush to get back to the airport. He didn't turn to look, though. He was too focused on what was in front of him.

The weekly hotel wasn't as nice as he'd liked, but he tried not to let the peeling paint or burnt-orange carpet bother him too much. It wouldn't be long before he found a job, made some money, and rented an apartment closer to campus. He wanted to be right in the heart of it all. He wanted to suck the marrow right out of the quaint little college.

There was something powerful about being the dark spot in a world of bright. The shadow, he thought, as he laid down on the damp bed to stare at the ceiling and plan. The darkness who tainted everything.

He could barely wait.

The next morning, he was up and out of bed by six, too eager to explore his new life to sleep any longer. The sun wasn't even over the tops of the towering palm trees, and the campus hadn't yet woken. The absence of other people made him feel powerful, as if he owned it all.

Blood thrummed through his veins, causing his black heart to beat faster in his chest. He felt strong. Capable. *Violent*. Coming down here was the right decision. He wasn't certain at first, but all doubts had melted away.

He was near the south end of the campus when he came across the first person. A woman—beautiful and in her early twenties, jogging along the track alone. The sight of another person interrupting the stillness of the morning wasn't what stopped him in his tracks, though. It was her hair. The long, golden trail of it bobbing behind her back as she ran in the opposite direction.

It called to him like a siren, and he found himself walking toward her, nearly running so he didn't lose sight of her. All the tension that had been growing since he decided to move to Florida . . . all the excitement and eagerness built to a near painful crescendo.

Maybe he would go say hi to her. Introduce himself. See if he could get her to talk to him. Hell, maybe she would even give him the grand tour of the campus. Women loved that shit. They loved helping a wounded man, and he learned very quickly how to play wounded when it suited him.

If she said no, then he would just have to be convincing.

The faster she ran away from him, the more the hunter inside him told him to chase. It was not really his fault. All men had an instinctual drive to chase women inside them. His was just... stronger than most. There was no way she would say no to him. It was almost fate that they crossed paths that morning. She wouldn't be here if she weren't meant for him.

He increased his speed to catch up with her. The resulting rush of endorphins buoyed his mood even higher. He was invincible.

"Hey," he called out once he got close enough for her to hear.

When she didn't answer, he ran faster. A few more steps and he could see the earbuds and hear the blasting music. A feral grin stretched across his lips. She couldn't hear him.

Even better.

He glanced around once more to be sure, but it was still too early for anyone to be on campus. Convinced she was put here for him to take, a gift, he moved up until he was right beside her. With her eyes still on the track in front of her, she didn't notice him until he leaned over and pulled out an earbud.

"Hey," he said, causing her to scream. "Sorry, didn't mean to scare you." He lied smoothly. Seeing their fear was one of his favorite parts.

"Jesus." The word was a wheeze as she pressed a hand to her chest and slowed to a walk.

"I tried calling out to you," he said.

Guiltily, she popped out the other earbud and wrapped the cord around her phone, then put it in the pocket of her hoodie. Inside, he glowed with triumph. She didn't realize it, but she just made it all that much easier for him to take what he wanted.

"Uh, hi." She glanced around, but her steps didn't falter. She was no longer afraid . . . but she would be, and he was so looking forward to it.

"I don't mean to bother you." He made sure to lay the reluctance on thick. "I'm new to the area. First time in Florida, actually, and I have no idea where I'm going. You're the only one I've seen so far, otherwise I wouldn't have stopped you. I'm just terribly lost."

The tension disappeared from her shoulders, and her smile brightened. "Freshman?" she teased.

He just laughed. He was surprised to find himself enjoying the buildup of it all. It was almost, almost, as enjoyable as the act itself. "Do I look like a freshman? Let me guess . . . you are?"

"No! I'm a senior!" She giggled, and he grinned back at her. "Where are you trying to go?"

He tried to appear repentant. "Not sure, actually. I'm trying to find a better place to stay close to campus. I'm looking at some places today, but I was hoping to find someone with more experience with the area."

She gestured in a circle. "Pick a direction," she said. "You can't go wrong."

She was, of course, very wrong. Just then the track veered to the left. To the right, the forest edged up to the asphalt—a welcome home present to start his new life.

Since he was on her left, it was simple, really. All he had to do was body check her hard enough that she was winded when she went down. He easily had at least fifty pounds on her, so hitting her hard enough wouldn't be a problem. He moved so fast that she didn't even have the chance to scream before she was thrown into the protective line of closely spaced palm trees, their bases lined with the thick spread of Elephant Ear plants.

He followed after her, the trees swallowing them both. The foliage was lush and thick with vibrant palm fronds that provided excellent coverage. She tried to get up, but he backhanded her with a vicious swing, his knuckles connected with her cheek, and she cried out as blood dripped from her full, beautiful, split lip.

While she was disoriented, he took her arm and dragged her deeper into the woods. She eventually collected herself to try to resist, his favorite part, so he turned and gave her two swift kicks to the ribs.

When they were so far into the woods he couldn't see the buildings through the leaves, he threw her down on the ground and straddled her waist so he could get a better look at her. It was, without a doubt, the best seat in the house.

Her eyes were bright and wide with fear. She was breathing hysterically, and her mouth was frothing with saliva. The moment she felt his weight on top of her she went wild, thrashing and fighting him.

He let her go about it for a while, enjoying the way she screamed, but when she got too loud with it, he wrapped his big hands around her throat until all that was left was a strangled cry. He watched the brightness in her eyes fade just enough, and then he let up the pressure—he was a God giving her a gift of her own. He repeated the pressure and release until she grew to expect it, and then he did other things that made her scream that he enjoyed.

When she was no longer moving, no longer fighting him, he grew impatient. He shook her, hoping to revive her, but she was too far gone, and all she could do was moan and twitch, the life nearly drained out of her.

Eventually, all she did was stare, which made him angry. It all happened so fast—too fast. It wasn't nearly as satisfying as he thought it would be. Angry with her, with himself, he reached out for something, anything, to expel his anger, and his fingers wrapped around a weighty rock.

He lifted it and then brought it down with a satisfying *thwack*. He did this again and again until he was almost too tired to lift his arm.

Blood spattered the ground in a dizzying pattern and air whistled from his lungs when he managed to pull himself off her lifeless body. When the blood stopped rushing in his ears, he detected the sounds of the slumbering school coming to life —the distant call of voices and the sound of cars against the asphalt. With slow, jerky movements, he began the final act with a knife he kept in his back pocket. He never used it on the women—knives were much too easy, but he did keep one on him for exactly this purpose.

Before he was finished, he was already fantasizing about when he could do it again.

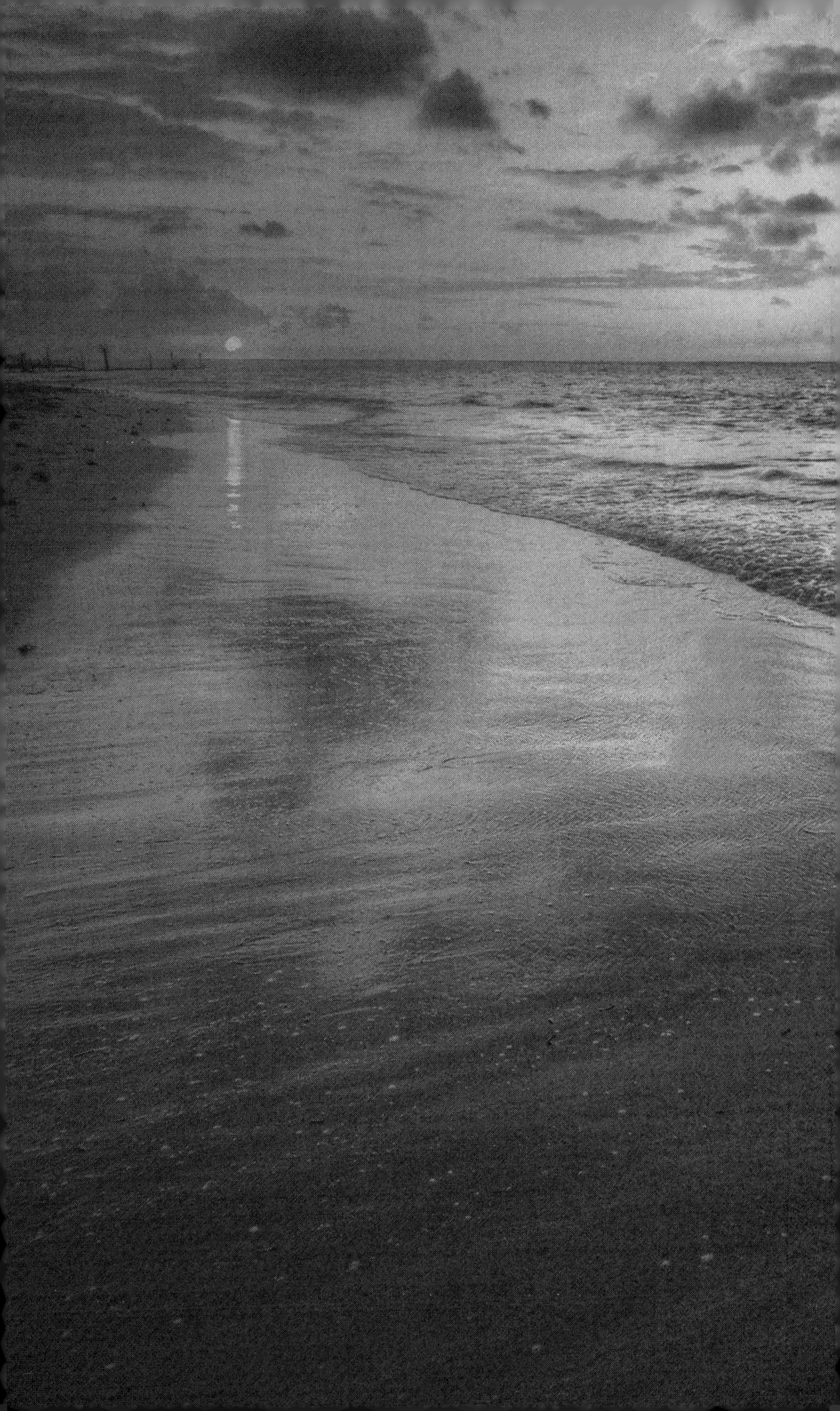

CHAPTER ONE

PIPER

"I CAN'T BELIEVE this is happening."

I glance up from my business admin homework at Paige, my identical twin, roommate, and best friend. It'd be like looking into a mirror if we weren't complete opposites in every way but the face we share. "You can't believe what's happening?"

She huffs and plops down on the side of my bed, bobbling my textbook and reams of copious notes. "Lennox disappearing." She rolls her eyes and snatches a paper, toppling a neighboring stack of flash cards. The contents make her frown, and she tosses the paper back down.

Her foot jiggles, shaking the bed and mixing my carefully organized study system. With a frown, I start lining the pages into neat stacks again. "She probably just ran off with a dude for the weekend. You know Lennox."

"Not during midterms." Paige runs both hands through her straightened dishwater blonde hair. It took her nearly two hours to perfect, so I know she must be more frustrated than I originally thought.

I close my textbook and sit up to give her my full attention. Her face is drawn and pale beneath her tan. When her lips quiver, I take her hand, my eyes catching on the tattoo on the skin between her thumb and forefinger. A sun. I have a small moon in the same place. "Hey, I'm sure she's fine."

Paige leans her head on my shoulder. "I hope you're right. I just worry."

"Mother hen," I tease, and she elbows me in the ribs.

A part of me is worried, too. Skipping her midterms isn't like Lennox, our roommate. She's a typical college girl—a bit boy crazy with a reckless streak. She's also on a scholarship and studies hard, never skips classes, and always attends the group sessions. I know I have a lot less faith in people than Paige does, but even I don't think it is normal for Lennox to just dip out on exams.

"Do you think I should try calling her again?" Paige says after a few seconds of silence. Her normally cheerful voice is quiet, soft. It quakes with unshed tears.

I squeeze her closer to my side and suck back the words I want to say. I'm glad it's Lennox and not Paige. Lennox and I are close, but Paige and I are inseparable, especially since we started college. Most twins grow apart as they get older, but not us. If anything, independence has only strengthened our bond.

"I have a business class later with her. If she's not there, we'll track her down and read her the riot act. It's Monday morning. She probably hasn't crawled out of whatever bed she landed in over the weekend."

Paige sighs and rubs a hand over her face. She punctuates this with a groan and then surges to her feet. "Ugh, you're right. I know you're probably right. I just don't have a good feeling."

"Send her another text." I get to my feet because her talk of bad feelings has my own stomach twisting with unease—and I'm already stressing about an exam I have on Friday. While Paige starts to pace in front of my bed, I distract myself with getting dressed. Just to spite Paige, I choose my rattiest pair of yoga pants and an over-sized T-shirt the same bright blue as my eyes. "Tell her I said she owes us a round for making us worry about her."

Behind me, I hear the click of Paige's nails against the screen of her phone as she taps out a message. I finish changing and turn around to sit on the bed to put on my socks and tennis shoes. After classes, I like to go out for a run to loosen up. Paige takes one look at my outfit and rolls her eyes.

Her brief smile fades, and then her eyes drop to the phone in her hands, which is still lit up and shows about a dozen unanswered texts to Lennox.

"It's just not like her," she says. "I'm worried . . . I'm worried she might be hurt."

"I know you are. And if she doesn't show up by tonight, we'll call her parents. The cops, even."

She chews on the inside of her cheek and seems to struggle over her next words. "You don't think she was kidnapped or something, do you?"

She doesn't have to say anything for me to know what, or who, she's talking about.

Three weeks ago, a pretty blonde senior went missing from campus. She just disappeared one morning during a run before classes. For a few days, no one suspected anything until her roommate reported her missing to the police. When they searched the area where her roommates indicated she liked to jog, they found none of her belongings. They did, however, find blood. It wasn't enough for them to say conclusively what happened to her, but it was enough to spur a county-wide search that lasted two weeks. Now, they're only anticipating finding her body and the searches are a fourth of the size they were at the beginning.

Most people are convinced she up and ran away, but who does that? I try not to think about how similar the senior girl is to Lennox. Lennox wouldn't run away, so there has to be another explanation. One she damn well better have by the time I get to class, or I'll be just as neurotic as Paige is.

I brush off both of our fears with a shake of my long ponytail. "You watch. She'll be calling us after lunch with tales of the dude she picked up."

My voice sounds confident, but Paige has known me our whole lives and doesn't buy it for a second.

"C'mon," I say with false cheer, "I'll pick you up a coffee at the cafe."

I'M NOT A NEEDY PERSON. In fact, I like to believe I'm self-sufficient. But when Lennox doesn't show up for class, I start spinning out of control with worry. I don't want to freak Paige out before I get back to the apartment, so I swing by the campus bookstore where my boyfriend, Gavin, is working the afternoon shift.

I step into the frigid air with relief, comforted by the familiar fragrance of the strawberry candles the manager likes mixed with the crisp, clean scent of new books. Scanning the check-out counters for Gavin, I frown when I don't find him assisting any of the customers. Normally, he prefers to be up front and right in the middle of the chaos, but he's not there or in the manager's office where everyone takes their break, which is strange.

There's a small café area to my right, so I take a seat on one of the benches to wait and pull out my phone. Lennox hasn't returned any of my or Paige's messages since Friday, which is odd, considering she keeps her phone glued to her side. I checked in with some of her teachers, and they told me she missed three important classes, which will have a devastating effect on her near perfect GPA. Then as I was leaving each of her classes, I stopped a few other students and asked if they had seen her, not a single one of them had.

The next rational step is to call her parents and the police. They would take it seriously and investigate or send out more search parties. It has been only a few weeks since the senior went missing, so I know the police wouldn't drag their feet about another missing girl. I don't want to cry foul play and look like an insipid college chick, but I'm also worried about my friend.

A few minutes pass and Gavin still hasn't shown up, so I push myself from the little table and stride across the room to the checkout counter.

"Hey, Joseph."

He looks up, his eyes brightening when they land on me. "Piper. Haven't seen you in a while."

"Midterms," I say and make a face.

He finishes checking out the freshman and hands him his change. He turns his attention to me and says, "Killer. Need help with something?" Flashing a teasing grin, he leans a hip on the counter.

His brilliant smile brings out my own if only for a moment. "Actually, yes."

"Anything."

"Have you seen Gavin around? I need to talk to him."

His smile falters just a little. "Yeah, I think I saw him go into the storage room. I can call him up here if you want."

Already pushing from the counter, I wave over my shoulder. "That's okay, I'll go hunt him down. Good to see you!"

His response is cut off by another customer.

I'm well acquainted with the large storage room off the back of the bookstore. On multiple occasions, we've made use of the space behind the towering shelves full of supplies with Gavin whispering words dirty enough to make me blush. The thought almost puts a little warmth back into my icy stomach.

I push through the throngs of students, who are too busy searching for last-minute testing study materials to care, and head to the large gray doors with black rubber trim. I don't bother looking around to see if the manager is watching or if anyone is going to stop me. I've practically become part of the staff and have gotten to know everyone during the long, often dull, summer hours I sat around with Gavin.

Thinking about him only makes me more eager to find him to allay my worries about Lennox, so I shoulder open the door. I skid to an immediate stop, as if I've run into an invisible wall.

My gasp draws their attention, and they break apart with an audible *smack*. Face is frozen in horror, feet epoxied to the floor, I can't even summon words to express the sudden bottomless pit my stomach becomes.

"Piper!" Gavin extricates himself from the arms of another

woman and takes a hasty step back. "What are you doing here?"

"I should go," the girl says, sliding past where I'm still frozen in the doorway.

"I can explain, Piper," he says as he takes a step forward.

"What? Did you accidentally shove your tongue down someone's throat?"

He winces and finally stops moving toward me. I'm thankful for that. I'm not sure what I would have done if he had managed to reach me. "You've just been so busy."

"Busy." My voice is flat. Hollow. He thinks I've been too busy, and this is what he does? I feel strangely removed from the situation, as if I'm watching it from above or from someone else's point of view.

"Ya know. Wrapped up in yourself. School. The future. We never have fun anymore."

I'm not blind to my faults. Whenever I get lost in tasks, Paige is there to pull me out and remind me to have some fun. I'm very goal oriented, some would say oblivious to others when it comes to my own aspirations. I can be single-minded and forceful in my own opinions, but I would never even consider cheating on Gavin.

"Fun," I repeat. The word sounds strange, not because I don't have fun anymore, but because he's using it as an excuse to cheat on me. "We don't have fun."

He shrugs, and I'm so consumed with the urge to wrap my hands around his throat, I have to turn around. With quick, clipped steps, I force myself to walk out of the storage room and back through the heavy doors. Compared to the dark, intimate lighting in the storage area, the LED bulbs are blinding. I shove my way through displays and racks of

Florida Southern University gear until I reach the automatic doors.

"Piper!" Joseph comes around the corner of the checkout counter, his mouth pulled into a frown. His head swivels when he spots Gavin storming out of the storage room.

"Thanks for your help!" I wave to Joseph and barrel through the door before it's even completely open. I try to lose myself in the afternoon crowd, but when I look back, Gavin is right behind me. He is reaching for me as if to grab me, but I don't let him. Whirling around, eyes flashing, I spit out, "Don't touch me!" in a voice more brittle than I'd like.

The crowd around us slows to watch, and I swear I can hear the *click, click, click* of a shutter as he steps forward with his hands in front of him. My teeth grind together as I shake my head. I do not want him to freaking touch me. When he steps toward me again, I step off the sidewalk, just needing to get him away from me, and a car honks. I don't know how close I come to being hit, because almost as soon as it happens, someone is pulling me to safety.

Joseph's warm brown eyes hold my blue ones and, for a second, I am thankful he's there. "Are you okay?"

Then I hear Gavin's shouts and I push away, needing the space. "I'm fine. Thanks."

The crowd continues on its way now that the drama is dying down. Gavin tries to elbow his way through a couple burly dudes, but they're too distracted by hitting on a couple of sorority sisters to care. I use the few seconds he's distracted to bolt in the other direction.

Joseph jogs to keep up with me. "Are you sure you'll be okay? I don't know what happened between you, but you shouldn't run off mad like this."

The light changes and traffic starts, so I stop at a crosswalk and stab at the button. "I'm okay, I promise, but I appreciate your help back there."

"Anytime."

My phone buzzes against my thigh, causing me to jerk. With a self-deprecating laugh, I pull it out and find a text from Paige. I curse under my breath, remembering I forgot to update her after my class about Lennox.

To think my biggest worry this morning was midterms.

I put my hand over the phone after I press the call back button. To Joseph, I say, "I owe you."

His lips spread in a grin. "Fine by me. You can treat me to lunch tomorrow."

Before I can say anything else, Joseph sprints back down the sidewalk, passes an open-mouthed Gavin, and disappears into the bookstore.

"Piper? PIPER!" Paige screams in my ear.

"Hey, I meant to text you back—"

Paige makes an impatient sound. "They found her."

Shaky laughter escapes my throat. God, what a day. "Thank God, is she at the apartment?"

"No—" A sob cuts down the line, and my whole body goes still. Every cell inside me already knows what she's about to say, but my brain refuses to acknowledge it. When she gathers herself, her voice is no more than a whisper, forcing the words into my ears and making the situation real. "I mean the police found her. S-she's dead."

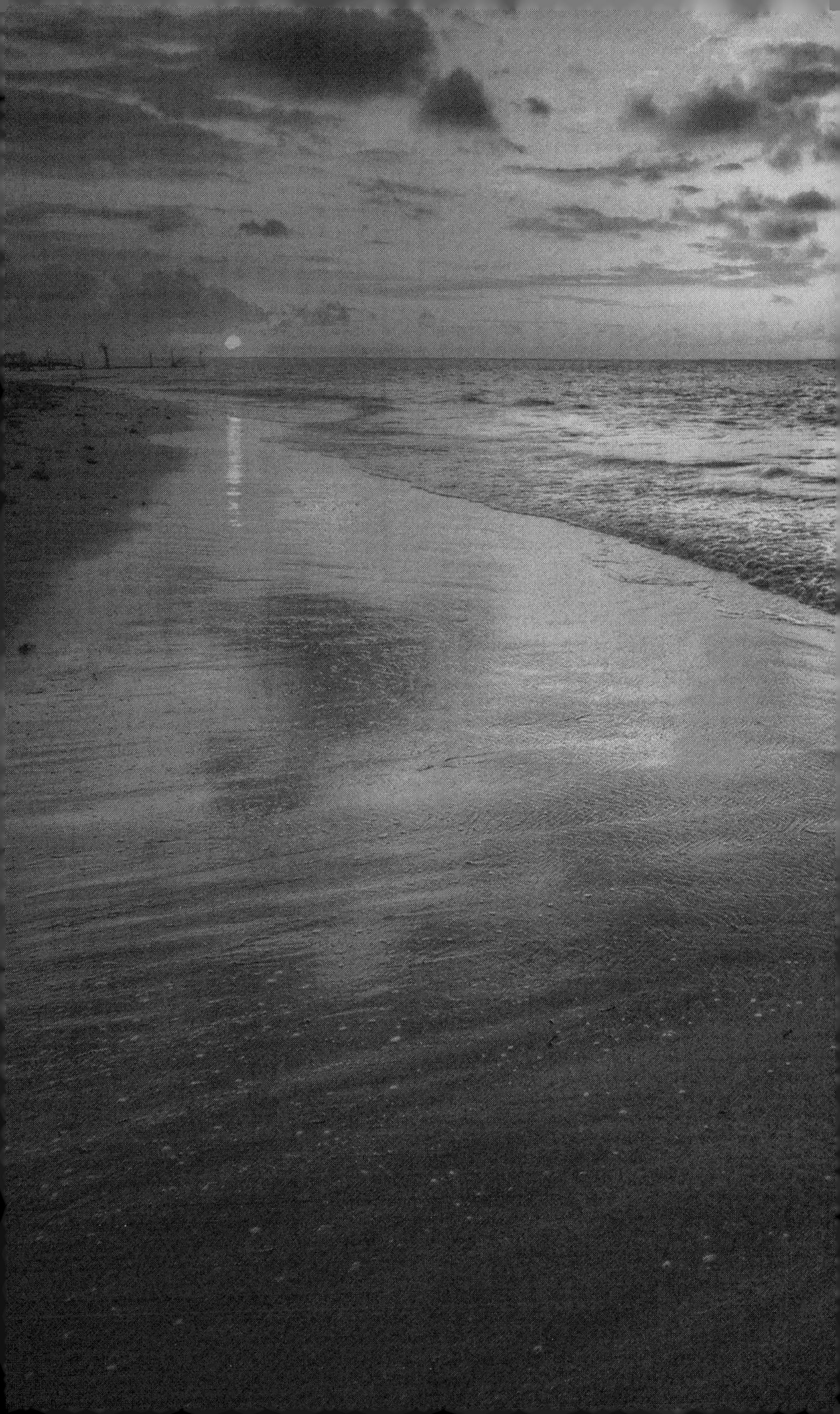

CHAPTER TWO

PIPER

I DON'T GET much sleep.

Paige, who was closer to Lennox than I was, cries for hours until finally passing out from exhaustion. I don't dare leave her side, so I spend the sleepless few hours until daybreak on a chair beside her bed in case she wakes up in hysterics. It gives me entirely too much time to think, and by seven, I'm contemplating waking her up. I don't, and it's another hour of having my own thoughts for company before she wakes.

"Time izit?" Paige sits up, rubbing at her bloodshot eyes.

"About eight."

She explodes from the bed in a flurry of blankets and shedding clothes. "I'm gonna be late for class."

"Paige."

"Why didn't you wake me?" She shrugs into a hoodie, which muffles her voice. "I have a lecture at eight thirty!"

"Paige."

Her head pokes out of the neck, her hair disheveled, and

her face pale against the dark blue material. "We emailed our professors yesterday. We don't have to go to class today. We're excused."

She frowns at me as she ties up her hair in a messy bun. "Why would you—" Then her eyes widen, and she claps a hand over her mouth. Fresh tears sheen her eyes. "Oh my God."

Even though my legs are weak with exhaustion, I get to my feet and cross the room to pull her into a hug. "We'll get through this."

"How?" she whispers. "How do we get through this?"

"Together."

Her arms come around me then and squeeze tight. "I just don't understand."

"I know." I have to pause around my own tears. "I know. I don't either."

When her tears abate, she pulls back and wipes her face. "You look worse than I do and that's saying something. Did you sleep at all?"

I shake my head and wince at the resulting throbbing. The headache I can't seem to shake pulses angrily behind my eyes. "I couldn't. I was worried about you."

Her face softens. "Why don't you go take a shower, and then it'll be my turn to take care of you. Maybe take a nap after?"

"A nap sounds like heaven, but we promised we'd go talk to the police today. They want to take our statement."

She shoves me in the direction of the bathroom. "Fine, take a shower, and I'll grab some coffee. Lots of coffee."

Twenty minutes later, she cracks open the door and thrusts

a hand holding a cup through. The scent emanating from it is enough to make me groan aloud. "Thank you."

Paige peeks her head in. "Thank *you*. You're a good person, you know that?"

"I'll remind you of this conversation the next time I forget to do laundry or wash the dishes."

She opens her mouth to speak, and then her eyes widen. I know without asking that whatever she had been about to say was about Lennox. Even gone, her presence is still all over our apartment.

"I ordered a cab," she says instead. "They should be here in about twenty minutes."

I nod and she closes the door. When I hear her footsteps recede down the hall, I lean my forehead against the wood. I give myself a few minutes to surrender to my own tears.

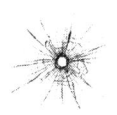

THE BUS STOP JUST outside our apartment is full of students and every single one of them glance over at Paige and I as we cross the sidewalk to the waiting cab. The news spread much faster than I thought it would, which is silly. I should have known something like this would reach every inch of campus.

"Miami-Dade Sheriff's Department, right?" the driver asks as we get in and buckle our seat belts.

"Yes, thanks," Paige answers. She leans against the seat and closes her eyes.

I pull out my phone, hoping to lose myself in the mindless, banal updates on my social media. Then the page loads, and all

I see are pictures of Lennox's face and posts from all of her other friends mourning her death.

I don't want to know the details.

I don't want the last memory I have of Lennox to be tainted with the bloody residue of her death, but social media has no conscience, and it only takes one swipe for me to see the gruesome reports of the last minutes of her life.

My eyes scan the words before I can tear myself away.

Lennox was raped repeatedly, sodomized, brutally beaten, and finally strangled. Her naked body was dumped like garbage in a wooded area not far from the venue where the party had been held. A place where we'd all gone for various get-togethers and parties. Her face was nearly unrecognizable and her hair had been hacked off.

A strangled sound escapes my throat, and Paige sits up in her seat. "Are you okay?" she asks.

I toss my phone into my purse, willing the images away. "I'm sorry." I clear my throat, hoping I sound more convincing. "Yeah, I'm fine."

She takes my hand in hers. "It'll be okay."

"Hey, I thought I was supposed to be the strong one."

Her hand squeezes mine. "You can't be strong all the time. You have to break a little."

"I'll break after we find out who did this to Lennox."

The ride to the police station is a short one. The receptionist takes our names and information, and we sit in a cramped little room until an officer with graying hair leads us to a freezing conference room with a battered table in the center and chipped filing cabinets lining the walls. We take a pair of seats and the officer, who introduces himself as Detective Manning, sits across from us.

He slaps a legal pad down on the table and uncaps a pen. "I'm sorry for the loss of your friend. I'll do what I can to be as brief as possible."

Paige smiles, but it's a ghost of her normal cheerful expression. "Thank you."

"How about we start with the last time you saw Lennox?" he asks, pen poised over the legal pad.

"Um, Friday," Paige answers but then looks to me for confirmation.

I nod. "She'd just gotten off work—she was a receptionist at a doctor's office—and she was going out to a friend's birthday party."

He asks for the name of the doctor's office and scribbles it across the notepad. "Did you hear from her the rest of the night? Maybe a text letting you know when she was coming home?"

"Around ten or ten thirty," I glance to Paige for confirmation and it's her turn to nod. "She texted me to let me know she was going to be late. The party ran long."

"Do you have the exact time?" Manning asks.

I fumble with my purse and pull out my phone. Lennox's face greets me as I open our last conversation. The reality that I'll never see her again hits me right in the gut, stealing the breath straight from my lungs. It takes a moment for me to remember what I am looking for. Blinking back tears, I tap our last message and provide him with the time stamp.

Manning jots it down on his legal pad, his brows furrowed. "And did she mention meeting someone there? A man she was going home with, maybe?"

Paige shakes her head and looks down at the table. "She didn't say. We didn't hear from her after that."

"If she were to meet someone, would she leave with them without telling you?" Manning asks.

"That was what we thought happened at first, but she would have let us know the day after. It's how we knew something was wrong." Realizing how it sounds, I add, "She wasn't . . . promiscuous or anything. She didn't go home with every guy she met."

"I understand."

Paige taps her thumb against the wood tabletop. "I don't even think she'd have gone home with anyone. We had important classes this week. It wasn't like her to be reckless and put her personal life ahead of school, not even for a cute guy."

Manning's impassive face softens. "Whatever happened, this was not her fault, and we're going to do whatever we can to find the person responsible."

"Thank you," Paige says.

He nods. "Now, was she involved with anyone? Did either of you notice anyone paying her a lot of attention that made her uncomfortable? An ex-boyfriend maybe?"

Paige and I share a glance. "She wasn't seeing anyone new that I know of," Paige tells him.

"Me either. Her last relationship was last year, and there hasn't really been anyone since. She was more interested in playing the field and her work."

"Around when was this?"

I rub at my temples and squeeze my eyes shut. "June, I think."

"We can get you her laptop, if that helps. I mean, if her parents say it's okay. I'm not really sure how this works. We just want to help find who did this to her."

He questions us for another half hour, and we tell him

everything we remember about Friday, her friends, and her habits, but to me, none of it points to who killed her. For all I know, she went to her friend's birthday party and was abducted the moment she left. Based on what he told us, no one at the party saw her leave with anyone, though one person did see her walking out to her car.

It's like whomever attacked her is a ghost.

"HOW ARE YOU HOLDING UP?"

Joseph pulls me into the dark recesses of a near empty coffee shop and guides me to a table in a corner. I let him because I don't have any energy to protest.

"I'm exhausted." I don't go into more detail, but I am running on three hours of sleep. Paige was a wreck after we got back from the police station, and I spent the whole night sitting next to her and making sure that she was okay.

"You wait here." Joseph plants me in a seat. "I'll go get us a coffee and something to eat."

"I'm not very hungry."

He just smiles. "You look like you're about to pass out. I'll get you a Panini to go with the coffee."

Overcome with gratitude, I smile. "Thanks."

I shed my purse and hang it on the back of my chair. My eyes feel like they're made of paper, and I could use about a ten-year nap, but when I tried to lie down, sleep wouldn't come. Every time I closed my eyes, I would end up replaying the last time I saw Lennox.

The sad thing, one of many, is that I can't remember what

we talked about or if she knew how much I cared about her. Tears fill my eyes, and I blink them away before Joseph comes back. Inhaling slow and steady, I try to focus on something else, anything else, to distract me. When Paige is able to make it through the day without bursting into tears, I'll allow myself the reprieve of dealing with my own emotions, but until then, she needs me to be the strong one.

When I look up again, I find the doorway full of students coming in from classes, their eyes all on me—each expression full of pity, sadness, and uneasiness.

Disgusted and unable to watch them while they watch me, I keep my eyes on the table until Joseph returns.

"Sorry. They took forever." He sets two plates with steaming sandwiches and two paper cups full of coffee on the table. He pushes mine in my direction.

"No, that's okay. Thank you." I sip the coffee but barely taste it. "I hope you don't mind if I'm not too chatty today."

He waves my concerns away. "I'd be more worried if you were. I just wanted to make sure you were okay after what happened with Lennox and then that shit between you and Gavin the other day."

For a second, I don't remember what he's talking about. Then it's all there again.

At my crestfallen look, he winces. "I'm sorry, I don't mean to bring it up—"

I take another sip of my coffee before I respond. "I completely forgot. Shit, what a couple of days."

"Don't take this the wrong way, but you look like hell. You need to take care of yourself."

"I haven't been getting much sleep," I admit, sliding the

sandwich he got me closer and picking up half. "It's been hard on Paige."

"Do the police have any updates?"

"Not many. They aren't even sure if it's related to the disappearance of the other girl." I say, forcing myself to take a bite. I can't remember the last time I ate anything.

"They'll come up with something soon. They'll find the guy."

"I hope so."

We both eat and chat some more, the topic turning from Lennox to other, easier, subjects. He tells me a funny story about work that I manage to laugh at, and I tell him about what happened with Gavin.

Joseph frowns. "What a dick!"

I wipe my mouth with a napkin. "Tell me about it."

"I hope you don't think what he did is a reflection of you."

"Right now, Gavin is the least of my worries."

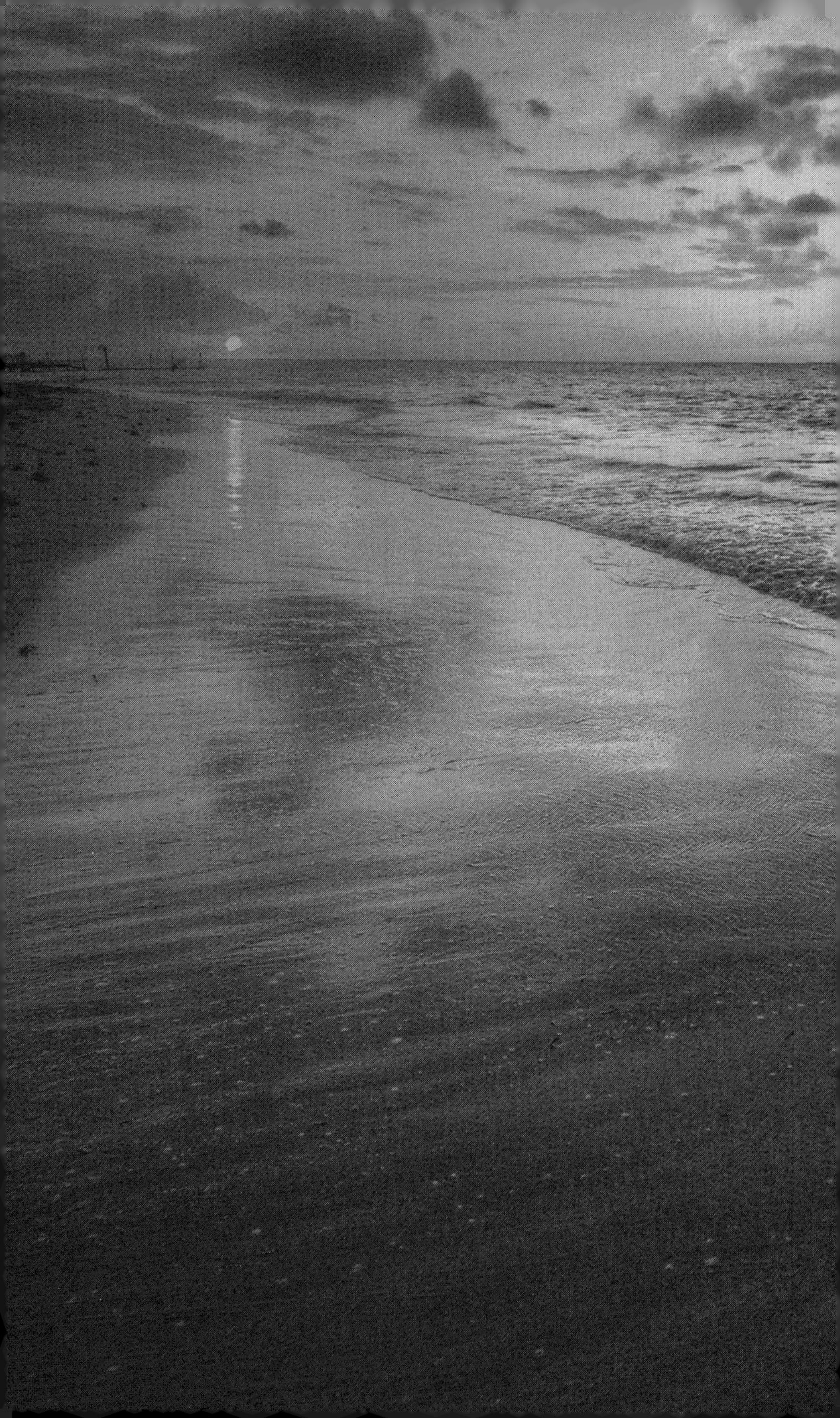

CHAPTER THREE

PIPER

THE RIPPLE of awareness slithers across my skin, and I shiver at its unwelcome caress. I steel myself with a sip of God-only-knows what cheap brand of beer they have on tap. It leaves a bitter taste on my tongue . . . or maybe that's just regret. Regret for coming out tonight. Regret for the sudden and absolute mess I've made of my life. Regret that, in spite of it all, I can't seem to muster up the energy to care enough to claw my way out.

The shadows shift to my right, and when I glance over, my ex-boyfriend Gavin rests his elbows on the deck railing next to me. I drown the resulting spark of attraction that ignites with another long gulp from my pint glass.

Gavin. Another regret.

I shouldn't have come out tonight, but I needed the change of scenery so desperately. In the three weeks since Lennox's murder, I haven't been able to focus. The fear on campus has abated. The prevailing opinion seems to be that she was killed by a drifter. Someone passing through. Since the body of the senior was never recovered, they don't think it is the same person and everyone has returned to normal.

Everyone except Paige and me, who are reminded every day that evil touched our lives when we pass her still-empty room. We haven't had the heart to rent it out again. Maybe in a few weeks when we aren't so raw. I turn to Gavin and look up into his familiar face. The pain from his betrayal is muted with the warmth of the alcohol in my belly and the sharp ache of Lennox's loss. His actions seem so very trivial in comparison.

"I'm surprised to see you here." His voice is smooth and low enough that I automatically want to lean closer to hear, to bathe in the comfort his closeness has always given me.

For my own safety, I put a few more inches of necessary breathing room between us while I still have the mental capacity to remember how much he hurt me.

"C'mon, Piper. Don't be like that."

My faux-casual posture belies the racing of my heart. "And how would you rather I be?"

"Pretty much any way but this."

I bark out an incredulous laugh, which feels just as hollow as the rest of me, and turn away from him. "Right."

There is a beat of silence, and then his front presses against my back, his heat warms my chilled skin, and his hands cage me between his body and the railing. The scruff of beard abrades my neck, and I shiver in response.

I'm disgusted with my own reaction, but at the same time, I'm grateful for the sense of control I finally feel. I can control what happens next. With the rest of my life spiraling, at least I have this. When he realizes I'm not rejecting his advances, he presses a soft kiss on the line of my neck.

I shouldn't want this. I should push him away. He's the one who hurt me and abused my trust. But even though I know it's wrong, I lift a hand to guide his mouth to mine. For the first time in too long, all the stress and pain melt away. I loved this man. I trusted him. I desperately want to bring back that feeling.

I'm comforted by the familiar taste of him, the way he knows how to nibble and deepen the kiss at just the right moments. I should hate him for what he did, but right now it feels like his kiss is giving me the first moment of sanity I've had in way too long.

"God, I've missed you," he whispers against my lips.

He shifts us around until we are in a darkened corner of the deck. Behind me, the walls vibrate from the bass and below us, the sidewalk is packed with red-rope hopefuls. Their chatter floats upward as Gavin lifts my leg to press into me at just the right angle.

He breaks the kiss and cups my face. "I need to talk to you. Come home with me? Come back to me."

I put my hands to his chest, unsure of my answer. It would be so easy to say yes, but I should say no. I'm saved from making a choice when my phone rings.

I tear away from him and jerk my phone from my pocket. It rings a few more times before my clumsy fingers can navigate the touch screen. "Thank God you called." I take a few steps away, shame flowing over me like a heat wave. "I was about to do something you'd probably kill me for."

"Piper," Paige, says, "Please tell me it doesn't have to do with that son-of-a-bitch."

"It may." I signal to him that I'm heading inside. "Would you mind coming to the bar on Second?"

He shakes his head and tries to follow, but I dodge his grasp. It's too loud and there are way too many people, so I head to the hallway leading to the bathrooms.

"I'm already on my way. Don't move a muscle. I'll be there in five."

The bathroom is blessedly empty. I pocket my phone and splash my face with water, then rip off a couple paper towels to blot away the moisture. When I step back out, Gavin is there waiting. I glance at him, but keep walking when I see the anger twisted in his features. Is he really that pissed that I wouldn't just take him back after what I walked in on him doing? I don't know, and I don't really care. I take a seat at the bar, order another beer, and wait for Paige. Somehow, I always feel steadier when she's there. The sun to my moon.

"That one's for you." I point to the identical glass and stool next to me when she shows up. "Consider it my peace offering before you read me the riot act."

"Smart move. Plying me with alcohol always works."

"I—"

"No." She covers my mouth with her hand. "You don't even have to explain. You forget that I live with you. Just shut up and drink. We're going to forget all about this and chalk it up to a weak moment."

"You're the best."

"You know it."

"Would it have been so bad?"

"If you'd slept with him again?"

"Yes."

She takes a contemplative sip of her beer. "This could be me being overprotective, but I think so. You deserve better. You deserve a man that worships you and puts you first. I don't think he could ever be that kind of person. What can I say? I have impossible standards."

"At least you have some."

"This is also true."

Truth be told, Gavin is the most recent in a long line of self-centered jerks I've dated. As much as I hate to admit it, Paige is right.

We finish our drinks, and I convince her to go out on the dance floor with me for a while. It's not often she can tear herself away from the books for a night out, so I take advantage of the time we have. A part of me knows once college is over, the best friend I've had my whole life will be one step closer to living on her own. So when she tugs her arm and signals she's going to go, I force myself not to protest. We have to cut the cord sometime. I mean, it's not like we can spend our whole lives living together, sharing everything. We're both going to have to get used to the idea that we'll be apart for the first time in our lives.

She nudges my arm. "Don't worry about it. You order another drink. Dance your ass off for a while. Then you'll come home, sleep it off, and I'll wake you up at the ass crack of dawn to do Pilates at the rec center or something."

"You aren't staying?"

"I can't. I have a project due tomorrow." She sends a pained look at the door, and I immediately sober a bit. "Are you going to be okay by yourself? You know you can always come hang out with me."

"Thanks, but I think I'll follow your suggestion." The last thing I want to do is interrupt more of her night. One of us needs to make our parents proud. "Are you sure you don't want me to walk you home?"

"I'm sure. And please call me when you get home so I know that you made it okay."

"I will."

She stands, and I give her a one-armed hug. "Thanks again for coming," I whisper.

"Anytime." She gives me a big smile and then is swallowed by the crush of college students.

An hour later, I'm walking the five blocks from the bar to the apartment complex where Paige and I have lived for the past year. I did follow her instructions, mostly. After she left, I downed two more glasses of beer and a couple shots, and I managed to grab a dance or two before deciding it was time to call it a night. My heart just wasn't in it anymore.

The streets are deserted, most students safely inside their builder-grade houses and tidy worlds. It's way past midnight, and not even the meager glow from the street lights penetrates the darkness that envelops the porches of our two-story walk-up.

Paige normally leaves the porch light on because, despite what she says, she's the most maternal, responsible person I know. So, it's a bit odd that it's turned off.

A figure in the space between our house and the next catches my attention. I squint against the darkness, but whoever it is disappears into the shadows. Immediately, I think about Lennox. About how alone and vulnerable I am out on the street. Too much beer has my vision hazy, and I struggle to pull my phone from my pocket, just in case. It takes four tries before I'm able to wrestle it out, and by then, my eyes are half-closed.

God, why didn't I just go home with Paige when she asked?

The first whispers of unease filter through my boozed brain

as I make it to the place where I'd seen the shadow. I glance around again, hoping to find someone out on the street, but there's no one. Lights flicker in the windows of the neighboring buildings, but the street is otherwise devoid of any sign of life. With my phone poised in my hand like a threat, I inch closer to our dark apartment, my steps now hesitant, and my heart thudding heavily in my chest. I can barely see through the shadows that engulf the alley, but I can feel it in my bones that something isn't right.

My thoughts are fevered and grow more so the closer I get to the yawning opening. I peer into the blackness as I pass, but find nothing out of the ordinary.

"You really need some sleep," I tell myself. It's probably just a stray cat or something.

After a couple deep breaths to clear my head, I clomp up the stairs and manage to get the key out of my pocket much more easily than I did my phone. I'm walking in the doorway, already dreaming about a twelve-hour hibernation, when a hand closes over my mouth and drags me backward. Instinctively, I try to scream, but it doesn't make it past the barrier. An arm clamps around my waist, trapping my arms against my side.

I fight a full body shiver when the person behind me leans closer. So close that I can feel the scrape of stubble on my neck and smell the sweat and an earthy cologne clinging to his skin. "Don't scream."

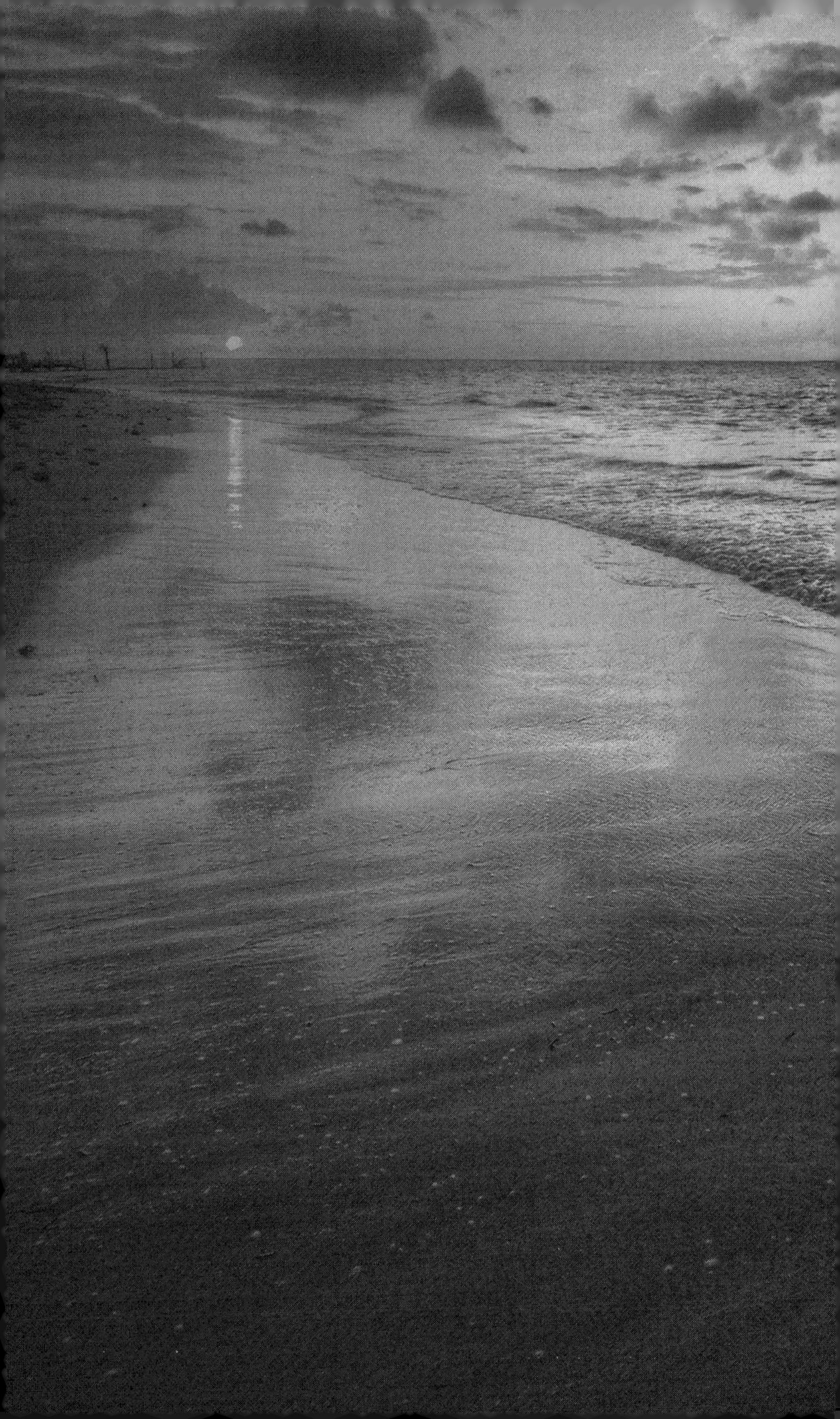

CHAPTER FOUR

PIPER

MY HEART DROPS to my stomach, and my first thought is of Paige. The last hug we shared at the bar and how the last thing I saw was her head bobbing through the crowd. Did she make it home before he got here? Please, let her be safe.

My second is of Lennox.

I struggle to make my brain fight through the exhaustion, the residual effects of too much beer, and fear. He maneuvers me through the front door, and by the time my brain catches up, we're already heading down the hallway toward Paige's room. I try to kick my legs to throw him off balance, but he's too strong. The arm around my waist constricts to the point of cutting off all my air. The fingers on my mouth flex, and I can feel the tender flesh bruising. As we near Paige's room, the dread in my stomach sharpens. By now I'm crying and struggling against his hold even more violently, twisting one way and then the other.

A strong metallic smell reaches my nose when we get to her

partially closed door. Through the opening, I spot thick drops of blood framing a hand on the floor. My entire body goes slack at the sight, and I struggle to catch my breath to no avail.

No, just no, no.

He nudges the door with a shoulder, and I clamp my eyes shut. I can't look, I won't. Inside my head, I'm screaming her name, but I can't seem to get my voice around the knot in my throat. He drags me into her room, where the scent of blood mixes with musk of sweat and sharp bite terror. I'm sobbing, and my brain is racing wildly to figure out a way to get the fuck out of there. To find help. To rescue Paige, even though a part of me already knows it's pointless.

We're two steps in, and I can feel my chances to escape getting smaller and smaller the longer he has me trapped in his arms. He releases the hand on my mouth, and I finally find my voice. I scream as long and as hard as I can. So hard that I feel my throat tear from the force of it. It breaks, and I heave a deep breath to scream again.

I scream until I can't scream anymore.

He whips me around, his face mostly obscured in shadows, and I flinch instinctively when he raises an arm. The room is dark, but the street lights shine through the window, outlining his body. I don't move fast enough to dodge the blow. The back of his knuckles connect with my cheekbone with such force that I'm knocked to my knees and land roughly on my hands. My wrist gives under the pressure and awkward angle, causing pain to streak up my arm. He jerks me off the ground, and I slip on the slick residue that coats the floor and tumble into him.

He's reaching behind him in the direction of the bed—for what I'm too terrified to even imagine. The pain in my wrist is blinding, and I can feel the bones grinding together as I struggle to break free of his hold.

He hefts me across the room and onto her bed, and I can see the bat—a leftover from Paige's softball days—in his hands more clearly than I've ever seen anything in my life. In the light from outside, I can see the dark smears on its thickest part. I remember the autopsy report I'd found online about Lennox. How she'd been beaten, and my insides turn to ice.

I'm grateful because the light isn't strong enough to illuminate whatever horror is on the bedroom floor. Thinking about what happened to Paige in unconscionable. Seeing it would break me.

He props the bat by the bed and studies me, the pause before the pain. I close my eyes, unable to watch what comes next. It takes me a minute to realize I'm talking, begging for him to please, please, please, please stop. No. Nonono. Mindless. Thoughtless. Complete and utter terror.

What's more terrifying than the bat, is his rapt focus. He hasn't said anything, not one word since he attacked me on the porch. Like I'm not human. Like I'm just a *thing* he's playing with. Less than a person. Not worthy of his words.

Anger floods over me in a hot rush, and I'm surprised it doesn't simply steam right out of my ears. As he twists his torso to reach for a section of rope sticking out of his back pocket, I snag the handle of the bat and swing. There's no time to aim, no time to second-guess myself.

The bat arcs through the air and connects with his shoulder. It's not enough to seriously injure him, but it's enough to distract him, if only momentarily. He shouts in pain and jerks backward. I take advantage of it and surge forward, hoping the combination of the hit and the shift in balance are on my side.

His hand comes up to grapple for something to counter his weight and his fingers snag in my hair. Whole chunks come away with his fingers as he falls backward and tumbles to the ground.

It takes every ounce of strength that I have to open my eyes. I can barely see through the tears and the sting of mascara, but I manage to clamber to my feet. I scoot by the bed as fast as my feet can carry me and inch around the periphery of the room. The man, who is dressed in black, gets back up to his feet. I don't look down because I can't. I won't. I block that out, too.

My sobs have subsided, and I look around wildly for something, anything, I can use to fucking hurt this guy with so I can escape. I grab the first heavy-looking thing next to me—a metal bookend. As he moves to open the door, I raise the bookend in an arc above me, my wrist screaming in pain. By the force of sheer will, I manage to bring it down as fast and as hard as I possibly can across his head. The resulting, wet-sounding *thump* makes me cringe, but I force myself not to give in to the fear and panic.

He crumples in front of me but isn't unconscious like I'd hoped.

By now, my wrist is throbbing fiercely, but I gather my strength and use both hands to throw the bookend at the assailant who is scrambling to his feet and picking up the discarded bat as he advances. The bookend bounces off his back, and he momentarily loses his footing but rights himself before I have a chance to move. The man turns and body checks me. I fall back back, landing on the floor in a pool of blood and knocking my head against the corner of Paige's dresser.

Head throbbing and thoughts muddled, it takes precious

seconds for me to regain my footing. In that time, he raises the bat above his head and swings, the bat whistling through the air. I duck on instinct and feel the air ruffle my hair. Unable to connect the hit, he spins, and I rush across the room to shove him the rest of the way out of the open door. He lurches to his feet just as I fling the bedroom door shut. He throws his weight against the door once, and I grunt. As he reaches a hand through the door, I take the opportunity to slam it shut, closing it on his fingers, once, twice, three times in rapid succession. The sound of someone's pain has never been so satisfying.

He shouts and pulls the hand back. I throw the door closed and use sweaty, bloody fingers to flip the lock. I fumble and flounder for my phone and manage to pull it from my pocket. It takes me precious moments, and I'm crying in frustration and fear by the time I'm able to activate the touch screen and dial.

"9-1-1 what is your emergency?"

"She's dead!" I shout. "He killed her!"

"Ma'am, are you saying there was a homicide?"

"He's still here. He's trying to kill me, too."

"We're going to send help. Can you tell me your address?"

I choke on my frantic gulps of air and scream when the door jerks behind me. The ringing in my ears drowns out my voice as I relay my address and phone number in case they need to call me back.

"You're doing just fine. Can you tell me your name?"

"Piper. My name is Piper. Just please help us."

"They're on their way. Can you tell me if you're hurt, Piper?"

"My hand—I think he broke it. But Paige, my sister. I

think," my voice breaks with a sob, but I force myself to continue, "I think she's dead."

"Is the person who attacked you still there?"

Another shove comes at the door and a scream tears from my lips. "Yes," I say to the operator. "I locked him out of the room, but he's here. He's trying to get in." Tears pour down my cheeks. "Please." I don't know if I'm talking to her, to him, or to God, but I say the word so many times it becomes one long chant.

"We've got officers and paramedics en route. Stay inside the room until they call for you."

"I will," I tell her.

Then, I close my eyes because the adrenaline gives way to shock, and it's the only way I blot out the reality.

There, surrounded by the scent of my sister's favorite perfume and blood—*her* blood—that stains my skin, I finally succumb to mindless panic.

The sound of my name being called in a familiar voice shocks me out of the stupor. "Piper!"

I twist around, realizing I slumped on the floor against the door at some point. It's still dark out, and I have no idea how much time has passed. It can't be long because the police haven't arrived. Still clutching the phone in my hand, I get back to my feet, but I'm too scared to open the door and check to see who is outside.

"Piper!" The person yells again, this time the voice sounds closer and is followed by the sound of splintering wood and shattering glass. I press my ear to the bedroom door and hear the thunder of footsteps coming down the hall. "Piper, where are you?"

Recognizing the voice, my hand reaches for the doorknob.

"Gavin?"

"Thank God," he says through the door, his voice muffled. "I heard you screaming. Open the door, baby. Are you okay?"

I almost do it. I almost open the door, then I remember the man and my hand stops mid-air. "What are you doing here, Gavin?"

"What the hell, Piper? Just let me in!"

Caught between the need for someone familiar, someone safe, and the devastation of what I've been through, I freeze. Gavin bangs on the door, and I jump backward.

"Piper? Piper, c'mon, baby. Open the door." His voice is achingly familiar and causes sobs to rise in my throat.

"No," I think I say, but I'm not sure if the words actually make it through my lips. It's too coincidental. Too soon. He couldn't be the man who attacked me, but I can't seem to make myself move to let him in.

He keeps banging on the door until other voices join him, then another knock comes, but this time it's a woman on the other side. I glance out the window and find the parking lot full of flashing lights.

With tentative movements, I open the door and peer around the side.

The officer on the other side lowers her weapon. "You're safe now, Piper. Help is here."

A HAND WRAPS around my wrist, and I come up screaming, fists balled and swinging.

"Ms. Davenport! Ms. Davenport," says a frantic, shrill voice. "Calm down. You're in the hospital."

I open my eyes and blink, chest heaving from the sudden rush of adrenaline. A wary, unfamiliar face peers down at me. "I just need to check your vitals," she says and takes a measured step toward the bed. "Is that okay?"

Nodding makes my head throb, and I press a hand to the thick bandage covering it.

What the—

Then it hits me. All of it.

Paige.

My fingers wrap around the metal arms of the hospital bed when the force of it threatens to simply wash me away. The nurse puts a hand on my arm, and I jerk away again, lost in the throes of the memories. A harsh sound is coming from somewhere, and it takes me a minute to realize it's my desperate, broken sobs.

The nurse rushes out of the room and comes back. I cover my eyes and sink into the bed as she pushes God-only-knows-what into the IV snaking into my arm. Whatever it is, I hope it'll take the pain away. He didn't kill me, but I almost wish he did. I wish he'd taken me instead.

Living without Paige is simply incomprehensible. I reject the very thought of it.

Whatever the nurse gives me swallows me slowly, taking me under into the blessedly empty depths where there's no such thing as pain at all. I give into it gleefully.

A few hours later, after a visit from the doctor and a bevy of nurses, my parents appear. I can hardly bear to look at them. They remind me too much of Paige. My mother flutters about the hospital room arranging all the flowers already filling every surface while my father stomps around glaring at everyone. They're trying to keep it together, trying to be strong for me, but I can read the strain between them. I can see how they're struggling with the fact that they just lost a child, but at least they still have the other. It doesn't escape my notice that they can't stand to look at me either. Then, I realize it's because Paige and I shared a face. It must be like looking at a ghost.

I ignore them both and feign sleep. The police are supposed to come by for an interview, so the nurses and doctors are giving me enough medication to help with the pain, but not enough to knock me out. I can't even move without being reminded of my own anguish.

A broken wrist, various lacerations, a concussion, and shock are my new bedfellows. And I am grateful. The combination blurs most of what happened after I locked myself in Paige's room. I have only a few recollections of being wheeled from the apartment to an ambulance. Flashing red and blue lights. A huddle of curious onlookers scenting blood. Flickers of the ride to the hospital. Feeling grateful I didn't have to see them take Paige away. The blood smeared on our floors is the only image that is crystal clear.

The finality.

"Piper," my mother says from the doorway, her voice watery with tears. "The officers are here to talk to you."

I nod, though I keep my gaze on the lone window of my hospital room as I sit up.

Detective Manning, who is dressed in a worn suit that is hopelessly wrinkled, steps into the room. Paige deserves that kind of dedication. He was tireless with Lennox's case and kind to us. He's the only one I feel understands what I'm going through. The moment his eyes settle on me, I want to burst into tears and throw my arms around his neck.

As he draws into the room, I nod to the chair my mom had been sitting in. He obliges and sits with one ankle crossed over a knee, a kind of familiarity borne from tragedy. He takes my hand for a second, then pats it and sets it on the bed. He pulls out a legal pad about a third of the size of the one he used when he interviewed us the first time, which almost makes me smile. When he speaks, his voice is soft and full of compassionate understanding. "Start wherever you can, with as much detail as you can, Piper. Whatever you can remember will help us figure out just what happened. Take your time."

I have to clear my throat repeatedly to get my voice to work. The screaming damaged my vocal chords. "It was late, probably past midnight, although I don't remember the exact time. I'd been drinking. I was coming back from a bar. She'd been there with me about an hour before. Around eleven o'clock. I'd seen my ex-boyfriend, and she was talking me out of rekindling the relationship."

"His name?" he asks.

"Gavin Lance," I reply absently.

"The same Gavin Lance we found at your apartment?"

I nod, and Detective Manning shuffles through his notes. "So you were at the bar together around eleven o'clock and you went home about an hour later. How did you get home?"

"I walked. It was only five blocks, so I didn't bother calling a cab. When I got home, I thought I heard something in the alley beside the house." I look up at him and blink back tears. "I was scared. I thought it could have been the same person who attacked Lennox, which is stupid, right? Anyway, I went up the steps and started to unlock the door when he—he came up behind me and put his hand over my mouth. He told me not to scream."

"Did you get a look at him? Recognize anything?"

I shake my head. "No. He pushed me inside before I knew what was happening."

Manning nods and gives me an encouraging smile, which bolsters me for the next part.

"He pushed me into P-Paige's room," I manage before my voice breaks.

My mother chokes on a sob somewhere across the room, and I squeeze my eyes closed to rein in my wildly fraying emotions.

"It was dark. There was a little light coming in, but I couldn't see much. Then he pushed me down on the bed and picked up Paige's bat she kept from high school."

"Could you tell how tall he was? Short?" Manning prompts.

I force myself to remember the feeling, his arms around me and the scrape of his beard on my neck. His chest against my back. A shudder of revulsion rolls down my spine.

"Taller," I croak out. "I'm five eight so he would be about six feet tall, I think. Muscular. Strong enough to lift me easily. Pin me down."

"Did he say anything? Did you recognize his voice?"

"He didn't say anything else, but no, I didn't get a good look at him. It was too dark and everything went so fast. I'm sorry."

"You're doing just fine. Do you think you would be able to recognize his voice if you heard it again?"

I press my lips together and shake my head.

"That's okay. Was there anything else about the attack that you can remember?"

I forced myself to remember, to track through the nightmare for any detail that could help. "During the struggle, I knocked him out with a bookend. He was only down for a few seconds, though. I also managed to slam his fingers in the door. So, he'd definitely be injured today, and I think he had dark hair. His was wearing cologne, I think, but I can't tell you the brand. It wasn't familiar."

"Can you tell me more about your boyfriend, Gavin Lance?" Manning asks.

My brows furrow. "Ex. We broke up around the time Lennox was . . . around the time Lennox was found."

"You said you saw him at the club? Did you argue?"

"We talked, like I said. He wanted to get back together, but I blew him off."

"Was he upset?"

I glance between him and my parents and sit up a little straighter. "What's going on?"

"Honey, just answer the question," my mom says.

"He seemed a little angry when I wouldn't stay and talk with him, but he couldn't . . ." I brush a hand through my hair. "He couldn't have done anything like this." I don't know if I'm trying to convince Detective Manning, or myself.

"We're just covering all bases," Manning reassures me. "Did you change your mind? Make plans to meet at your house later?"

I shake my head. "No, not at all."

"Do you know what he was doing at your house last night?"

My hand goes to my forehead to rub at the dull ache

growing just behind my eyes. "No, I . . . I have no idea. He probably came by to try to make up with me." My voice is small and choked with tears. "He's not. . . a suspect, is he?"

Manning shares a look with my parents.

"What aren't you telling me?" I demand.

"You said you injured the man who attacked you?" Manning flips through his little notebook. "Smashed his hand?"

"Yes," I say slowly. "I hit him over the head, too."

"What does that have to do with Gavin?"

"Mr. Lance has a broken hand," Manning says. "And he's pretty beat up. He says he got in a fight at the bar, but we're still conducting interviews. It'll take some time to process the scene and compare blood types. . ."

I tune out after that and wonder how much more pain I can possibly take.

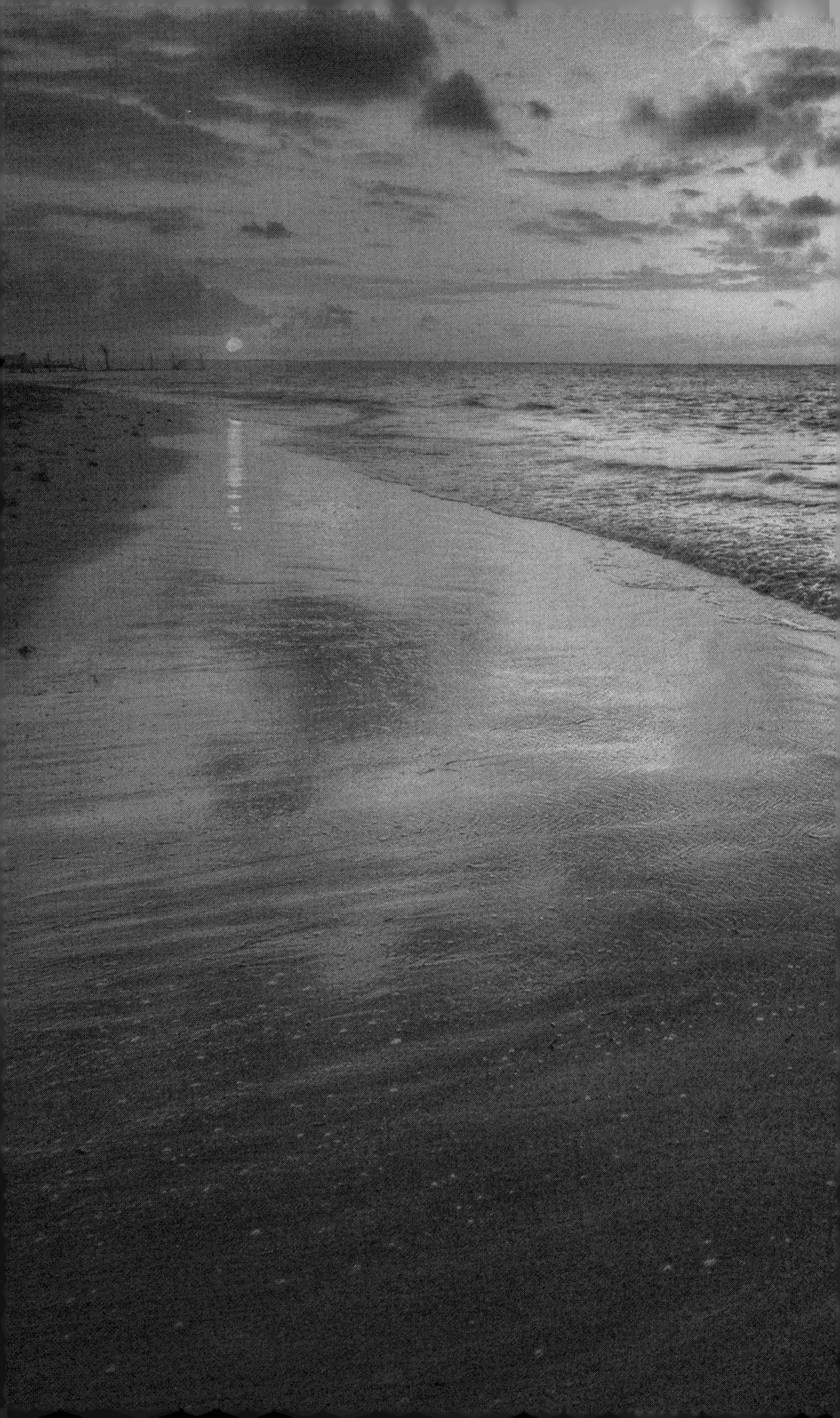

CHAPTER FIVE

SIENNA

AS THE GREYHOUND bounces and groans its way through the flat Florida fields, thatches of paradise peek through the expanse of pine and palm trees. A familiar sugar-white beach is first, much to my delight. It is already full to bursting with pink tourists and shrieking children. A postcard-perfect picture. I can't help but sigh at the sight. I've missed the ocean.

Along the front of the beach are tourist attractions, putt-putt golf, go-cart rentals, places to rent beach equipment, and a couple of diving shops and boating places. Farther down the beach are brightly painted buildings gathered in groups. The whole scene makes me smile, and the muscles in my cheeks protest. I'm so used to wearing a scowl.

I've been coasting on gut impulses and luck since the night Paige was murdered, and so far, they haven't done me wrong. After that, I'd given in to the pressure to pursue therapy. Hours and hours of therapy at my mother's request. It may have given me some tools to deal with the night terrors and depression, but it did nothing to help with the fear, the overwhelming guilt, or paranoid need to look over my shoulder. The journalist covering the murders, Phil Exeter, had somehow shadowed me wherever I went, hounding me for a story, which I refused to give.

    Finally, when I realized that the anxiety was going to suck what little there was left of me, I decided to leave. I just hopped on the first bus out of Miami—the place I'd begun to consider home—and decided to make a fresh start. My parents gave me the money from Paige's insurance policy and encouraged me to start over. I picked Jacksonville, where I opened my own business. It worked—for a while, until Phil caught up with me again. After that, I moved around a lot, hoping to run from him—and myself.

    I'd stuck to Northern cities like Boston, Chicago, and New York, hoping to lose myself in the anonymity of the crowd. For the past two years, the memories have been crushed by the day-to-day obligations. Being on the move meant having to find a new job to support myself in each city. The old me had been a little too wild. Too reckless. Careless. Working and worrying about paying for rent and food hadn't been too high on my list of priorities. Now, endless, menial work serves to distract me from the ghosts of my past.

    My phone rings, and I find Chloe's name on the caller ID. "I'm almost there," I say without greeting. Chloe is the only person in the world who really has any idea of the trauma I've been through, my other life, other identity. A couple years ago, she was taken hostage along with a couple dozen other people on a ferry and strapped with bombs. She was my sole employee at the little travel agency I'd opened in Jacksonville and my closest friend. When I started to feel the fingers of the past reaching out to drag me back, I decided to put Jacksonville in my rearview and passed the agency over to her very capable hands.

"You're going to love it," she says.

I'm not quite so optimistic, but I force myself to be cheerful. "So you've said. Repeatedly."

"I wish you could have seen it in summer, but the country air will do you some good."

"I think I remember saying something similar to you before I made you take the ferry from hell."

Chloe just scoffs. "Best and worst time of my life. At least I got Gabe out of the nightmare."

She ended up marrying her rescuer. Now, the two of them and his little girl live together in Jacksonville. I make a mental note to go visit them the next time I can now that we're so close.

"You never know, maybe you'll meet a guy there," she says.

I roll my eyes at the seat in front of me. "Not a chance."

I don't have any plans to date, but maybe I can finally relax, finish school, and make friends again. Find some way to put together the tatters of my old life. It may not be perfect, but it will be mine. And it is time I take my life back. It is time I have any life at all. I know I will have to face my family and my faults eventually, but before I do that, I know I have to come to terms. Perhaps Nassau is just what I need to lay those demons to rest.

The thought is comforting as the bus pulls into the depot across the street from a pewter blue lake. Even if I can't make this paradise my temporary home, I can at least enjoy the brief respite from traveling. What could be better for that than some

Florida sunshine? That's one thing I missed from living in Miami and Jacksonville. The constant sun. So much of the past few years had been spent in gray, dreary places.

I promise myself every day that I will take joy from anything and everything that I can. Life is, as they say, way too short not to enjoy every moment of it.

"I'm getting off the bus now," I tell Chloe. "I'm going to try to find a place tonight and get settled. I'll call you as soon as I can, and we'll make a date."

"I'm going to hold you to that!" Chloe says. "Miss your face."

"Miss you, too. Thanks again for recommending me to your friend about the job and everything. If I haven't already said it enough."

"No need to keep saying it. That's what friends are for. Don't forget to call me!"

"I won't. I'll talk to you soon."

"Later," she says.

I tuck my phone into my pocket and grab my bags down from the empty seat next to me—two well-worn duffels, which hold everything I own.

The verdant air wafts through the bus the moment the doors open. I have to steel myself against the scent of earth as it throws me back into the memories of that night. After a few breaths, I manage to calm myself and try to enjoy the warm air. It lifts my long blonde hair and whips it around my face and shoulders. I'd grown it out in the years since I left Miami, allowing my shoulder-length hair to grow down past my waist. Not to mention I wear it like a shield. I'll never forget the feeling of his voice as it curled around my neck, the scruff of his beard on my bare nape. The mere thought of it makes me shiver and glance around the occupants who dawdle as they disembark, oblivious to my sudden bout of paranoia.

No. He's not here. He'll never hurt me again. The only thing I have to be afraid of is my own memories. And that's plenty to keep me zigzagging around the country.

I give one last once over of the other people on the bus, but there is no sign of a tall, dark haired man. And there won't be, I remind myself. As many times as I explain it to myself, I still look around every corner. After all this time, I still don't think the nightmare has ended. My heart begins to race, regardless of how many times I tell myself to be calm and cool. I take deep breaths. In four seconds, hold, out four seconds, and hold. I repeat it until my heart rate goes back to normal.

By that time, the other passengers have cleared the bus. Feeling foolish, I lift my bags to my shoulder and follow the last of them down the steps and into the depot.

The sun beats down on my shoulders as I walk along the main street that goes around McCormick Lake toward the bundle of businesses. I make a mental note to invest in some sort of sunhat or my pale skin will be burned to oblivion in no time.

Nassau couldn't be more different from the places I have called home for the past year. There are crowds here, but they are nothing compared to the mobs of New York and Chicago. The tourist attractions and the lakefront center most of the activity along the water. From the trip in, I know that going two or three miles beyond the city limits will dramatically decrease the amount of civilization, and any farther than that is nothing but fields and farm land. A good place to get lost in.

I reach the cluster of buildings and follow the footpaths down the charming main street lining the lake. Cute little bungalows dot the road across from it and are interspersed with towering cypress and pine. Each house is a different color, and I wonder if this place is seriously a wonderland. I smile at the thought as I walk between two buildings and turn onto a boardwalk of sorts, which is lined on one side with restaurants and gift shops. Any one of the shops will need help as summer melts into fall, and the thought of working right on the lake is appealing.

I keep walking until the boardwalk ends and the dock begins. The dock sports dedicated fishermen who are intent upon their lines and lures; their coolers for their catch line the walk. Teenagers in cutoffs and T-shirts walk hand in hand. Younger kids attempt to throw their own lines over the lip of the pier, and their screams of elation or disappointment ring all around.

I reach the end, which is far out into the diamond-studded lake, and rest against the wooden railing with my duffle bags at my feet. In the distance, a group of brave teens race and splash, spitting water into the sky. The buzz of sea planes flying overhead competes with the crash and hiss of gently rocking waves below me. Back on the manufactured beach, herds of people shift along the sand with colorful umbrellas and blankets hoping to leech the remnants of summer before it gets too cool.

One day, I want to be like them—surrounded by the love and compassion of good friends. People who care to know what I'm doing and where I'm going. For so long, I'd squandered the attention of friends and family who only wanted the best for me. Hopefully, if I got the opportunity again, I wouldn't let the same thing happen. You never know what is most important until it—against all reason—is taken from you.

I make my way back down the dock, and my eye catches on

a bright white building at the far end of the main line of businesses. It's situated so it has a direct view of the lake, is flanked by rows of beautiful flowering bushes, and has a sign just to the right of the walkway that reads: Nassau Bed and Breakfast. Drawn by the beautiful picture it paints, I sift my way through the throngs of people on the boardwalk until I'm standing in front of it. Even if Chloe hadn't put out feelers, I would have immediately been drawn to its classic lines and charming decorations. There's love here, and it almost emanates from the place.

Heavy pieces of furniture, crafted from driftwood, sit on the expansive wrap-around front porch. The front door is open, so I take the opportunity to duck in for a peek before I find the owner for introductions. The foyer is empty of guests and surprisingly quiet for what I'd expected of midday. The only sound is the soft ticking of the grandfather clock situated at the base of the stairs in front of me and the waves crashing in the distance.

I crack open a set of double doors to my right just enough to see the library on the other side. A rainbow of spines decorate floor to ceiling shelves. A grouping of comfortable-looking chairs is placed in front of a delicately crafted stone fireplace. The windows are open to a garden of colorful flowers. To the opposite side is a closed door, where I assume the dining room must be located.

On my left is a little gift shop with more driftwood lining the walls as shelves for knick knacks, books, and a variety of tongue-in-cheek shirts. I turn in a slow circle, taking it all in. The space needs no music or scent because the unique scent of fresh air fills the space. It's peaceful and quaint. Finally, my eyes land on a large hunk of wood with elaborate, delicate branches that serves to hold the checkout counter and register.

A colorful chalkboard on the wall behind it details an enticing lunch menu. They must serve the occasional foot traffic as well as those with reservations. I walk slowly through the gift shop and out a pair of French doors. They lead out onto a spectacular veranda with the most beautiful lake views I've ever seen, which includes the two weeks I'd spent getting wasted on the shores of Mexico with Paige our freshman year in college.

The memory spears a fresh wave of pain, so I turn from the view and nearly run into a woman with a short cap of white hair. She joins me, leaning her arms against the deck. "Beautiful, isn't it?"

Awestruck, I can do no more than offer her a baffled smile. "I've never seen anything like it."

"That's what we like to hear." She straightens and turns to me. "I'm Rose. Were you looking to book a room or order something for lunch? Our fresh fish is to die for."

"Actually, I would kill for some caffeine. You wouldn't happen to make coffee here would you?"

"You're in luck. We have the best cappuccinos in the state. Mostly because you can sit out here on the deck while you drink it."

I couldn't argue with that.

I follow the woman back through the gift shop and hall to an open room with a grand staircase and dining room on the far side. I conclude based on the lake views there as well that the back of the house must jut out toward the water, offering a million-dollar panoramic view. The dining room opens up into a spacious kitchen that is bright and airy, all light wood and soft cream accents. There is a central island with a sink and stainless steel stovetop, two commercial-grade ovens, and two identical stainless steel microwaves. It is like something from a design magazine.

As I step into the kitchen, I hear a curse coming from another side entrance that is followed by a lot of feminine grumbling.

My guide's mouth pulls into a frown. "Excuse me for a moment."

"Of course."

She hurries from the room, her heels clicking against the tile floors as she goes. Curiosity piqued, I follow, though only to the stools situated at the bar, which is plenty close enough to hear the conversation going on down the hall.

"What in the devil is going on in here, Diane?"

I jump when three bangs sound in rapid succession from the hall. "Mrs. Cleary has decided she doesn't want the Lily Suite after all. Too sunny."

"Did you mention she specifically booked the Lily Suite because it gets a lot of sunlight?"

The woman sighs in response. "Of course I did, Mom, but that woman doesn't listen to reason."

"Well, we have customers in the other room. You can't be throwing things about in here, now. We'll take a look at the other rooms and see what we can do."

"Of course. You're right, but sometimes a body just needs to let off a little steam."

I hear Rose laugh. "Next time you need to blow off a little steam, why don't you just take a dip in the lake. It's right cold enough to cool that temper of yours."

"I may take you up on that offer," Diane says. "If I don't, I may drown that damn woman."

"Language, Diane. We have a guest in the kitchen."

"Well, why didn't you say so?"

"What do you think I'm doing here?"

The sound of shuffling feet jerks me from my eavesdropping, and I snatch up a menu from the counter and pretend to study it. It offers a variety of light meals that I'd find in a gourmet café. Soups and sandwiches. A selection of coffees and fresh salads, plus the aforementioned fish, probably freshly caught.

I glance up as they enter the kitchen and have to blink twice at the sight. The women could have been identical were it not for the marked age difference. They both have the same heavily lidded tawny eyes and smooth cocoa-and-cream skin. The same slashing cheekbones and Cupid's bow lips. The younger woman, presumably Diane, has a thick mane of hair so brown it is almost black and looks to be in her forties. She is easily one of the most beautiful women I have ever seen.

She offers me a warm smile as she crosses the kitchen to the sink where she grabs a dishrag to run under the cold water. "Welcome to Nassau Bed and Breakfast. I hope we didn't bother you. Bit of a complication came up."

"No problem at all." I indicate the menu and hope that my stomach doesn't growl. "This all looks so great."

"Thank you." She rinses her hands in the sink. "What can we get you today?"

"Rose mentioned a cappuccino? That sounds perfect, thank you."

Diane moves across the small bar to the cappuccino

machine. Her gait is easy, confident, and her movements as she prepares the drink are efficient and capable.

She hands me a steaming mug with a complimentary pastry. "So what brings you to Nassau? Vacation?" Diane nods toward the duffle bags at my feet.

I take a moment to blow on the drink and sip before answering. "Of sorts. More like a fresh start. I'm—" I have to pause and remember I use my middle name now. It helps with the questions. As the death toll rose, so did the coverage of the case—especially when I made it out alive. Even now, years later, I still tense up when I say my name, expecting someone to recognize it. "My name is Sienna Davenport. Chloe said she talked to you about maybe giving me a job."

They share a look. Finally, Diane exclaims. "Thank goodness! Lord have mercy, we could use some help around here."

My mouth drops open and I remember to shut it after a few seconds of stunned silence. "Really?"

"Mom and I have been trying to find someone to help out around here for months with no luck. If you want, we can go up to the office to discuss hours and pay."

My heart beats a little faster. "That sounds great. You wouldn't also happen to know of anywhere I could rent, would you? I'll be staying in Nassau for the foreseeable future, but just got to town and haven't had a chance to look yet."

Rose is pulling cookies from the oven and the smell overwhelms the room, reminding me the pastry was delicious, but small, and I can't remember the last time I'd eaten before that. My mother had never been very skilled in the kitchen, but there is something about the smell of baking that makes me feel at home.

Diane perches on one of the bar chairs and nabs a cookie,

juggling it around as it cools. "Chloe mentioned how handy you are, and based on the resume she forwarded, my mother and I could use you around here. There's always something that needs to be fixed or some errand to run. We also manage the bungalows across the street. We're renovating them as we go. Same goes for our tenants there. I'm assuming you have experience?"

"Believe it or not, I was raised by a general contractor. I can do just about anything that you need doing. My father insisted on it. In addition, I've also done just about every job under the sun. Waitress, secretary, cook, maid."

"Have you ever been fired or committed any crimes?"

My mind flashes back to that night, but I force myself not to let it show on my face. "No, I haven't."

She studies me for another minute before grabbing another cookie and indicating for me to follow. She leads me through the hallway and out to a solarium that opens out to a side road with a fence on either side.

"We are open year round but do most of our business during the warmer months. At the moment, we have all of the seven rooms occupied, and I expect that we'll stay at full capacity throughout the end of the month as people take last minute vacations. If you decide to take the position, your duties will include light housekeeping, some paperwork, general Q and A for our guests about the area's activities, and maintenance as needed. I do most of the cooking here in house, and I may need a hand from time to time. My mother does a little bit of everything else when her health allows."

"What would the hours be like?"

"I'm obviously here around the clock, but I would need you from eight to five, sometimes longer depending on what activities are planned that day. In any case, if that happens, you'll be paid overtime. Are you going to school out here?"

"No, I haven't made plans to. Well, not yet anyway."

She gives me an assessing look as we cross the street toward the bungalows. "If you do, Nassau College has a great selection of night classes, and if need be, we can work around your schedule."

"Thank you, that's kind of you to mention."

"Well, it works in my favor to keep you around."

The main road that separates the bed and breakfast from the bungalows is heavy with traffic. As the sun starts its slow descent down the horizon, the soft blues paint the white shell driveway in pastels. Lights from the passing cars dance spots over the windows and lawns. Gathered in a loose semi-circle are a dozen or so modest houses with matching porches and carports. Each has a little fence framing the sidewalk that leads up to the front door. Diane guides me down the road to the farthest one. The house is like a fairy tale tucked away under a pair of palm trees. It's a faded lavender color, but not in any way that makes it look old or worn, just lived in. The front window is large and bare, framed by a flowerbox of struggling impatiens.

"It's nothing special." Diane takes a ring of keys from her pocket and unlocks the door. "It has a bedroom, kitchen with attached dining room, and bathroom. The yard isn't much to speak of, but who needs one with paradise across the street, right?"

I step in and take in the second hand-furniture, oddly charmed by the mismatched pieces. "Right. Does this one need some cleaning or fixing up?" I'm eager to get started, I realize.

To prove myself worthy of the two kind women taking a chance on me.

"If so, I'm sure you'll be able to fix it in no time."

"What do you mean?"

"Well, while you're helping us, you're welcome to live here. I'll speak to my mother about a reasonable deal for rent and utilities, but if you want it, this place is yours."

I turn in a circle, dazed. "This place?"

"Unless you'd prefer another?"

"No!" Giddy laughter bubbles in my chest. "No, this is great, I'm just caught off guard. I wasn't expecting you to offer me a house."

"You need it, and we need you." I shift my weight from one foot to another at her frank appraisal. "I can tell that you've had a hard life. Trust me, I can relate. Just consider this Southern hospitality."

I raise a hand to shake hers. "I can't thank you enough."

"You're welcome. Besides, you'll come to know everyone is family here."

I turn in a circle, taking it all in. "I don't know what to say."

"You don't have to say anything. I'll let you get settled in. You can start first thing tomorrow. Pleasure to meet you, Sienna."

CHAPTER SIX

LOGAN

THE BEER IS warm and flat, but it is wet enough to wash the sour taste of vomit from my mouth. My father always said a beer in the morning was the cure for a hangover. As a veteran drunk, I guess he knew best. Can drained dry, I toss it in the general direction of the overflowing garbage and wince at the clatter it makes against the tile floor.

The reflection in the chipped mirror above the leaky sink, which is stained with rust that I've been meaning to clean, reminds me more and more of that old bastard each day. Sweat and a slew of other indiscriminate stains camouflage what was once a white T-shirt. My beard has far surpassed the five o'clock shadow stage and has grown in patchy and unkempt. But what most reminds me of my father are my eyes. Light green, ringed by red, watery—as if I'm drowning myself in alcohol as well as drinking it—and angrily bloodshot.

I flip open the medicine cabinet and hunt for a bottle of ibuprofen. Empties rain down into the sink, along with a dull razor, empty mouthwash, and squished tube of toothpaste. A singular rattle leads me to a lone pill. It won't kick the headache completely, but it's better than nothing. I twist the stiff knob on the sink and use my hands as a cup to drink water.

    I half stumble, half trip my way to the kitchen, bypassing a mountain of laundry and a stack of unopened bills. Dishes are piled over every available surface, so I opt for a reasonably clean one I find next to the fridge. I give it a quick rinse, fill it with water, nuke it in the microwave and then dump in some instant coffee. It tastes like ass, but it helps eradicate some of the cobwebs that took up residence in my head during the night. There's some leftover pizza from three or four days ago that I throw on a paper plate and heat up as I suck back the remains of coffee. I've found coffee—like beer—is best consumed quickly and without mercy.

    After inhaling the pizza as I stand over the counter, I make a second cup of coffee and amble through the dark hallway that forks off to the only bedroom and bathroom to the living room. Normally, I'd sit on the couch in front of the flat screen and ferment in the haze of the blue light until the sun went down, but it's starting to cool off, and I could use the fresh air. Since it's hotter inside my house than it is outside, I head out to the porch. I don't mind the heat, but I don't want to sweat to death, either.

    I spent the last decade in the desert. A little Florida sunshine is pitiful in comparison. The heat almost makes me a little homesick for the dusty trailers and hundred-degree weather.

    The ancient wooden swing on equally ancient chains creaks audibly as I sprawl over it with one foot planted on the floor so I can sway myself back and forth. A fan circulates the humid air in lazy rotations above me.

A car door slams in the distance, but I ignore it. I'm almost asleep again, and the throbbing in my head is finally fucking off.

Someone's shouting over the whir of the fan, but I ignore that, too. A good nap to sleep off the last chokehold of this hangover is my number one priority.

I reach that point where all my muscles are lax, my breathing is slow and even, and the specters of the man I used to be are quiet. Then a woman screams, and I bolt upright, knocking my head against the arm of the swing and nearly blacking out for the second time in twenty-four hours—a record even for me.

My hand comes away smeared with blood. "Fan-fucking-tastic," I croak.

I use the hem of my shirt to staunch the bleeding, but that leaves me hunched over, so I just yank it off and press it to my forehead. When I sit up, the world tilts, and I have to grab onto the chains to keep from swaying like a reed in the wind.

I keep my eyes closed until the urge to yak all over my shoes —again—passes, then I get unsteadily to my feet and hobble down the steps. There's a fifty-gallon container I keep near the water hose beside the house that's already filled with rainwater. I duck my head in it to wash away the blood, and it also serves to cool me down and clear my head before I do something rash.

Like kill someone.

With the blood gone and streams of water flowing down my chest and back, I feel reasonably calm when I turn to face the source of the scream that gave me the concussion.

I knew when the FOR RENT sign wound up in the neighbors trash a week ago that my little slice of solitude wouldn't be so for much longer. After spending a large chunk of my life packed like a sardine with fifty other men while I spent eight long years in the Marines, I've grown very protective of my privacy.

The little blonde—really she isn't little, but I'm over six feet and would dwarf her—is standing on her own porch steps nearly identical to mine, glowering at a man in a suit that must have cost more than everything I owned.

They don't pay me any mind, even though I must look like a psychopath all shirtless and swaying from side to side with bloodshot eyes and blood running down my face.

"You shouldn't be here," she says. One hand is pressed over nondescript breasts and the other gripping the railing. "Leave now, or I'm calling the cops."

"I just need five minutes of your time," suit says. He leans forward as if he wants to get closer, but pussies out and straightens back up. "I can make it worth your while."

Blondie doesn't notice. The hand on her breast moves to her cocked hip. "Clock's ticking. I asked you to leave."

"You can't keep running from this."

Her eyes flash, and if my head weren't throbbing so much I may have grinned. "Don't tell me what to do, Phil."

"I'm not."

"Why can't you leave well enough alone? You've followed me all over the state. Probably all over the country. You won't wring one more thing out of me. Let it rest, for God's sake, and stop harassing me."

The sour taste in my mouth multiplies. I shake my head before I remember the headache.

There's maybe a twenty-foot spread of weed-choked grass

between our bungalows, but even with the distance, I catch the pleading look on pretty boy's face.

"Pi—" A swift, fierce look has his Adam's apple bobbing. "Sienna, let's talk about this."

I wince for him. Begging never works for a man. A woman doesn't want to be begged. I can tell I'm right when her full, pink lips pull into a frown. Loser never had a chance.

"I don't want to talk. I've done enough talking. Don't ever bother me again. Next time you do, I'll put the concealed carry to good use. Understand?"

Pretty boy deflates under her fierce stare. He tugs at his limo tie and runs a hand through his hair. "I'll call you," he says.

"I won't answer."

She watches until his sporty little car kicks up dust down the dirt road to the highway, then she turns and catches me staring at her.

"Your head is bleeding," she says and then she goes into her house and shuts the door behind her. I hear the unmistakable sound of the lock slamming home.

It takes me a good five minutes of staring after her before I clear my head enough to navigate on shaky feet back to my spot on the swing. I pop open the cooler by my side and flick open the tab on an ice cold beer.

It's never too early for a drink as the old man would say.

AFTER STEWING AWAY MOST of the morning, I shower, shave, and make my way down the winding driveway to my grandma's. She and my grandpa started the little bed and breakfast on Lake McCormick just after they got married. Unlike my parents, whose favorite past time was getting into yelling matches with each other, Grandma Rose and Grandpa Deacon loved each other to distraction.

For thirty years, they operated the Nassau Bed and Breakfast together, and their patrons always came back because the love they had for each other showed in the way they ran their business.

After Grandpa Deacon died from cancer, which no one saw coming, I made it a habit to stop by and check on her. Once she started getting sick and moved Aunt Diane in, I gave up my shabby one-room apartment and, after my transfer was approved, moved into one of their available bungalows to keep a closer eye on the both of them. They practically raised me, so I considered it my duty to help them around the property when I'm able. Today that duty extends to finding out more about the woman Diane is letting rent the cabin.

The long walk clears my head somewhat, even though it's still throbbing from the earlier abuse. The scent of crisp bacon wafts through the open screen door, and I let myself in, following my stomach to the kitchen where Grandma Rose sits at the table with the newspaper. Behind her, Aunt Diane is flipping bacon in a frying pan.

I pass Grandma Rose who tilts her head up for a kiss. Obediently, I place one on her forehead, and she squeezes my hand. There's a plate of bacon next to the stove, so I nip a piece and take a bite before Aunt Diane has the chance to slap my hand away.

"Boy, if you don't keep your hands out of my food," she warns, spatula raised like a threat.

"You could never hit me." I grin at her, but she shakes the spatula.

"Just try me."

Hedging my luck, I turn and fill a cup with coffee from the waiting pot on the counter. "Even when I came home at sixteen thinkin' I got Jenny Anderson pregnant, you didn't raise a hand to me."

Aunt Diane snorts. "Maybe I should have. If I'd been an advocate for corporeal punishment, maybe you wouldn't already be divorced."

I take a sip of coffee, opting to burn my tongue instead of having to answer. My marriage to, and divorce from, my ex-wife is a spot of contention for both of us. We'd gotten married when we were both too young and too stupid to know better. Aunt Diane has always refrained from saying the actual words "I told you so," but I don't need to be a cop to detect the meaning behind her attitude.

The tense moment passes, and I take another casual draw from my coffee cup. "Saw you rented out the cabin next to mine."

"Yes," she says succinctly. I wait for her to elaborate, but she doesn't. Woman wouldn't even crack under the most experienced interrogator.

"Were you going to tell me?"

She snorts as she plates the rest of the bacon. Then she crosses to the other counter to drain most of the grease into the little canister she keeps hidden behind the toaster, keeping only enough in the pan for eggs. "And let you scare the poor girl away? I don't think so."

"I wouldn't scare her away." She levels a look at me. "Fine, but you can't take in every stray."

"I wish I would have taken that advice when I took you in all those years ago. Would have saved me a hell of a lot of trouble."

"I'm serious, Aunt Diane." My firm tone doesn't even cause her to turn from the task of cracking eggs into the pan.

She merely turns to me and pats my cheek. "You worry too much."

"And you don't worry enough."

As the eggs sizzle, she pulls out silverware from a drawer to her right, and I take out plates from the cabinet and set them on the counter. Grandma Rose winks at me as she settles in to work on the crossword puzzle. She's heard these arguments a million times over and likes to watch us go at each other's throats. She told me once it replaced her soaps for entertainment.

I take my seat next to her on a wooden stool, and Diane sets a plate of eggs and bacon down in front me. I spent most of my life at her counter. She doled out punishments, advice, and food in equal measure and is more a mom to me than my own.

"Maybe I should run her background just in case. Did you at least check her references? Have her fill out an application?"

Aunt Diane points her spatula at me, grease dripping onto her pristine floor. "You'll do no such thing Logan Elias Blackwell."

I polish off a piece of bacon and then reach for another, but Grandma Rose steals it from my plate with a cackle. "There's something off about her. Did you know she carries a gun?"

Diane just laughs. "You'd say the same thing about Mother Teresa if she moved next door. Besides, I suspect whatever is 'off' about her has more to do with what's in your pants than whatever is in her past. Besides, what young, single girl doesn't carry a gun in the South?"

Wincing, I push away my empty plate. "Low blow."

She takes my empty dish to soak in soapy water in the sink. "Always knew how to shut that mouth of yours."

I stand and round the counter just as she reaches for a sponge to wash the dishes. She barely reaches my chin, but she's just tall enough for me to rest it on her head. The mop of curly dark hair tickles my chin.

When I speak next, it's soft. "I just want to protect the most important women in my life. Can't you let me do that?"

She sets down the soapy dish, and grabs a kitchen towel to wipe her hands, and turns to me with a patient smile, which makes me scowl down at her. Hands dry, she reaches up to cup my cheek. "Sweet boy, you have nothing to worry about. For now, if you go pestering that girl, it'll be a different story."

Resisting the urge to growl, I block her path as she tries to move around me to gather Grandma Rose's cleared plate. "I won't promise to leave her alone because I plan on keeping a close eye on her."

"I'm sure you do."

I ignore her twinkling eyes and knowing smile. "The first time I see something suspicious, she's gone."

Aunt Diane's smile fades, and I remember why the younger, more belligerent teenage version of me used to cower in her presence. "Don't threaten me, Logan Elias. She's a sweet girl looking to find her roots. You, of all people, know well enough about needing a place to feel safe. If you go interrogating her, you'll scare her for no good reason other than to soothe your male ego. So you're gonna leave her alone, you hear?"

The tone is a familiar one, and I know I've reached the point where she won't bend an inch more. "I'll leave her alone," I say and pull her into a hug, knowing it will break down some of her resistance.

She wraps her own arms around me for a second and then pushes me away. "I have guests to feed so you stop with all this nonsense and get."

I kiss her forehead, and her smile softens. Turning to Grandma Rose, I give her another kiss and her knowing eyes flash up at me. She grins, and I just shake my head. Why I thought it was a good plan to go up against them both, I'll never know. Dealing with women, especially if there's more than one of them, requires a great deal more intestinal fortitude than I possess.

"You remember what I said, Logan. Don't you cause her any trouble," Aunt Diane calls out behind me.

I lift a hand because we both know causing trouble is what I do best.

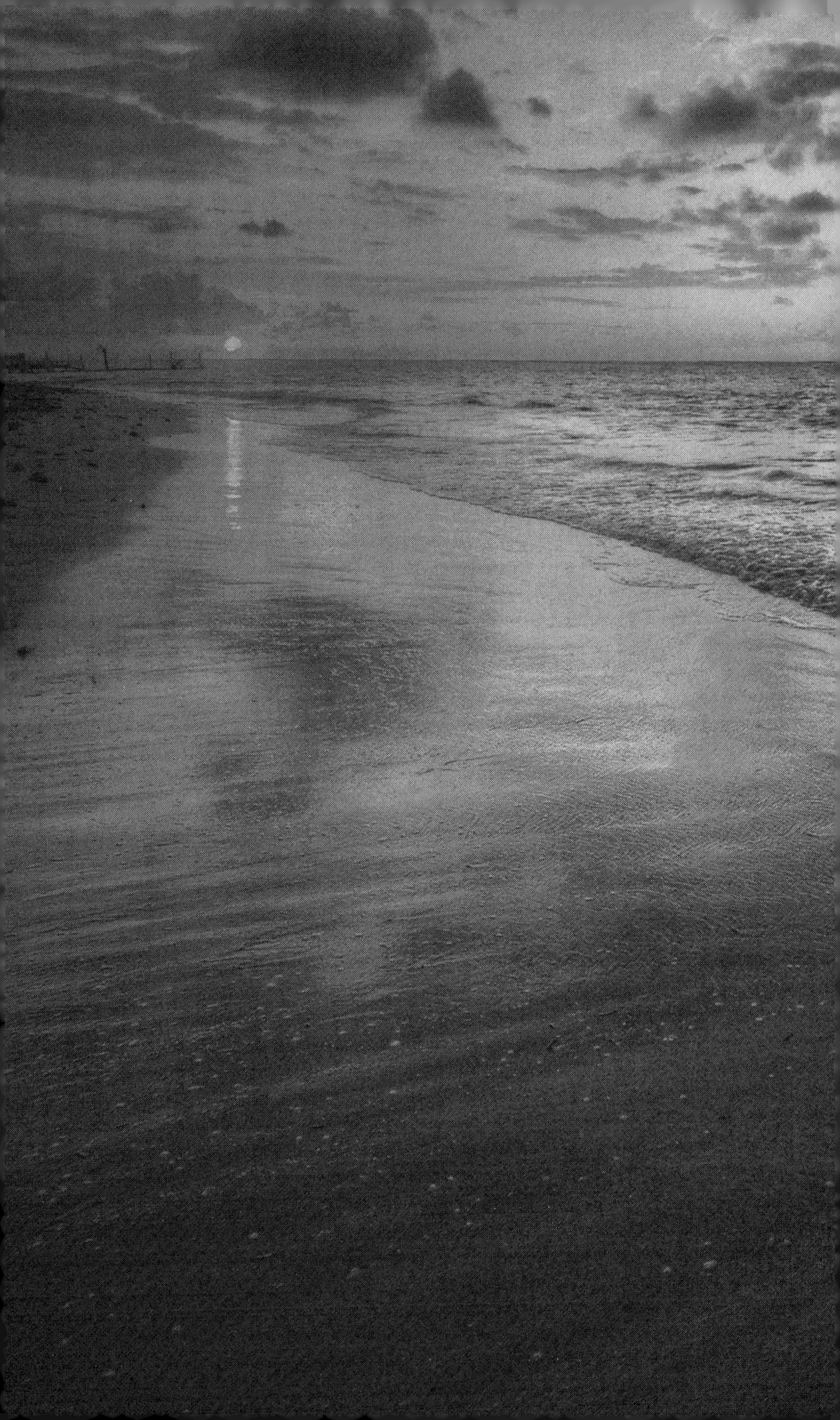

CHAPTER SEVEN

SIENNA

I DON'T WANT to be that person. I'm not that person.

This is a new start, a new me, and the new me isn't confrontational and doesn't believe in stirring up drama. Especially not with a brand new neighbor who I haven't even met yet. That would be a hell of an impression. Since Diane is my boss and this is her place, I want the first impressions with my neighbors to be good ones.

Besides, I am too damn tired to move let alone tromp across our yards to confront the man who thinks that the middle of the night is the perfect time to be revving his motorcycle.

Great, now I sound like my mother.

Really, it's none of my business. Who needs sleep anyway? Certainly not me after deep cleaning the house all day and helping Diane at the B&B. She kept telling me to get settled in first, but I couldn't stand the emptiness of the bungalow—no matter how cute and quaint it is—so I spent the afternoon and evening hours helping to check in new guests, planning outings, and cleaning up after check outs.

It's just a new house, that's all. A new place. It always takes a while to get settled somewhere new and learn all the sounds and idiosyncrasies.

Including new, inconsiderate neighbors who drive ridiculously loud motorcycles at two in the morning.

Old me would have asked for a ride . . . I don't want to speculate which type of ride that would have been, but suffice it to say, old me wouldn't have hesitated either way.

New me is all about the hesitation.

Sometimes, I don't like it at all, but what am I gonna do?

The motorcycle revs for what seems the hundredth time right outside my window, and I choke back a scream of frustration. Then, the guy laughs, and I give up my plan to be the nice, understanding neighbor.

Almost as an afterthought, I grab my robe and tie the belt loosely around my waist before swinging my bedroom door open. Shadows blanket the space between my bedroom door and the living room. For a moment, I hesitate, contemplating the length of the hall. My fingers grip the wood frame, and a shiver that has nothing to do with the temperature wracks my body. Then, the motorcycle revs again, breaking me from the moment and allowing me to shake off the fear as it's replaced again by annoyance.

I open the front door and squint against the bright light from the naked bulb above my head. When my eyes adjust, I'm able to discern a shadowy figure standing beside a massive chromed out beast of a machine.

"Excuse me!" I yell, but my voice is drowned out as he punches the gas.

Gritting my teeth, I start down the porch steps and cross the white-gravel drive. He doesn't look up until I'm nearly standing right next to him, and when he does, my words of protest whither into nothing as our eyes meet.

Without a change in his expression, the man unfolds himself from the seat of the motorcycle and comes to stand at his full height in front of me. I immediately take a preemptive step back just to look at him without straining my neck. I know I'm not ridiculously short, but I've never felt as physically small as I do standing in front of this massive man. He's six foot and change with broad, formidable shoulders, slim hips and thick, muscular thighs. Even though every female part of me recognizes his raw masculinity, it's his eyes that give me pause. I've never seen such a beautiful color, and I have spent many days staring at the ever-changing color of the ocean. They're blue-green—almost jewel colored. They are framed by long, thick lashes that stand out against the caramel tone of his skin.

It would almost be unsettling if the rest of his features didn't soften the stunning effect with rough edges. The dark slash of his brows and the distinct line of his jaw from a Roman nose and full, enticing lips, which are currently pulled into a frown.

Remembering why I got out of bed at such a god-awful hour, I draw myself up and set my features into what I hope is a careful balance between friendly concern and firm admonishment. I would offer my hand, but I am afraid I might not get it back, so I just wrap both of them around my waist.

"Need something?" he asks before I can say anything.

"I . . . uh, yes, actually. I was wondering if you could keep it down." I make a pained face. "It's really late."

He glances over my shoulder at my house and then back at

me, his eyes pinning me to the ground. Without saying anything, he reaches back and removes the keys from the ignition. The resulting quiet is nearly deafening.

"Thanks," I say. By sheer force of will, I manage to unglue my feet from the ground to turn and walk back to the house. Relief blankets me. Still feeling chilled, I rub at my arms and resolve to get back in bed and never leave.

But his voice stops me before I can make a full retreat. "That's it?" he asks.

I really should ignore him and get back to the warm comfort of my bed. New me should, anyway, but apparently, there's enough old me left somewhere deep inside, because I find myself swiveling around to face him. "What's that?"

He ambles closer, his eyes intent upon me. I'm going to have to start wearing full body armor when we're in the same vicinity, which could be a lot considering we live less than twenty feet from one another. It's either the armor, or living with the daily feeling of his eyes caressing my bare skin. He looks at me like a man who looks at a woman in preparation to devour her.

I take an automatic step back. I'm too damn tired to be devoured. "Well?" I ask a bit more testily than I mean to, but dammit, it's two a.m., and I'm exhausted. It's his own fault.

He follows after me automatically. "I said, is that it?"

"What else would there be?" I ask as my feet make it to the bottom step on my porch.

His lips twitch in what could be a smile. "Introductions," he says. "Since you're new to the area and all. I'm Logan. Logan Blackwell. You're Sienna, right?"

"I think your motorcycle was doing that well enough, Logan," I say without thinking. I want to ask how he knows my name, but something tells me prolonging this conversation isn't in my best interest.

I switch my weight from my right leg to my left and run a hand through my hair. The action causes my robe to slip down the side of my arm, baring my shoulder. Before I can fix it myself, his hand lifts, catches the material, and drags it the long, slow journey back up my arm.

Our eyes catch as he reaches the top, where his hand pauses on my shoulder. I take another step back and cross my arms over my chest, ignoring the tingling from his touch. "Good night," I say, mostly out of habit, and then reach for the screen door.

When it doesn't budge, I look up to find his hand above me and frown. I blow out a breath and shoot him a look. "You mind?"

"When someone introduces themselves, the polite thing to do is to give them your name in return."

"You already seem to know my name. Besides, I don't think you have any room to talk about manners. After all, you were the one trying to wake the entire state at two in the morning." I tug on the door, but it doesn't budge since he's still holding it shut.

"I didn't say I was polite." I realize that with his arm up blocking the door he has me pinned against it and his big, towering form.

"Apparently not," I snap, trying desperately not to sink into the debilitating fear that is rolling just under the surface. This guy is not going to hurt me. "Look, it's late and I haven't had much sleep tonight. Can we not do this now?"

"Do what?"

I turn to face him and wave a finger between us. "This. Us.

Whatever seduction routine you've got going on here. I'm not interested, and you're just wasting both our time."

His hand finally drops, and I open the door just enough to slip through before closing it soundly behind me. Unfortunately, it doesn't give me the sense of security I'm hoping for. I have a feeling it will take more than a door to stop this man from getting what he wants.

For a minute, he just looks at me through the tightly woven black mesh, and I think he may actually press the issue. My heart doesn't know if it's excited or frightened at the prospect. Then he takes a step back, though his gaze doesn't leave mine, and I release the breath I was holding.

While he's moving backward down the steps, I lock the hook for the screen door. Though I didn't have a reason to do it earlier, I have the sudden urge to secure everything in the house.

He reaches the bottom of the steps and then glances back up at me. "Nice to meet you, neighbor," he says before disappearing into the darkness between our two houses.

I retreat to my room and wrap myself up beneath the covers. There isn't a peep from next door all night, but I don't sleep a wink.

I GET into a good routine at the B&B. It's easy, familiar work. When I left the travel agency to Chloe, I thought I'd miss being the one to give orders and be in control of everything. In fact, it's nice not to be in charge all the time.

Two weeks pass, and I start to feel like maybe I can have the normal I've been craving. It didn't seem like such a big deal to me a year ago, but now, as I watch happy families and lucky in love couples come and go, I'm reminded each day of what I'm missing.

I force a smile at one such couple as I check them out at the reception area. "Did you two have a great time?" I ask.

"The best," the perky blonde gushes. "The absolute best. I told John here we have to come back this time next year."

"We'll see," he says, but he indulges her with a quick kiss, and I can tell if I'm around next year that we'll be seeing them again.

"We hope you do consider coming back," I say by rote. "Fifteen percent off booking for return customers."

The woman squeals and they walk off, already chattering about their next vacation together. I spend the next half hour straightening brochures and wiping down counters and table tops, wondering if we have any more customers checking in or out today. I don't think we do, but I stay close to the front just in case anyone needs me.

It's just after two when Diane comes through the back door with her arms full of grocery bags. I rush to the kitchen to help her, taking all the bags she has dangling from her right arm.

"Thanks. It was a madhouse!" she says, shaking out her now free arm. "An absolute madhouse. I don't know why I keep going on Friday afternoon when I know it'll be so busy."

"You should let me come with you to help next time."

She makes a shushing sound. "Please, you do enough around here, and I'm perfectly capable of going on my own. You are certainly welcome to help me unload and put them away, though."

"I'm on it!"

I head around the large center island to the inside garage door. Already thinking about the delicious menu for the night, I don't notice until I'm halfway across the garage that someone's already standing by Diane's car.

"What are you doing here?" I ask before I can think to stop it.

Logan straightens from the trunk with his arms full of dangling grocery bags. "I could ask you the same question."

I take a tentative step toward Diane's car. "I work here."

"And I would tell you what I'm doing here, but I don't even know your name," he says and then passes by me and disappears inside.

It takes me a few seconds of frantic thinking before I remember I'm supposed to be helping. By the time I make it back inside, Logan's helping Diane unload the bags and putting groceries away into cabinets. Wanting to question him about what he's doing here but not wanting to invite questions, I decide to bite my lip to keep my interrogation from spilling out.

To distract myself, I make two more trips back to the car for the rest of Diane's haul, set everything on the counter, and help unload. All the while, Diane and Logan chatter in the background.

"Have you met our new hire, Sienna Davenport?" I overhear Diane say. "You've been away training and may have missed her. She moved into the bungalow next to you."

My shoulders stiffen, and I pause for a second, one hand outstretched as I put a can of diced tomatoes away. There's a moment of heavy silence while I wait for Logan to answer, and then he says, "Sienna?" and I swear I can feel him glaring at me. "Yes, we met."

When he doesn't add to it, I set the can of tomatoes on the shelf, relaxing marginally.

"I don't know what we'd do without her," Diane continues. "I hope you don't mind that I put her into the house next to yours. If we were further along with the renovations to the others, I wouldn't have. I know you like your privacy."

I hear Logan kiss her cheek and then say, "It's no problem, Aunt Diane."

Stifling a gasp, I take extra care setting the next few cans in an orderly line on the shelf in front of me. I never would have pegged them as related, but now that he's mentioned it, I can't help but see the resemblance. Well, hell, I went and insulted my boss's nephew. I have to resist the urge to slap my forehead as I gather all the empty bags and put them in their storage container. God, I'm such an idiot.

They continue to chatter behind me, though I doubt chatter is a word many have used to describe any activity involving Logan's deep, rumbling voice, and I pretend it doesn't affect me at all by getting out all the ingredients Diane will need for tonight's dinner. The kitchen seems much smaller with him in it, though.

"You know I just worry about you," Diane says while I gather the spices from the top shelf over the commercial-grade range.

"So you've said," Logan replies. "Many times."

"I thought your deployments were hard—"

"Aunt Diane." There's no mistaking the warning tone in his voice.

I move to the fridge to grab the defrosted chicken, not

because I'm somewhat intrigued and certainly not because I want to know more about him. When I look back at them, Diane is waving away Logan's protests. "I don't want to hear it. I'm allowed to worry about my favorite nephew."

Logan smiles down at her, and it's quite possibly the most perfect smile I have ever seen. I must have made some sort of strangled noise, because his eyes find mine. My. Good. God. He is beautiful—so much so that my whole body refuses to listen while my brain screams for me to turn away. Diane flutters about, unaware of the tension that suddenly fills the room. After a moment, he breaks the contact and pulls Diane into a hug.

"I just don't like it. That's all." She pulls back to put a hand on his cheek. "You promise me you're careful?"

He kisses her forehead. "I promise."

"If your momma were alive, she'd have kittens. Still can't believe you've been a cop for going on four years. A cop!" Diane exclaims. "After all the trouble you got into as a teenager. She'd never believe it."

The heat growing in my belly extinguishes, and my whole body runs cold. Without looking back toward the pair of them, I cross the kitchen and set the chicken on the counter next to the other ingredients, hoping it doesn't slip out of my now trembling hands.

Of all things, I never expected him to be a cop. A criminal maybe, but a cop?

I almost would rather he be the outlaw I thought he was. A cop asks too many questions, and I'd really prefer the past stays where it belongs. Already I can sense them ticking around in that brain of his.

I school my expression to a sunny smile and turn back, my

attention on Diane. "Is there anything else you need before I take off?"

Diane turns to me, one arm still slung around Logan's waist. "You don't want to stay for dinner?"

"Thank you, but I have something at home and a good book calling my name."

"All right," she says. "I'll make sure to save you a plate for lunch tomorrow."

I give a silent prayer of thanks for Diane's undemanding nature. "I'd love that."

The hairs on the back of my neck prickle with awareness as I turn and stride out of the kitchen. Even though I can't see him, I know Logan's watching me all the way back to my house.

Keeping secrets is hard, but keeping them around a cop is going to be even harder. I should strangle Chloe for even recommending I move to Nassau.

My phone vibrates against my pocket on the short walk home, and I take it out, glancing at the screen.

Speak of the devil.

"I couldn't wait for you to call me anymore. Are you settling in okay?" Chloe asks without preamble.

I harrumph into the phone. "Yeah, but you could have told me Diane's nephew is a jerk."

"Awe, honey, I'm sorry about that. The job is going all right, though, isn't it?"

"Absolutely. I couldn't be happier. Thank you again for referring me."

"Thank God. I told Gabe you'd be fine. And it's no problem at all, sweetie. You did the same for me. Now, tell me what Logan did to piss you off."

I try not to let my sigh of disappointment turn the line to static. "It's okay. I can handle him."

I've been through worse things than having to ignore a gorgeous cop, right?

"Are you sure? I bet we can get Gabe to rough him up if he's such a big pain in the ass."

"No," I rush to say. "No, please. You've done enough already. I'll figure something out."

"Are you sure?" she asks, concern softening her tone.

No.

"Yes, I'm sure. It's not a big deal."

"If you say so." There is a beat of silence before she says, "Well, I'll see you around sometime."

"Hopefully soon. Maybe a hurricane will ruin business, and you'll be able to take some time off," I say then wince. "I didn't mean it the way it sounded."

Laughter bursts from her side of the line. "Sure you didn't. I'll let you know if something starts going around."

"I'd appreciate it, thank you."

"Bye, Sienna."

"Later," I say then tuck the phone in my pocket for the remainder of the walk.

Once upon a time, I had a thriving business and employees. Back then, I'd felt a modicum of safety. Now, I know better. Now, I take whatever job comes my way, keep my head down, and aim for simpler things—make sure my bills are paid and there is a roof over my head and food in my stomach.

Of course, none of that will take away my painful memories or protect me when my past catches up with me, but I'll figure something out. Hopefully Phil, the journalist who's followed me all over the country waiting on his next big scoop surrounding the murders, will take a hint and leave me the hell alone.

I can't even comprehend what will happen if he doesn't.

So, I force myself to think of happier things instead. As I near the drive of my new little bungalow, I remind myself that this is a new start.

The past can't touch me here.

I think of how easily Phil found me and hope my new start isn't just wishful thinking.

CHAPTER EIGHT

LOGAN

"BLACKWELL," I say without looking at the caller ID.

"You sound tired." I'm a little surprised it's Aunt Diane, considering how late it is.

"Probably because I am." I turn away from the speaker when I can't suppress a yawn. All I want is a shower, my recliner, and a good action movie to turn off my brain. I could also use a beer so bad my hands nearly shake with the need.

"I wouldn't call if I didn't have to," she says.

I hold back a groan as I watch my evening of relaxation circle the drain. "It's okay, I'm just pulling up the drive. Do you need me to come by?"

"I take back all the unpleasant thoughts I've had about you. You're a good boy." I refrain from pointing out this boy is on the dark side of twenty. "Sienna called this morning to let us know the air conditioner is out in her unit. I tried to call the repairman, but he said he wouldn't be able to get it until next week. I can't let that poor girl die of a heat stroke!"

The temperature gauge on my dash says the temp is a cool seventy degrees, but I bite my tongue, mostly because arguing with Aunt Diane is futile. "I'll stop by and see what I can do."

"Just don't pester her," she reminds. "Do you hear me?"

"I hear you," I say wearily.

I end the call and put my truck in park. All the lights in her house are on and most of the shades are up, allowing me to see right into her living room.

I've gotten into a sick, sad habit of just watching her. Though, it's hard not to when the girl has every light on all the time and every blind in her house open. It's practically an invitation. At first, it was out of habit and concern for Aunt Diane and Grandma Rose just hiring a stranger, even if Chloe knows her. When the most exciting thing she did was read books after work, I realized there had to be another reason why I always looked to her window before I went to sleep.

Through the living room window, I find her curled on the couch, an empty plate on the coffee table in front of her, and a half-full glass of wine to her side. She's reading again, though this time from a tablet she has propped on her knees. She's not very big to begin with, but in her curled up position, she looks tiny.

I turn away and open the door to my truck, shoving away all thoughts of what it would be like to curl up next to her. I'm going to go in, fix her air conditioning, and get out. Then I'll take that shower, only now I think I'll need to make it a cold one. I know she hears me walking up the porch steps, her whole body tenses, but she doesn't look up until after I knock.

"Logan," she says as she stands and moves to the other side of the screen door. She doesn't open it.

"Aunt Diane said you were having trouble with the air conditioner." Impatience roughens my voice.

Her lips purse, and she crosses her arms over her chest. "I'm fine. I tried to tell her I could fix it myself, but she wasn't having it."

I nearly roll my eyes, but manage to refrain. My aunt is one damn interfering woman. "Let me in, I'll fix it, and then I'll leave. It shouldn't take more than fifteen minutes."

An internal struggle wages across her face, and I wonder if she knows how transparent her expressions are. Frustration, anger, impatience all give way to acceptance. Finally, she takes a step back and allows me inside.

She's barely been here a month, and already she's put her stamp on the inside. Even if I could turn the cop off inside me, I'd still be able to get a sense of her from the house alone. It's neat, almost meticulously so. When I close the door behind me, my eyes land on the top-of-the-line deadbolt and security chain. Those sure as hell didn't come standard with the place. I have no doubt it will be the same for the back door. The shades are open, but a quick glance confirms all the windows are locked tight.

"It's just through the back." I nod and follow her down a dimly lit hallway to the small kitchen, which is identical to my own. Even the light in the small bathroom is turned on.

"I'll let you know if I need anything," I say as I unlock the door, smiling because I had been right about the lock situation, and head out to the back porch.

She flips on security lights—new—and they illuminate the entire backyard all the way to the tree line. Shaking my head, I get down on my knees and inspect the unit. Her footsteps retreat into the house, but I know she'll be watching. Something tells me people being in her space makes her nervous. I can't help but wonder why that is.

The air conditioner turns out to be an easy fix, and I'm done within the quarter hour like I told her. She's waiting for me in the kitchen when I walk in. Her hands are free and loose by her sides, but she's still radiating a nervous energy.

"You should be good to go," I say. "Your condensation drain was clogged. Just had to shop-vac it out."

She blinks her big blue eyes up at me. "That was fast," she says after a few seconds.

I shrug, nodding to the roasting pan sitting on her stove. "What is that?"

"Dinner." When I don't move, she adds, "I had a pot roast on today while I was at work."

"Smells good."

She glances at me and then at the door, and I can tell she's struggling not to tell me she wants me to leave, which only makes me want to stay. "I can make you some to take home," she finally offers. "As a thank you. I know you just got off work. I didn't mean to bother you."

I gesture dismissively. "Not your fault. I help Aunt Diane out on occasion when I can. And I'd appreciate some pot roast. I was going to get down on my knees and beg, but you saved me the trouble."

Laughter dances in her eyes for a second, and all I want to do is make her laugh again to see her face brighten with it. "I wouldn't want to make you beg."

"Thank you, I'd appreciate it."

While she pulls out a Tupperware, I get my first close up

study of her since she started making it a point to avoid me. Her frame is deceptively slight. Since she's moved in, I've watched her moving around furniture at all hours, so I know she's stronger than she looks. She tries to hide behind simple, dull colors and faded clothes, but her face is striking, her intelligent eyes too alluring to be forgotten.

I'm admiring the shape of her legs and the jeans that are almost painted on when I notice a familiar shape beneath her thick cardigan. My brows pull together as the two thoughts collide: her ass is altogether too good to be true, and she's packing another dangerous weapon under those clothes.

The sight reminds me of the conversation she had with the suit on her porch and renews my interest. What is she doing carrying a gun?

I barely have time to control my expression before she turns back to me and holds out the container. I take it automatically, noting her own tense look.

"Thanks for coming by so late."

"You're welcome."

I don't want to make her uncomfortable or cause her to clam up, so I walk to the front door, considering my options. She opens it for me, and I walk through. I don't know what happened to this girl, but it's obvious that something did. The locks, the lights, the gun . . . my gut twists at the possibilities. Suddenly, the last thing I want to do is make her feel uncomfortable, but I have to know . . .

"I got a few things to say, and the way I figure it, you've got a couple options."

She licks her lips. "Oh?"

"You can either tell me to go to hell and slam the door in

my face, or you can hear me out." Before she can speak, I raise my hand. "Before you slam that door, let me elaborate. The only two people I care about in the world are giving to a fault. They're the type who'd give the coat off their back and so on."

She softens just a bit. "Yes, I'm aware."

"Good, then you know that there are people in this world who take advantage of kindness like that."

"And you think I'm one of them?"

"I'd like to think not, but in my line of work, it pays to be cautious. When it comes to them, I'm probably overly cautious."

"If you think I'm going to object, you're wrong. Look, I realize you don't know me, and maybe we got off on the wrong foot, but I do understand the concept of protecting your family."

"Then I hope you'll understand when I ask outright if there's anything I should be worried about when it comes to you."

Her eyes flash, but she doesn't slam the door in my face. "There are reasons why I like to maintain my privacy, but no, there's nothing you need to worry about."

"Bullshit," I say without preamble.

She blinks. "I'm sorry?"

"I said, 'bullshit'."

"I think it's time for you to go now." All traces of understanding are gone from her face now, and she moves to swing the door closed. When I stop it with my foot, she sends me a fierce look. "You really need to stop."

"I want to know what you're hiding, and don't give me any of that bullshit. There's a reason why a woman carries a gun on her. If you're in trouble, I can help you."

"Am I doing something illegal?" she asks with forced calm.

"Are you running from something?"

"Isn't everyone?" she counters smoothly. "Besides, you should know better than anyone that there's evil in this world. I'm a single woman in a new place. Why wouldn't I protect myself?" Before I can say anything else, she takes a deep breath and her shoulders slump just a tiny bit. I feel like the biggest dick ever, but I have to know. "I am no threat for your family, Logan. I just came here for peace and quiet, and I have a right to do so. Now, if there's nothing else you need, I'd like for you to go now."

"You'd tell me if you were in any trouble, right?" Even as I ask, I already know the answer.

She takes a step back, and I wonder if she's distancing herself from me or from the question. "There's no need for you to come and rescue me. I'm not a damsel in need of saving."

Realizing I won't get any further with her tonight, I move my foot, and she closes the screen door between us. "Well, we both know I'm hardly chivalrous."

The cell on my belt interrupts her response and she closes her mouth.

"Blackwell," I say to the caller.

Our dispatcher Eileen answers, her voice brusque and efficient. "261A at Lawson's Park. Victim is responsive. Suspect left on foot and may still be in the area."

"Be there in ten."

I look to Sienna, whose face has gone white. "Go," she says. "Hurry."

I don't ask how she knew it was a serious call, or why she looks like she has seen death. There isn't any time. I make a mental reminder to check back in on her as I dive into my truck and spin out of the driveway.

On the way, I get additional details from Eileen. According to the victim, the suspect has already left the scene and emergency medical services are en route. All fatigue drains away as adrenaline spurts into my blood. Sirens flashing, I speed through what little traffic there is at this time of night and make it to the park in five minutes flat. My thumb drums against the wheel as I scan the nearby sidewalks for the victim, finally spotting her sitting on the curb half hidden in shadows.

I throw the gear into park and surge from the truck. The woman is pretty and can't be older than twenty, but when she sees me, she seems to shrink into herself—the movement making her look younger. I pause and make sure to keep my hands loose by my side.

"I'm Officer Blackwell with the Nassau County Sheriff's Department. I'm going to reach for my badge." When she doesn't object, I move slowly to my back pocket and pull it out for her to see. "What's your name?"

Her wide eyes don't seem to take in anything I'm saying, but when I hazard a step forward, she doesn't back away. I take another.

"Are you hurt?" I say softly. "Do you need medical attention?"

When I'm within touching distance, her eyes focus on me, and she whispers, "E-Elizabeth Gallagher," in a broken voice.

"Elizabeth, I'm here to help you. You're safe now."

After a few moments she steps to me, and I wrap my arm around her to lead her to the tailgate of my truck. I lower it so she has a place to sit and then quickly grab a blanket I keep in the cab. She's shivering when I wrap it around her, and I scan the surrounding streets for any sign of the ambulance. The girl is going into shock. I speak words of comfort as the adrenaline gives way to shock. I tell her everything is going to be okay.

What's more important is what I don't say.

I don't tell her the nightmare is just beginning.

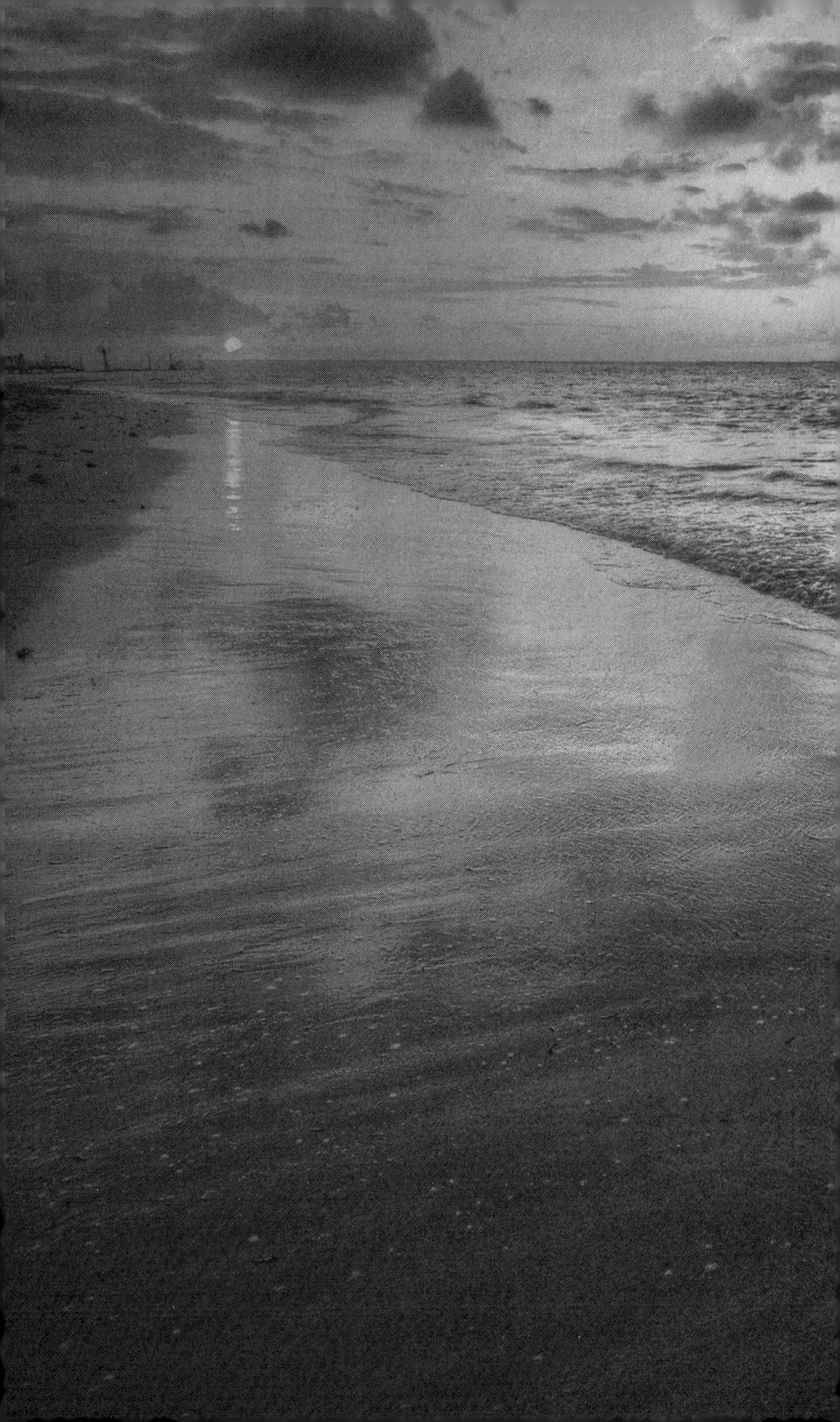

CHAPTER NINE

SIENNA

AFTER LOGAN LEAVES, I can't seem to find a comfortable position to sleep. I twist and turn until four a.m. before I finally give up on sleep and move to the kitchen to make a cup of coffee. Might as well get the day started if my brain won't shut off. Anything will be better than positing different scenarios with the one man I should be avoiding.

I fill up the water reservoir and select my single serving of chai latte. As it percolates, curiosity gets the better of me, and I peer through the window over my sink that looks into Logan's kitchen, a mirror image of mine. The windows are dark and his driveway is still empty. I don't want to admit it to myself, but I couldn't go to sleep because he hadn't come back. I wanted to hear the growl of his truck or the roar of his motorcycle coming down the drive to let me know he's okay.

After he left, fear clenched my belly so tight that I had to sit under the scalding spray in the shower until the water ran cold to get myself to calm down. I shouldn't have listened, but I couldn't help but overhear the attempted rape call and be thrown back into my own living nightmares.

I distract myself by belting a robe and stepping out into the cool morning. I'd started a small vegetable garden off my back porch, something I'd always dreamed of doing. Tending it, according to one of the many therapists I was forced to talk to, encouraging the little sprouts to grow is supposed to help me process the losses I'd experienced. I thought he was full of shit, but nothing else has worked and a couple plants won't take much time.

So one of the first things I did after I got settled and received my first paycheck was borrow Diane's car to go to the local hardware store chain to pick up seeds. After consulting with a gardening associate, I settled on broccoli, cauliflower, lettuce, carrots, and spinach for a nice fall garden. If I am still wracked with loss at the end of it, at least I'd have a salad to drown my sorrows.

When he still hasn't returned by the time I've polished off my chai latte and weeded the garden, my worry is replaced by irritation—at myself. I have no interest in indulging Logan's curiosity about me or my past. I have no interest in indulging Logan in any capacity whatsoever, so my concern about his well-being is useless.

I have no desire to become entangled with a man, emotionally or otherwise and something tells me Logan is all about the entanglements.

Brushing off the dirt from the hem of my robe as though I can brush thoughts of him off just as easily, I get to my feet and head back inside to change and get ready for work. I resolve to keep my routine. It'll be the best way to keep from inciting his own natural curiosity. Once he realizes I'm no threat to his family, he'll lose interest, and I'll go back to being invisible, which suits me just fine.

Unfortunately, Diane and Rose don't agree with my plan, and they pounce the moment I step through the door.

Diane plies me with another desperately needed cup of coffee first. "You look like you could use this," she says and hands me the steaming mug.

"Thank you."

"Logan came over, didn't he?" She asks, a little too innocently. "To fix the AC?"

I sip my coffee, considering my answer. I feel like I'm trapped in a sea of quicksand and taking the wrong step will mean a slow excruciating death. "Yes," is all I offer.

"Good." Diane pats my arm. "That's real good. He's a sweet boy, our Logan." She makes a face. "Well, when he puts his mind to it. He didn't say anything out of line, did he?"

It almost makes me smile. She knows her nephew very well and obviously cares for him a great deal. "No, he was very nice."

That seems to give her pause. "Nice. Hmm. Yes, well. I hope you had a chance to talk with him. There seems to be some tension between you two."

I sip my coffee again. Is it so obvious? "Everything is fine. We did talk for a bit before he had to go."

Diane straightens. "Go?"

"He had to take a call. I gather it was urgent." Coffee finished, I rinse the mug and set it in the dishwasher. Diane harrumphs behind me, and I hide a smile. Wanting to change the subject, I say, "I was thinking about getting a dog, and I wanted to check to see what your policy is on pets in the cabins."

"A dog?" Diane slaps a rag on the counter.

Lifting my shoulders, I round the bar intending to head to the hall to grab my cleaning supplies. Over my shoulder, I say, "To protect me from your nephew."

That surprises a laugh out of the two women. Diane grins. "Have one in mind?"

"Not yet, I haven't really had the chance to look around yet. My new boss likes to keep me busy."

Diane grabs a pen and paper from the organized area underneath a landline. "Here. This is the number for the pound. Next time you get a day off, you should go by. There's always a good stray in need of a home."

I pocket the paper and send her a grateful smile. "I take it I can have one in the house?"

She just laughs. "Honey, if you haven't learned it of me yet, you soon will. I can't say no to a soul in need. You haven't said it yet, but you look like you could use some kindness."

Swallowing around the lump in my throat, I say, "Thank you. I appreciate it."

The bell at the front desk rings, and she rubs my arm as she moves around me. "No thanks needed, child. It was worth it to see the look on your face."

"Do you need a pet deposit or something?" I call out to her almost as an afterthought.

She waves it away. "Just bring 'em by from time to time for me to love on. That'll be enough."

AFTER WORK, I go back and forth with myself on the way to the shelter located just inside Nassau proper. I don't *need* a dog, but it makes sense to have one at home for protection. Before I moved around too much for it to be practical, but now I can afford to lay down some roots. It's a small step, but an important one.

"Afternoon!" a bright voice greets me. "How can I help you today?"

The voice belongs to a cheerful but disheveled-looking blonde woman in her late twenties who is hefting an oversized bag of dog chow onto a counter. Her dark blue shirt is covered with dog and cat hair of every imaginable color, and her tattered jeans are spattered with indistinguishable stains.

"Hey, yes actually. I'm looking to adopt a dog." A quick glance around the room tells me it's a neatly kept place, probably as clean as it can be considering the occupants. The scent of antiseptic, animals, and dirt is strong, but the place isn't dirty.

"My favorite kind of customer." She smiles at me and reaches a hand across the cluttered countertop for me to shake. "I'm Jillian."

I take her hand in mine. "Sienna, nice to meet you."

"Why don't you follow me on back, and we'll go meet your new best friend."

She pushes through a door to a room behind the counter, and we are immediately assaulted by the excited barks and yips from its inhabitants.

Jillian moves to the closest kennel and puts her fingers to the wire mesh. "Yes, hi, precious boy. I know you missed me." The large terrier mix jumps up and bathes her fingers in slobbery kisses. "Feel free to look around and meet them. If you spot one in particular you'd like to get acquainted with, just let me know. They're all fixed and house trained."

Nodding, I take another step inside and turn toward the closest kennel. Inside is a sweet-looking long-haired dachshund with warm chocolate eyes. Even though every cell inside me is screaming to drop to my knees and give it a cuddle, I have to move on. If I'm going to get a dog, I need something big enough to train and protect me. The next few kennels prove to be an excitable Chihuahua, a smash-nosed Boston Terrier, and a Pomeranian, all of which are incredibly adorable, but I keep moving.

Then my eyes fall to the last of the kennels on the row. It's inhabitant, unlike the rest of the animals, doesn't make a peep. Curious, I draw near with careful footsteps so I don't spook it. When I peer through the front of the crate, a pair of soft, honey-colored eyes meet mine, and I fall ass over teakettle in love with the mangiest, most pungent ball of fur I've ever met.

Without thought, I straighten and turn back to Jillian, who is already crossing the room to join me. "We have some others out back in the exercise kennels—"

"I want this one." I jerk my thumb back at the matted mass of brown fur.

The look on her face can only be described as abject horror. "O-oh," she stutters, "I don't know. Rocky there hasn't been fully treated. His owner beat him up pretty bad, and he was found wandering the highway just yesterday." Noting the determined look I send her, Jillian rocks back on her heels. "Since he's new, he'll still need to come back in a week or so for a checkup and to receive another round of shots and schedule an appointment to get him fixed."

As she speaks, I crouch down again and scoot closer to his cage. "Hey, there," I say in a soft voice. "Hey there, Rocky."

He whimpers and beneath the tangled mess of his fur his whole frame shakes. He shrinks against the back wall of the crate.

"Are you sure you're up for this? He's going to be a lot of work. He'll need to be supervised for a couple days at least, and he howls something terrible when he's left alone."

I nod. "I understand. I work right next to my house, and I have a very understanding employer. I'll take good care of him."

"Why don't you two get acquainted while I round up the paperwork?"

I hunker back down next to his cage as she pushes back through the door to the receptionist area. Even though there are dozens of other dogs, I only have eyes for this one. I won't know what breed he is for sure until I can give him a proper bath and probably a good cut as well, but he looks to be some sort of Lab / Shephard mix.

"Hey, Rocky," I say again, cooing at him in the gentlest voice I can muster. "Hey, boy. Do you wanna come home with me?" His ears twitch at my voice, but he doesn't move. "We'll get you a bath and some treats. I'll even let you sleep on the bed with me. I bet you're a good cuddler, huh?"

Jillian enters, her hands full of papers. "I'll just need you to fill out the adoption information and there's a thirty-dollar application fee. Since he's still looking a little rough, I can throw in a bath before you leave and a quick grooming. He's not injured as far as the vet can tell, but he is a little skittish and malnourished, so you'll need to be very patient with him."

"Thank you, I appreciate your help." I take the offered clipboard and application and settle on a nearby table to fill out the paperwork. After a year of signing my new name to things, I don't even bat a lash anymore. I fill in the bungalow address, my place of work, and the landlord information. Since I don't have any other pets, I hand the clipboard back to Jillian.

She beams at me. "Let's get you some treats and let the big guy out so you two can officially meet. Then we'll give him that bath." She heads to a line of cabinets and pulls out a handful of treats, which she then hands to me.

While she unlocks his cage, I get down to my knees so I'm on his level and hold out a hand. "Hey, Rocky," I say again, but this time he lifts his head and sniffs. "C'mon, boy, do you want a treat?"

I place a treat near the entrance to his kennel, and he inches closer. Not wanting to spook him, I slowly ease back to give him some room. With a careful, guarded look at me, he lifts onto his haunches and delicately takes the treat between his teeth.

When he is done munching, he scoots a bit forward, and I hold out another treat on my palm. His body trembles, but he takes a step out of the cage in my direction, scenting the air for the treat I hold in my open palm.

"It's okay. I'm not gonna hurt you, baby." As much as I want to inch closer, I hold the same position until Rocky takes a tentative step forward. Then another and another until his wet nose sniffs at the treat in my hand. He glances up at me, then nips the treat with a swipe of his tongue. He doesn't retreat back into his cage, so I offer him another. "Good boy, Rocky. Good boy."

"That's the closest he's gotten to another person aside from me." I grin up at Jillian and she crouches down to pet him. "Looks like you made a friend."

When I offer him another treat, he abandons all traces of restraint and launches himself at me. I bury my face in his fur, ignoring the dirt and grime because he's not the only one who needs a friend.

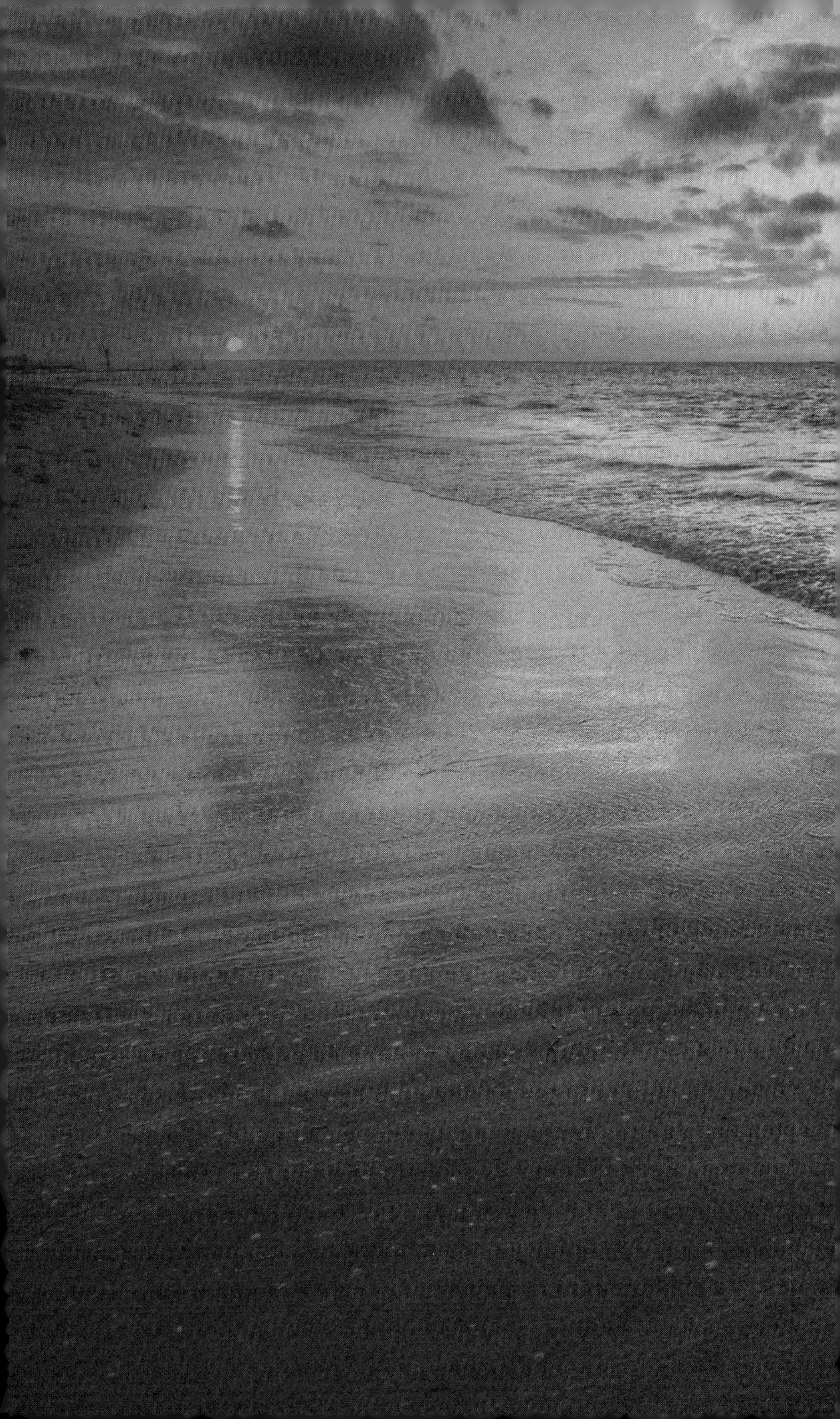

CHAPTER TEN

LOGAN

SOFIE MEETS me at the department to interview the assault victim, Elizabeth Gallagher, the next day. She'd been put through the humiliating misery of the evidence collection and documentation and now she'd have to relive the worst night of her life in front of an audience. Sometimes my job sucked, and now is admittedly one of those times, but not as much as it sucks to see the vacant expression in Ms. Gallagher's face as she walks in the station.

"Has she said anything yet?" I ask Sofie.

"She's responsive. Seems a little steadier today."

Glancing down at her, I'm struck by how small she seems. She's wearing a sweater and a pair of jeans tucked into dark boots. She may be tall for a woman, but at six-two, I still tower over her.

I look away. "I hate bringing you here."

Two uniformed officers guide Elizabeth to a secluded

conference room. She keeps her eyes on her shoes to avoid the inevitable stares the entire way.

Sofie puts a reassuring hand on my shoulder. "Don't be," she says. "The way I look at it is that I get to help people the way I wish I'd been helped."

When Sofie was younger, just a teenager, she was attacked and raped by someone she considered a friend. She never told anyone—not even her boyfriend, who happens to be her now husband, Jack. For ten years, she could barely stand to come back to Nassau, let alone confront what happened to her. When her mother died, leaving her two brothers, Donnie and Rafe orphaned, she moved back to take care of them. In doing so, she also had to face the man who brutalized her.

I kiss her hair. "You're one of the strongest people I know, you know that, right?"

She smiles up at me. A couple years ago, I would have been hard pressed to think she could be so happy when she'd always been so haunted. "Quite the compliment coming from you."

"Are you sure you won't leave Jack and run away with me?"

Laughter dances in her eyes. "You'd better be glad he's deployed or you'd have to take that up with him."

"How is he doing?"

"Happiest he's ever been, I think. You've talked to him. He missed it."

I think back to my time in the Marines as a sniper. Most of my job involved waiting, lots of it, and the rest was choosing whether or not the target on the other end of my scope was going to die on that particular day. Unlike Jack, when my second tour was up and my marriage crashed and burned, I was ready to get out. Ready for a change. Being a cop is the best thing to ever happen to me. I get to help save lives instead of taking them.

One of the officers comes out to greet us. Sofie shakes his hand and then looks to me. "Ready?"

The conference room isn't cozy, but we do what we can to make Ms. Gallagher feel comfortable. Sofie takes a seat next to her and I offer her a cup of water.

"Thank you for coming in today," I tell her as I take a seat in front of her.

She nods and the smile she sends my way is wobbly and doesn't reach her eyes.

"I'm going to keep this as to the point as possible. I know Sofie has explained the process to you. Do you have any questions?"

Ms. Gallagher nods after a quick glance at Sofie for reassurance. "N-no, thank you. She was very clear. I just want to get this over with."

"I won't take up much of your time. Why don't you start with what you were doing yesterday evening?"

She takes a sip from the paper cup and wipes her lips with trembling fingers. "Uh, it was a Tuesday, so I had an evening class—bio. I didn't get out until eight or so."

"At the community college?" At her nod, I note it down on my pad and look back up at her. I don't want to pester her with questions and I've found it best to let them retell the events in their own words. It helps with recall and allows for greater detail than a question by question interview.

"My car was parked on the other side of campus, and it's easier to cut through the park. Faster. So I was walking through the main sidewalk there when this guy comes up to me."

"Was there anyone around?"

She bites her lip, looks down at her hands. "Um, maybe? A lot of people choose to take that shortcut, so there should have been. I wasn't paying much attention. I have a Spanish exam Friday and I was studying flash cards on my phone. I should have been paying attention. It was so stupid."

Sofie places a hand on Ms. Gallagher's. "It wasn't your fault."

"He came at me from behind, surprised me. At first he—I mean, he was nice. He was cute." She buries her face in her hands. "I was *flattered*. I can't remember what he said because he hit me." Her fingers probe the bandaged area on her head. "Then I was in the woods and I couldn't see anyone."

I make another note to contact her class and others who may have been walking on the same trail. She may not have seen them, but there could have been a witness.

As I write, she continues, "I know I should have fought, should have called out for help, but I was just so scared."

"I know this is hard, but every detail may help catch the man who did this to you."

She nods and wipes her eyes. "The more scared I got, the more he . . . liked it. Jesus." Sofie makes a sound of encouragement. "There was a sound, there must have been something that spooked him because he turned back like he heard something. I didn't even think about it, I just pushed him and he lost his balance. I got away. I just ran. I could barely see, couldn't even recognize where I was."

"I know it's not easy to remember these things, but do you remember if you hit him? Scratched him, maybe?"

While she thinks, she digs her knuckles into her eyes. "I don't, I don't know. Maybe?"

"You're doing just fine," Sofie says next to her.

"Were you able to get a good look at him? Was there anything about him that was familiar?" Most victims know their attacker. In a high number of date rape and sexual assault cases, the offender is someone they knew. Like in Sofie's case. The thought makes me gnash my teeth, but I focus on Ms. Gallagher's response.

She shakes her head. "It was dark, but he didn't have his face covered. I'm sorry, I didn't recognize him, though. I just remember that he was attractive, like I said."

"Would you be up for sitting with one of our sketch artists?"

A shrug, then a sigh. "Sure. I don't know how much help I'll be, but I'll try."

I hand her my card. "If there's anything else you remember, anything at all, or if you feel like you're in danger, please don't hesitate to give me a call."

"Thank you, Detective Blackwell." She stands and rounds the table, coming to a stop in front of me. "Thank you," she says again. For a second it looks as if she wants to give me a hug, but then she turns and leaves.

"Doesn't get any easier," Sofie says, once the door closes behind her.

I glance back at my notes, the file with the crime scene information. If she hadn't gotten away, I can't even imagine what would have happened to her. Even though she got away, I know the man who did this to her is still out there.

"No, it doesn't."

I see Sofie safely out to her car. "Give the boys a hug for me," I tell her.

"I will." She pauses before she gets in. "You take it easy, okay?"

"I'll do my best."

She smiles and waves as she drives off.

As I'm walking back to the station for paperwork, a man loitering by the entrance catches my eye. At first, I don't recall why he looks familiar, then I remember him from Sienna's porch. He was the one she was having the heated conversation with.

Frowning, I come to a stop beside him. If I didn't recognize him from that day, I wouldn't have paid him any mind. He's around thirty with a budding paunch and thinning hair. The kind of man who's gone to pot. Up close his suit is faded and worn and the easy charm I thought he had comes across more like desperation.

"Something I can help you with?" I ask, looping my thumbs in my belt.

"My name is Phil Exeter. I'm a journalist out of Miami. I'd like to talk to you about a person you may be involved with, a Sienna Davenport."

My eyes narrow. It's been a long night and I don't want to deal with him right now. The mention of Sienna, though, keeps me from walking away. "What about her?"

"I'd love to talk to you sometime. I have information I think you'd find valuable about your new neighbor."

"What do you want with Sienna?" I ask bluntly.

"Professional interest. Like I said, I'm a reporter."

"Pleasure meeting you, Mr. Exeter, but I have nothing to say to you." When I start to leave he quickens his pace to match mine and grabs my arm. I give him a look that stops him in his tracks.

"Tread carefully, there," I say.

He holds up his hands. "No offense meant. Here," he says

and dips into his pocket, coming out with a business card. "Why don't you call me if you have any questions. I'll be in the area for a few days if anything comes up."

"If anything comes up?"

"When you're ready to talk, call that number," is all he says before smiling thinly and then walking off.

I look at his card again, then toss it in the trash.

Hours later, I stagger to my truck, my feet dragging and my brain a throbbing mass of images I can't seem to forget. I toss the folder with the Gallagher case information onto the passenger seat and chug a can of soda I got from the vending machine. Then, without looking back at the station, I start my truck and back out of the parking lot.

I should go straight home, take a shower, eat some real food, and park myself in front of the television for a couple hours. I should get a good night's sleep so I'll be ready for a long day of interviewing the college students I managed to track down who were in the park around the same time Elizabeth was.

I know if I go home to that empty house, the only thing I'll think about is turning right back around and heading to the first open liquor store. For a while, I just drive aimlessly, but before long, I end up pulling into my driveway, my focus turning to my neighbor's house.

Tonight, she has the front window open, which is different, but all the lights are on again. What is it with that woman and turning every light in the joint on?

I tell myself to just go inside my own damn house, but a sound from inside distracts me.

I slip from the cab of my truck and shut the door quietly.

Making sure not to walk on the gravel, I make my way to her front porch.

"What am I going to do with you?" she's saying. "Look at this mess! First you jump all over me and then you get me all wet. No, don't kiss me anymore!"

My brows damn near into my hairline, I bang on the screen door. "Sienna?"

She doesn't answer me, but I hear her say, "You stay right here or I'm not going to give you a surprise later."

Anger, irritation, and plain male stupidity burns away every trace of exhaustion. Now I know I don't have any claim to this woman, but I'd be lying if I said I hadn't entertained the idea of seeing if she tastes as good as she looks. The thought of her with another man plain makes me want to hit something—or someone. When she appears in the hallway with her hair askew and clothes rumpled as if she just threw them on, I scowl at her.

The angry look stops her in her tracks a few steps away from the door. She frowns, those lips I'd been daydreaming about only make me even more irritated. "What did I do now?"

"Well, for one thing you can tell me why a reporter was looking for you at the station today."

Her brows furrow. "A report—shit!"

"A Mr. Phil Exeter?"

"You didn't talk to him did you?" she eyes me warily.

"I told him I didn't want to hear anything he has to say and I had no comment."

The tension leaves her shoulders and only incites my curiosity. "Wanna tell me what that's all about?"

She sighs. "Not really."

"Gonna have to open up to me one day, Sienna."

"Not today, okay?"

Before I can answer, a brown, furry mass darts down the hall and heads straight for Sienna. "What is—"

She shrieks, throwing up her hands to block the wet dog barreling at her. "Rocky! You were supposed to wait in the bathroom so I could dry you off, silly boy."

Struck dumb, I can only stare as she crouches down to run her hands over the dog's soaking wet fur. "You have a dog?"

She glances up at me, one hand still stroking over him. "I do now. I adopted him from the shelter today."

"I'm an idiot."

"Most men are," she says offhandedly. "Did your aunt need something?"

"No, she uh—" I pull my gaze away from the dog and catch her curious look. "I wasn't going to come here," I say, still standing on the other side of the screen.

"Then why did you?"

I rub a hand over my closely cropped hair and then over my neck and roll my shoulders impatiently. "I wanted to see you."

She opens her mouth. Closes it. Shakes her head with a confused laugh. "You wanted to see me? Why?"

I take a step closer. "Do I have to stand on the porch talking through the door? This is becoming a bad habit of yours."

"What?"

"Keeping me out."

She takes a step back. I wonder if it is intentional or instinctual. All I know is that it makes me want to follow. "It's the smart thing to do," she says, and she's probably right.

I pull the screen open then remember the locks and wait

for her to undo them. When she does, I take a step forward. "Let me in, Sienna."

"Logan, I—"

"I'm not here to get in your pants." I grin at her when her mouth presses into a thin line, the color drains from her face, and I swear I see the walls around her fly back into place. Something about what I just said has her closing off again, and I don't like it. "Well, that's not true, but not tonight." I try to back pedal, but she just closes into herself a bit more. I'm screwing this all up, so I switch my approach. "I just need to get out of my own head for a while. Will you help me do that?"

She hesitates for a second, arguing with herself. While she thinks it over, I hunker down to offer the dog a hand to sniff. He does so hesitantly, unsure of me. "What's his name?"

"Rocky," she says.

"That's a good name for such a manly guy, huh?" I stay down until he licks my hand, ignoring the scent of wet dog. "He looks like he could use something to eat."

"He was abandoned. They gave him a bath at the shelter, but when I got him home, we decided to do another just in case. He is in pretty bad shape."

"I've always wanted a dog." I give him a gentle rub, which is all he allows, and then stand.

"What kept you from getting one?"

I shrug. "I joined the Marines right after high school. Moved around too much and wasn't home enough to keep one. Then after I got married, my wife never wanted one."

She blinks at me. "You are married."

"Was. Young and stupid," is all I say. "We got divorced after I left the Marines. She didn't believe fidelity applied when I was overseas."

She studies me for a few long seconds, her blue eyes thoughtful as Rocky butts up against her legs. "I have some leftover casserole. Are you hungry?"

"I could eat, but only if it's not out of pity."

Her lips pull into a reluctant smile, and I know I'll be finding more excuses to come to her house after work in the coming days.

"Pity you?" she teases. "Never."

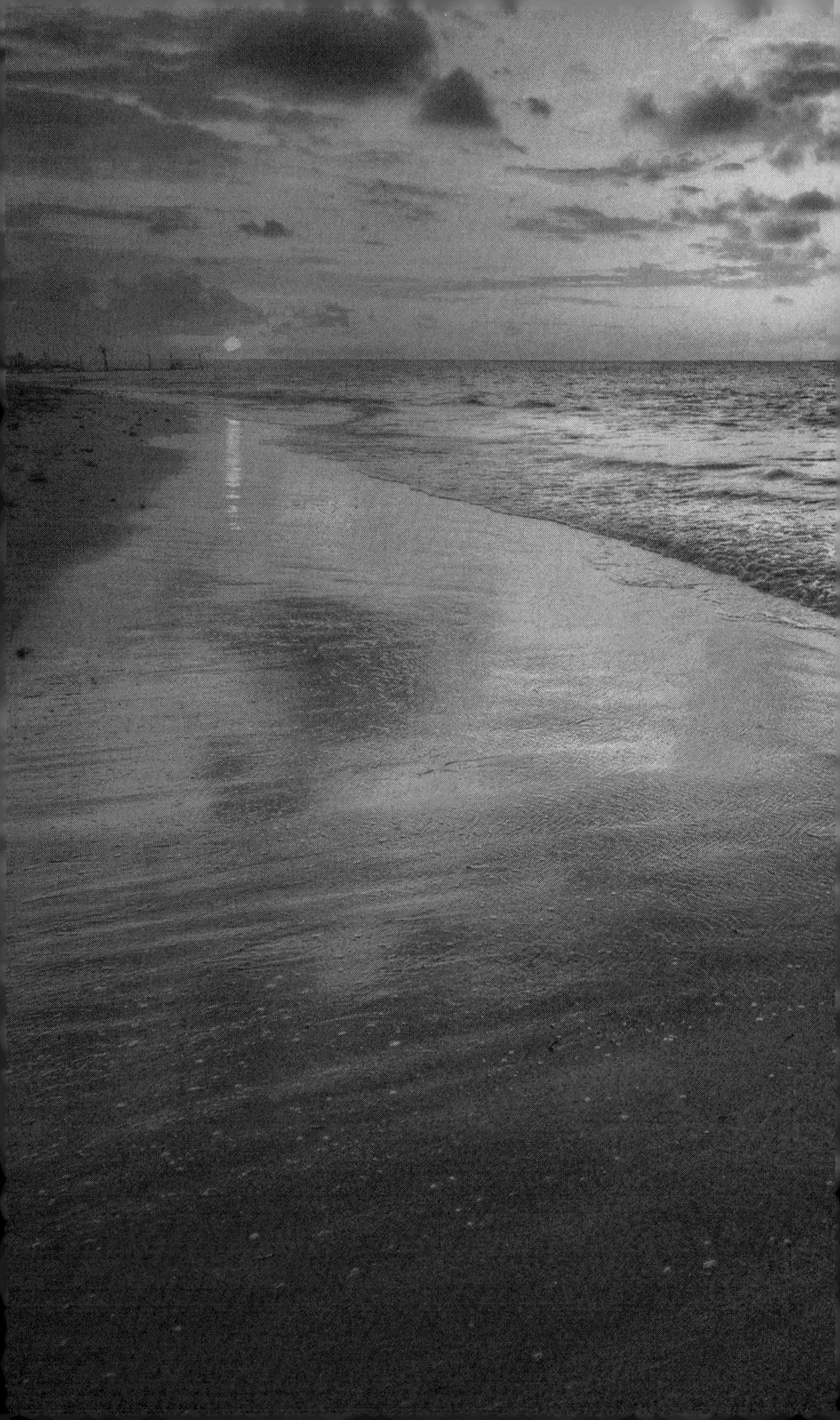

CHAPTER ELEVEN

SIENNA

I OPEN THE FRIDGE, grab the dish, and glance back over my shoulder to find his eyes on me. "You want a beer?"

"What?" He refocuses on my face. "Oh, sure."

My expression makes him grin, changing his whole brooding, devilish face into a younger, more boyish version. "I'm not going to jump you, Sienna."

I glance down at the bottle in my hand. "I, uh . . ."

He laughs. "Relax. I won't bite."

Shaking my head, I hand him the beer. "You're crazy, you know that?"

He just smiles.

The kitchen is only big enough for a small table and two chairs and with Logan's huge form standing in the middle, it seems even smaller. He takes a place at the table and makes an appreciative noise when I set a beer in front of him.

"Thanks. You know, you've only been here a couple weeks and already this place feels more homey than mine."

I pull dishes from the cabinets and set them on the counter. Glancing back over my shoulder, I say, "Why's that?"

"Probably because I've never unpacked."

"How long have you lived there?"

"Three years," he says, and even though I can't see him, I hear the smile in his voice.

I sputter, laughter bubbling in my throat. "Three years and you haven't unpacked?"

"I figure boxes are practically ready-made storage."

Rocky bumps his head into my legs when he scents the casserole I'm spooning onto the plates, and I idly pat his head with my free hand. "I bet it drives Diane crazy."

He smiles behind the beer. "Oh, yeah. She hates it, but she refuses to unpack it for me, too."

The microwave beeps, and I pull out the first plate. "Good for her. She shouldn't be doing those things for you. You're a grown man."

When I set the plate of food in front of him he grins. When he reaches out and wraps his long fingers around my wrist, I freeze. "What?" I ask.

"Got you to make me dinner, didn't I?"

I pause and then my eyes widen. "You little sneak! So that's the real reason why you came here. You're worse than the dog." Rocky, who's been begging for food since I opened the casserole dish perks up. I roll my eyes at the pair of them.

With my own plate in hand, I sit across from Logan. Rocky settles in between our feet under the table. It's . . . cozy, which is funny because Logan and cozy don't seem like they'd correlate, but I forgot how nice it is to just hang out with another person. I take a fortifying sip of my own drink. "Why'd you need to get out of your own head?" I ask.

He glances up at me and chews his bite of food slowly before swallowing. "I'm sure you've probably figured it out."

"Rough call from last night?"

"You can say that."

"I'm not sure it's worth much, but I'm sorry."

"You're feeding me, so at least something decent came of it."

I wave it away. "I'm just being neighborly."

"For someone who habitually carries a gun, you're being very hospitable."

Shrugging, I take a bite of casserole. "Turning over a new leaf."

He studies me. "Is that what you're doing here? Turning over a new leaf?"

"Trying to."

"I'm not going to ask, but I'm here if you need to talk about it."

I look down at my plate, afraid his finely tuned senses can read my eyes. "Thanks. Same goes, apparently."

"Make sure to tell Aunt Diane about this conversation. She thinks I interrogate you every chance I get."

I surprise us both by laughing. "I'll do that."

"What made you come to Nassau?" he asks.

"My friend Chloe. I used to own a travel agency out of Jacksonville."

"Used to?" His eyes are intense and assessing. I remind myself to be careful with details. It's easy to let down my guard around him, to forget he's also a cop.

I lift my shoulders in what I hope is a casual gesture. "She's managing owner now. I was ready for a change."

"So you're from around Jacksonville?" He shifts, and I spot

an arm going under the table and the happy slurps from Rocky. Logan looks back at my incredulous expression. "What?"

"Are you trying to teach him bad habits?"

He grins. "Are you trying to avoid the question?"

"Don't feed him from the table. He'll learn to beg whenever I'm eating if you keep it up."

"I'm going with my gut, and I'm gonna say if you're not originally from Jacksonville, you're at least from Florida. Am I right?"

To cover my surprise, I take another bite of casserole. Another drink. He sees far too much. "Your aunt was right to think you interrogate me."

"Not an interrogation." The implied "yet" doesn't need to be spoken. "Just neighborly conversation."

"Originally Alabama, but I've lived in Florida, yes." There, close enough to the truth. Not specific enough to point to my real identity.

"There? That wasn't so hard, was it?"

"Why do you care so much?"

"Natural curiosity."

"Is that why you became a cop?"

"Partially."

I raise my brow when he doesn't elaborate. "Now who's dodging questions?"

"Touché."

Plates cleared, he stands and takes them to the sink and surprises me by washing them instead of leaving them for me. I let Rocky out back, where I've staked off an electronic fence to keep him from wandering. Then, out of sheer habit, I leave Logan in the kitchen while I check the locks on the doors and double check that the windows are secure. When I return, I find him watching me with his patient gaze as he sips from another beer.

"Making yourself at home?" I tease.

"Afraid of something?" he counters, and my smile falls.

He sets his empty bottle on the table and crosses the room to where I'm standing. Everything inside me goes on alert. With a man like Logan, I would have to be dead not to respond. For a long time, I thought I was, but as he grows closer my whole body comes back to life.

"What are you doing?" I ask. The words are barely discernible over the loud rush of my breathing.

I don't realize I have been moving backward until my back touches the wall. I bring my hands up automatically, and they come in contact with the expanse of his chest. My eyes dart to his face, which is surprisingly close to mine. Then, I stop breathing altogether.

"Don't be afraid of me."

Then he draws me close. The move is so smooth, I go with him. His lips are so soft and so unexpected, I sigh into them. He doesn't move other than to rub his lips against mine, nipping at them with a gentle bite of his teeth. When his tongue presses forward and caresses my own, I snap out of my stupor and pull back.

I press a trembling hand to my lips. "I can't." Furious at the tremble in my voice, I slide out between him and the wall, desperate for cool air to clear my thoughts and take away the heat licking at my insides.

He takes a step to the side and blocks my departure. "Seems like you just did."

Shaking my head, I say, "No, you don't understand."

When I try to move around him again, he sidesteps. "I'm a pretty intelligent man, Sienna. Why don't you try to explain it to me?"

Blindly, I run a hand through my hair, tugging at the ends and hoping to regain some common sense. I grasp for the first explanation I come across. "You don't even know me."

"I know enough." He moves closer, and it's as if he sucks all the air from the room. "I'll get to know more."

"No you don't." I gasp for air. "You won't."

One hand comes to rest on my hip, searing through the material of my jeans. For one white-hot second, I imagine those hands on my skin without a barrier, and my heart leaps inside my chest. When I refocus on his words, I wish I hadn't. "I know you've got secrets. A past. I know you tremble when I touch you. That you sighed just a little when I kissed you. I know you like to garden, love my family, and, despite your initial skittishness, you're kind to everyone."

"We've barely met." Even to my ears, my voice sounds desperate.

"What? Are you fishing for compliments? Do you want me to tell you that you're the most beautiful woman I've ever met? That I dream about you and the way you looked at me the first night I saw you? About getting between your thighs and hearing those sighs in my ear as you're holding on to me? Do you want me to tell you how much I want to know what makes you look so sad sometimes?"

I close my eyes, trying to block out his words. "I don't want you to say any of those things. I don't want you to feel any of those things."

"You can't control me any more than you can control the world around you—no matter how hard you try."

"I'm not ready for this. It's too fast." I look away from him, but he takes my chin gently between his thumb and forefinger and turns my attention back to him. I want to tell him to stop, but the words won't come, and he presses a soft kiss to my lips.

"Fair enough, for now. We won't get into it all until you're ready." He moves away, and I resist the temptation to follow after him. The cool air swirling between us clears my mind somewhat. He takes another step toward the door and then grins at me, breaking some of the tension. "We'll save it for the second date."

He's halfway out the door when I realize what he said. "This wasn't a first date!" I call out after him and he turns back to me, his hand still on the doorknob.

"Are we going to argue over semantics? There was a dinner if I recall correctly. Conversation. I even kissed you good night, though you can get credit for walking me to the door."

I grasp blindly for an excuse. "Logan, just a few days ago, you thought I was trying to pull one over on your family."

This finally gets him to come back, but now all the playfulness has been replaced with a serious expression. "Pretty sure I was just being stubborn."

"Stubborn isn't really how I would describe it."

He shrugs. "It's not every day a man meets a woman who stops time just by walking into the room." With a tug of my hand, he pulls me closer. "That's what you do for me, Sienna. You stop time."

He kisses me again, and this time, I don't push him away.

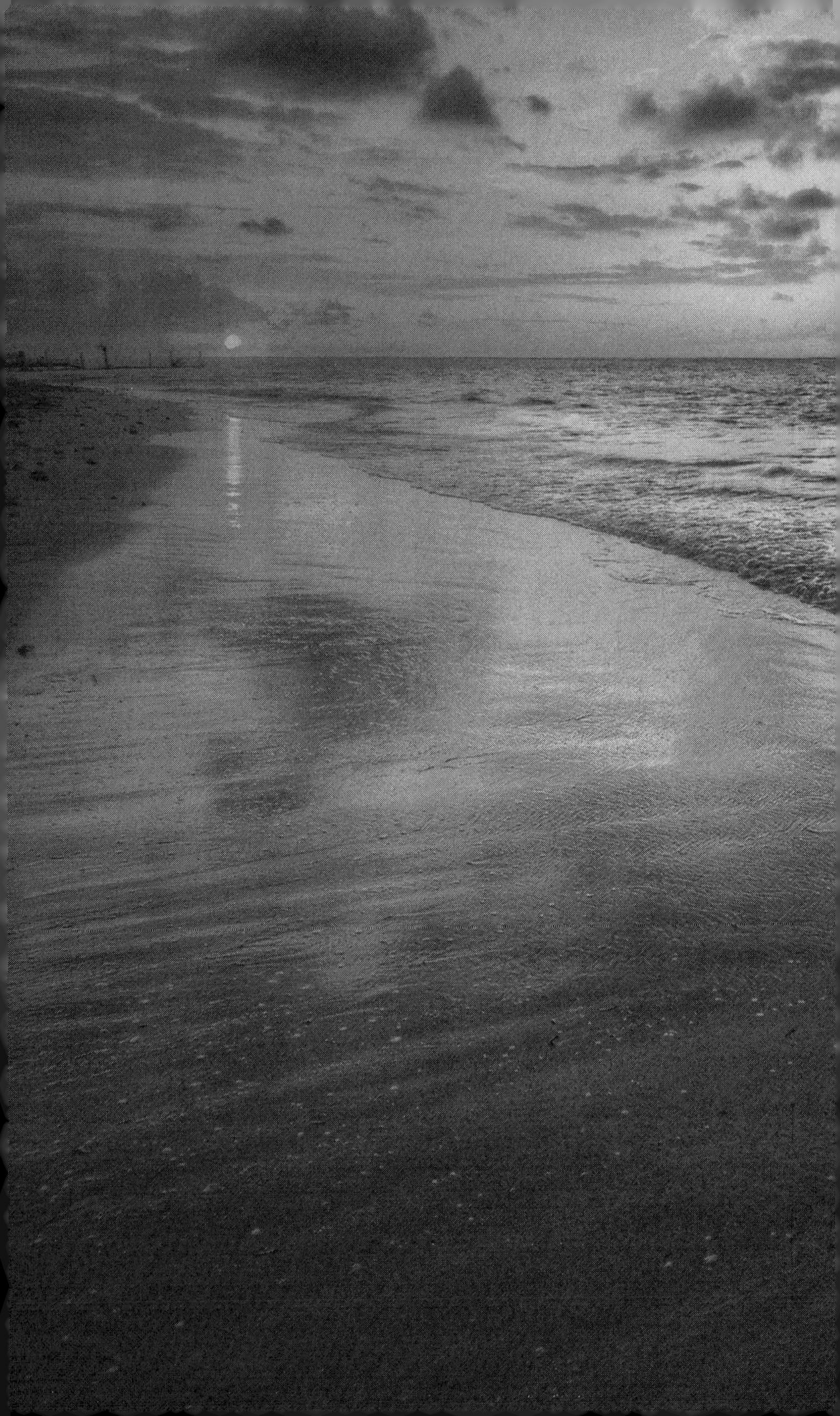

CHAPTER TWELVE

LOGAN

FOR THE NEXT FEW WEEKS, I give her time—not only to think about us, but because I'm so swamped with the Elizabeth Gallagher case I don't have time to pay her attention properly. Besides, with a woman like Sienna, I shouldn't pursue it until I can go all in. I still make sure to stop by the B&B more regularly, grab a cup of coffee, fluster her a little bit, get her used to seeing me.

She's not always pleased to see me, which only tells me I'm making progress.

On one such morning after a long night, I tromp up the mud-splattered walkway to the back entrance of the B&B, but Sienna's already waiting by the back door with a fierce scowl. The sight of it just makes me smile.

"What are you doing here?" she hisses.

"Why? Aren't you happy to see me?"

She tugs my arm and pulls me into the hall and pushes me inside a walk-in-sized pantry, then slams the door behind us.

"What? Are you stalking me now?" She glances over her shoulder and keeps her voice low, probably worried someone may overhear us.

There isn't much room to maneuver in the small space, but I think I can make it work for me. "Is that what you think?" I ask, my voice is equally low to match hers.

Her scowl deepens, and I take a second to think about tracing the lines of her lips with my tongue. She snaps her fingers in front of my face. "One kiss doesn't mean you can harass me at work, Logan."

I turn, using my grip on her arms to pull her into me as I lean against the shelves. They dig into my back, but I'm much more interested in how she feels when she loses balance and falls against me. She blows her hair out of her face, and I grin. "This isn't me harassing you, but I can if you're into that. My aunt owns the place. We live next to each other. You're gonna have to get used to seeing me."

She rolls her eyes and tries to wiggle out of my grip, but it's only a halfhearted attempt. "You can't keep coming to see me at work like this."

"Oh, I can't?" I twine my arms around her and dip my head so the next words are muttered against her lips. "I think you like it."

A surge of triumph crashes through me when she sighs and her hands twist around my neck. I'm sure she will deny it later, but she is the one who closes the tiny distance between our mouths.

In our urgency, we knock over a tower of cans, and they tumble to the floor with dull thuds. Sienna pulls back, cheeks flushed and eyes wide. "Do you think they heard us?" she whispers.

We listen for a few tense seconds. When it appears they haven't, I tug her back to me. "Go out with me."

Her dazed eyes blink up at me. "What?"

"Go out with me. Date two, remember?"

I kiss the resulting frown off her face.

"I don't know." Despite her protests, her head tilts to the side, giving me access to her neck. I would have to be completely dense to pass up the offer. Since I'm not, I drop my lips to her soft skin and suck and bite until her nails are digging into my arm.

"We won't call it a date. You have to eat, right?"

"Hmm?" I take her earlobe into my mouth, and she shivers against me. When she can breathe again she adds, "Oh yeah, mhmm."

"Then let me take you to dinner."

She swallows thickly, and I twist so she's pinned between me and the wall. Her eyes are overbought and half-closed. "I have to stay late tonight. Your Grandma has a late doctor's appointment so I'll be closing up and finishing dinner here so Diane can take her."

My groan is muffled against her throat. "What about after?"

"After?"

I chuckle, but even to my own ears, it sounds thin and desperate. "Yes, after dinner. After work."

"We've been over this," she says as her hands fist in my shirt. "I can't."

This time, my laugh is dark. "Oh, I think you can," I say, kissing her again.

She sinks into me, into the kiss, and I can't remember ever enjoying the taste of a woman so much. I'm not even sure she realizes how much she gives herself over. Based on how much she's been holding back, how much she's been hiding, having her give in is a reward a man like me doesn't deserve. But I take it, and I demand more. Her mouth is my new battle ground, and I use every weapon in my arsenal to make her surrender.

When I pull back, she's limp in my arms. "So," I say between breaths, "I'll pick you up after your shift?"

"What?"

"I'm gonna pick you up after work. We'll take Rocky to the park and let him run around."

"He'd like the park."

"What time do you get off?"

There's a soft knock, which startles us into silence, and then Aunt Diane says through the door, "Sienna, when you're done, can you fetch me a couple cans of peaches? I think we'll have cobbler for dessert later."

Sienna stuffs her face into my chest, her shoulders shaking under my hands. When she can control herself, she says, "Yes, ma'am." She pauses and shoots me a worried glance. "Do you think she knows what we're doing in here?"

Before I can answer there's a polite cough. "Logan, when you're done badgering her, there's food out here for you if you're hungry."

Sienna looks up at me wide-eyed and flushed. *Oh my God* she mouths in shock. She starts to pull away, but I keep her in place with one arm. When I open my mouth, she slaps a hand over my lips and frantically shakes her head.

I kiss her hand and then pull it away. "Yes, ma'am," I say to Aunt Diane, who chuckles as she shuffles back down the hall.

"Kill me now," Sienna says into my chest.

"I'd rather not."

"What is your aunt going to think of me now?"

I tuck a piece of hair behind her ear and tip her chin up with a finger. "She's gonna think you have great taste."

Sienna growls in the back of her throat and pushes away. "You're going to go now so I can make sure I still have a job." She scans the rows of canned goods and selects a couple of canned peaches. "You have to stop dropping by while I'm at work."

While her hands are occupied, I take advantage and kiss her again, causing her to suck in a surprised breath. "I like starting my day off with seeing you."

She shakes her head. "You're impossible." Despite her words she steps up to me and kisses me. It's the first she's ever initiated.

Inside I'm crowing because I know I've won this round, but I don't let it show. Don't want to spook her off. "I'll pick you up around six? It doesn't get dark till about eight."

She opens the door and looks back. "You aren't going to stop until I give in, are you?"

"Now you're learning." I follow her out into the hall and wave at Aunt Diane and Grandma Rose who are sitting at the kitchen counter with smiles the size of the Mississippi on their faces. "I'll see you at six."

"Yeah, yeah," she says as she walks away.

"Don't think you can run," I say to her back.

She waves a hand over her head.

As I leave, I hear Aunt Diane say, "He's right, you know. If you run, it'll just make him chase you."

"THIS IS A MOMENTOUS OCCASION," Jack says from the phone attached to the dashboard as we video chat.

Because I'm an adult, I ignore him. Ben, who is in the passenger seat beside me, does not. "The last of the single men. We should light a candle or some shit. Throw a party. Something."

I pull out of the gym parking lot and resist the urge to lay out both of my best friends. "I'm going to lock the both of you up."

Jack snorts. "I'm way the fuck in the desert. If you can find me, you're welcome to lock me up."

"Don't tempt me," I mutter darkly.

Chloe's cousin Ben laughs and punches my shoulder. You'd think after our time in boot camp after the three of us joined the Marines and countless sparring sessions would have made me immune to his right hook, but nearly a decade later and he still packs a helluva punch. "We all went through it, man."

"Yeah," comes Jack's warbled voice from the video chat. The picture fades in and out, but all of us are well used to the shoddy connection. "'Bout fuckin' time you met a nice girl. You deserve it after all you've been through."

"So who is she? My cousin Chloe's been pretty tight-lipped about her," Ben adds.

"Since when did you become such a chick?" I ask Ben, who angles his head toward me, reminding me to be sensitive to his single-sided deafness. During his last deployment a couple years ago, some of the men in his unit had been hit by rockets. When he went to help provide cover, concussive grenades killed nearly everyone. Ben managed to haul the only survivor, a man named Scott Green, out of the wreckage, nearly killing himself in the process. Green lost a leg and Ben lost his hearing in one ear, but they both lost what they used to love the most—being a Marine.

Ben just laughs and I know his family—his wife Livvie and their son Cole—help him cope with the life he lost in the explosion. "Sue me," he says. "After the last woman you were with, I'm a little overprotective."

"It's his overdeveloped father instinct," Jack chimes in. "Ever since he became a dad, he can't help it."

Ben flips Jack off, who laughs and I sigh. "She's a little gun shy right now, so I don't need the two of you fuckwads ganging up on her."

"Hey!" Jack protests. "What can I do? I'm thousands of miles away."

I shoot him a look. "Wait until you go on leave. What is it? A couple weeks."

Jack mimes zipping his lips. "As if I'd tell you. I want some alone time with my own wife before I get an ass kicking."

"She in some kind of trouble?" Ben asks, ignoring the two of us.

"Uh-oh," Jack says. "Here we go."

Rolling my shoulders, I change lanes to head to Ben's house. "I'm working on it."

"It's like he doesn't even know what he's walking into." Jack cackles into the phone while looking at Ben.

I scowl at him. "It's a good thing you're deployed."

"I miss you, too, asshole."

I glance back at Jack and find his expression has turned serious. "Something wrong?"

"No, I'm just worried about Sofie. Worried she may be pushing herself too hard."

"What do you mean?" Ben asks.

"I can tell when she has a case is all. She gets tense."

Both of their eyes turn to me. Calling our police department small is an understatement. There aren't many other cops aside from me, so even if I weren't working on the case, I'd know about it.

"She holds her own," I tell Jack.

"I know she does. She has to in order to put up with the idiots," he says, referring with male fondness to the two younger brothers they adopted after Sofie's mom passed. "But I just want you to keep an eye on her. Make sure it doesn't open old wounds."

"You don't even have to ask, man."

"Thanks. I never would have re-upped if I didn't think they'd be in good hands when I deployed."

"She's stronger than you think she is. I think it helps her to be there for other women going through the same thing."

"Livvie's the same way. She says it helps her process. Sofie gave her the idea."

My head jerks as I break at a stoplight. "What?"

"She is?" Jack asks.

Ben shrugs. "She volunteers with an advocacy group for families with children who have heart conditions. Not necessarily HLHS like Cole, but similar birth defects."

I remember when Ben came home from the deployment. A broken man, to be truthful, but learning he'd fathered a child with Livvie—Jack's sister and the one woman he always wanted—was the turning point that brought back the man I've always known.

"When the hell did she start doing that?" Jack demands. "She's my sister. How do I not know about this."

"Since Cole's heart transplant. It was a rocky time for her and when we thought it was going to fail, she needed an outlet to take her mind off the stress. When he got better, she kept at it." He lifts a shoulder. "She's happier now, so I don't get on her shit about it."

"It's not too much for her?" Jack asks, the consummate big brother, even continents away.

"Nah, and you know Sofie's got a lioness packed inside that little body. If she were in over her head, she'd let you know."

Jack snorts, and he and Ben share a commiserating glance. Then Jack says to me, "Just wait, your time is coming. If you play your cards right, you'll finally have a woman to worry about."

"I was under the impression you hated all the women I brought around."

Jack groans, and Ben says, "Tag chasers. You brought tag chasers home. Even before you got with your ex, the women you brought around were only in it to bang a man in uniform."

I grin. "You say that like it's a bad thing."

"Well, look who you married."

My grin fades. "Not cool."

Ben holds his hands up. "I'm just sayin'. It's about time you found someone real."

"You two are worse than your wives," I say.

"Just wait until they find out you're dating someone."

Ben laughs, and I consider banging my head against the steering wheel.

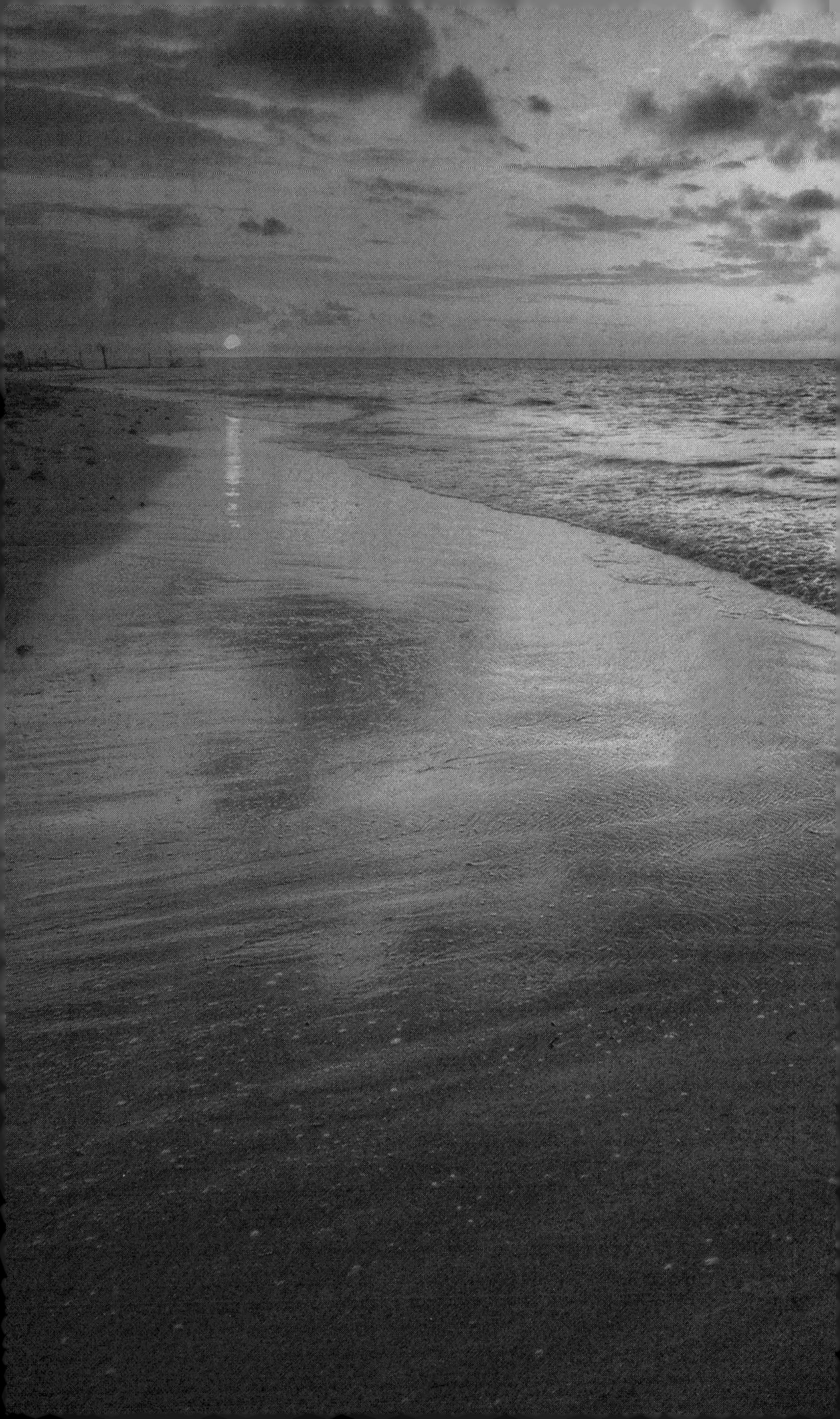

CHAPTER THIRTEEN

SIENNA

"THIS IS JUST BEAUTIFUL," Lena, a newcomer at the B&B, comments that evening as she sits down at the table where the dinner I've spent the last hour arranging awaits the guests.

"I can't take all the credit," I tell her. "Diane is absolute magic in the kitchen."

In the time since I started working at the travel agency, I've learned vacationers become a sort of temporary family. There is a small, but intense, connection, almost a fantasy, that forms.

It has to do with memories, I've concluded. People go on vacation to make memories, so they're choosing to include you in them. There's something beautiful about it, especially to me, since so many of my recent memories are too bleak to recall. It's much more fun to run away from my real life and make all new ones.

"I'm a baker, and I can assure you, presentation is half the battle." Lena closes her eyes and draws a deep breath. "Smells amazing."

"I've sampled some, it tastes better than it looks—or smells." We share a smile as I arrange a rolling service cart with the beverages.

"Are you from around here?" Lena asks.

Without a pause, I say, "Alabama and South Florida, yes, but I've moved around quite a bit."

Lena groans. "I'm so jealous. I wish I had the time to travel. I bet you've seen a ton of amazing places." She leans forward on her elbows, her dark blonde hair tumbling over her shoulders.

I think back to those horrible months spent on the road, running blindly from city to city. I hedge the question with a vague, "Oh, tons," and hope she swallows down the lie.

"I'm so jealous. I've always wanted to get in a car and see everything. Just start on one side of the country and pick a direction. See what I'll see and all that."

"Why didn't you?" I ask, moving the conversation further away from myself.

She sips the wine I put in front of her and gestures with her free hand. "Oh, you know. I had college first—my parents wouldn't let me start the bakery without a degree in business."

I think of my own parents and wince. They were so excited when I got into college. We haven't spoken much since I dropped out.

Lena doesn't notice my expression. "Then after that, I went to train with the most successful baker in the country."

"I bet it was exciting."

She laughs, sips again, then snorts and starts coughing, which makes me laugh, too. "It was *horrible*."

I stop arranging the spoons and forks and shoot her a horrified glance. "Horrible?"

Nodding emphatically, she explains, "He was French and he was a bonafide *tyrant*."

"Sounds delightful."

"Nightmare," she insists. "Night-freaking-mare. I worked for him for two terrible years after I graduated. My blood, sweat, and tears went to perfecting the perfect ganache, the most delicious crème brûlée. And he never gave praise. There was always something I could have done better."

"Probably makes you the best damn baker, though."

She grins and points at me. "You're right about that. He may have made me want to kill myself at the end of every shift, but after my internship there, I went on to have the most successful bakery in the tri-state area."

"No wonder you never traveled. So, what brings you to Florida? More work?"

Her smile goes electric. "Actually, I'm scoping out honeymoon spots." She holds up her hand and flashes a ring the size of a small mountain.

"Holy Moses!" I scoot around the table for a better look. "Look at that!"

"Well, when he wasn't shouting at me, he was the hottest man I'd ever met."

My mind blanks for a second. "Don't tell me you're marrying him?"

"*Oui*," she says with a huge smile. "Next fall."

"Congratulations!"

"Thank you." She picks up an empty glass and fills it with wine before handing it to me. "Let's toast to me."

We clink glasses, and I say, "To the first of many wonderful vacations with the sexy French chef."

She raises her glass to sip but gasps, "Wait! What about you? I'm no bridezilla. What are we toasting for you?"

I think about it for a second and then blush. "Well, I did just meet someone and I don't know if it's serious, but I feel like it could be, if I let myself."

"Take it from me, the quintessential single girl: do it. It's the scariest, most death defying leap you'll ever take, but when it's the right person, anything is worth the risk." She raises her glass and I do the same. "To my sexy chef and to your..."

"Sexy Southern cop," I supply.

Her giggles are infectious. "That's what I'm talking about. To them and to us."

I clink glasses. "To us."

AFTER THE LAST guest has eaten, including the bubbly and very tipsy Lena, I clean up and take the short walk back to the bungalow. Rocky trots happily by my side, only deviating from the path to investigate a bush or to dart ahead and then come back to my side.

I finally broke down a few days ago and got a car to take me back and forth to town. Unlike most of the large cities I've lived in in the past few months, Nassau doesn't feature a large transportation system and I couldn't keep relying on Diane's generosity every time I needed to go into town for groceries or to run an errand.

It isn't anything special, just a six-year-old sedan that was in desperate need of another coat of paint, but it will get me to and from town. Like Rocky and the garden, though, it's another way for me to lay down roots.

Logan leans against it, smiling at me as I near the house. The sight of him almost stops me in my tracks, if nothing else, it slows my pace considerably.

He exchanged his police uniform for a pair of jogging pants and a T-shirt, but he could be dressed in rags and somehow make them look sexy. The pants hug his muscular thighs and the T-shirt accentuates his defined chest. I'm not going to lie. It's been a long time since I've been with a man. A long time since I've felt the kind of heat he stirs to life. After Gavin, I simply couldn't find it in me to trust anyone.

When I get close enough, he tugs my hand and pulls me to him. "Hey," he says, after kissing me senseless. He leans closer, and I feel his breath on my neck. "You smell amazing."

"I smell like I've been working all day." I pull away because the eager feeling in my belly is screaming at me to drag him inside and do some investigation of my own.

His eyes glint like he can see the truth behind my evasion, and it makes me want to frown at him. "Ready to go?" he asks.

"Let me just water the garden and grab his leash."

He follows me across the yard and up the stairs. "How was work?"

I glance back at him as I unlock the door. "It was alright. You?" I wonder if it sounds as awkward aloud as it does in my head. "How's the case going?"

"It's going. Haven't had much luck interviewing potential witnesses. Until we get another lead, there isn't much I can do, unfortunately."

I make a noncommittal humming sound as I turn on the water

to the hose and start spraying. I keep my face averted so he can't read my expression. The fact is, I know just how frustrating the waiting can be—except from the other end of the scenario. I know what it's like to wait and wait as the police valiantly try to dig up clues.

"You'll find the guy," I say, and I hope it doesn't sound as hollow to him as it does to my own ears.

"I'll grab Rocky, and we'll wait for you in the truck," he says.

I nod and finish spraying down the rest of my garden. I take extra care because I can use the time to settle my nerves. To think I used to be so confident when it came to men. The old me would laugh at my skittishness now. She would have eaten men like Logan for breakfast.

With her in mind, I wind the hose back onto its wheel and lock up the back door, triple-checking the locks out of habit. Then I move to the windows and do the same there. By the time I finish, Logan's already gotten Rocky into his truck and has moved it from his driveway to mine. Rocky has his head poked out of the door and I could swear he's grinning.

He makes room for me as I swing myself up. "Where exactly are we going?"

"A little park. It has an old closed off baseball field they turned into a dog park."

I scrub Rocky on the neck. "He'll love it."

Like any other place in Nassau, the park is only a short drive away. It's located just off the main road, but it's relatively deserted.

"You'd think there'd be more people here," I comment as I jump out of the truck.

"There is a more upscale park built near the center of town

a year or so ago. Skate park, basketball courts, the whole nine. This one kind of fell by the wayside."

"Based on the peeling paint and brown grass, I'd describe it more as badly in need of attention."

"Maybe that's why I like it so much."

I refrain from asking if that's why he was so attracted to me at first.

Logan lets Rocky inside the double gates and Rocky takes off with a round of cheerful barks. I lean against the fence and watch as he sniffs every plant and pole in the park.

"So are we going to talk about this?" he asks as he comes to stand beside me.

I look away, pretending to study an incoming couple with an excited beagle. "Talk about what?"

He turns, leaning back against the fence and crossing his arms over his formidable chest. "You can pick a topic at this point. Why you keep pushing me away. Where you're from. Why you carry a gun everywhere you go and never turn the lights off in your house."

All the fight goes out of me, and my shoulders slump. "Logan, I—"

"You don't have to tell me everything. Just give me one thing. One little thing about you that I don't already know."

Wind whips my hair around my face, and for the hundredth time since Paige died, I wish she was here to guide me. She was always better at this sort of stuff. "Why does it matter?"

"For one thing, did you just hear yourself? I'm trying to get to know you, and you're asking why it matters? Of course it matters. *You* matter."

"Why are you pushing this? Why can't you just leave it alone?"

He turns so his shoulder nudges mine as he gazes over the dogs happily running around the park. "You'd like that, wouldn't you? I bet that's how you've kept to yourself for so long. You show them that prickly side for long enough and they just don't put forth the effort." A long silence follows until he sighs. "Did I ever tell you what I did in the Marines?"

This man, I swear. I can't keep up with him. I blow out a breath and then turn back so I can look at him. "No, you didn't."

"Since you're being stingy about the personal details, I figure if I share some with you, you'll be obligated to return the favor." Before I can object, he continues, "I didn't join the Marines to kill people, but that's what I ended up doing."

My eyes flash to his, but he's not looking at me anymore. He's watching Rocky greet the beagle, but his eyes have a faraway quality that tells me he's not really seeing what he's looking at.

"I was a sniper, Sienna. I spent a lot of time waiting, and if you think I'm going to back off because you keep pushing me away, you can think again. Patience really is a virtue and probably the only one I actually excel at."

I scowl at the ground. I don't want to know these things about him. I don't want to think of him on top of a dusty building in the desert as he gets his target in his sights. I can picture his cool-eyed stare all too clearly. I don't want to feel sympathy for the man who had to make such terrible choices. I don't want to feel *anything* for him.

When I don't speak, he continues. "Shooting was about the only thing my old man and I had in common, aside from the appreciation for good whiskey or a cold beer. He was the one who took me out shooting for the first time. Who taught me how to clean and care for a gun. Practiced with me for hours. At first I went with him because I couldn't get him to spend time with me any other way. Then, I got good at it. Real good. When Ben, Jack and I joined the Marines, I got better at it. For a long time, it was the only thing that mattered."

Unbidden, words spill from my lips. "What happened?" I nearly wish I could suck them back in, turn back time, but then he glances over with his eyes so sad, I want to wrap my arms around him and never let go. The part of me who's running from all the horrible things I can never seem to forget recognizes it's likeness reflected in Logan's eyes. The kinship rises up in me so swiftly, so strongly, it's all I can do to keep my hands from offering comfort, from soothing away the pain.

"Nothing worse than anyone else whose been in my shoes," he says in a tone lighter than the subject, a tone that tells me the truth is anything but light. "I did my job, kept my men safe. I did what was necessary."

I go quiet, watching Rocky bound through the maze of tricks they have set up for the dogs to run through. He goes up and over a bridge, weaves through a line of poles, and picks his way through tires, his mouth spread in a wide smile, tongue lolling.

I don't have to ask Logan for details. It doesn't take much imagination to paint the picture. He'd gone to boot camp, then probably to his first U.S. duty station. After that, he must have gone back and forth with tours overseas. His lack of description tells me more than any long speech ever could. Without the explanation, I discern he's taken lives. I can only speculate how many or the circumstance. It only takes one look at the faraway look in his eyes to see it. It explains why he has trouble with drinking, why he often holds himself separate like he's both there and somewhere else at the same time.

And again, the words just tumble from my lips without conscious thought. "Phil, the man who you talked to that day? He's a journalist just dying for his big break. Some . . . things happened to me a few years ago and he likes to follow me around hoping there will be a change in my story. Something that will be his big claim to fame."

When I look up, he's got a frown playing around his lips. "He's not bothering you again, is he?"

I study him for a few long seconds. "You aren't going to ask what he's trying to scoop?"

"What are you afraid of?" he asks instead of answering my question. He turns to me, caging me between the fence and his muscular body.

"You're not the only one with a past that haunts you."

He leans closer and I have to tip my head up to meet his beautiful eyes. "Your ghosts won't scare me away."

"You don't know anything about them yet."

He brings his hand up to my cheek, tucks his fingers into my hair. "I don't need to. I already know you're worth it." With one last long look, he lets his hand glide down my arm to take my hand. "Getting dark," he says after a glance around. "We should round up Rocky."

The part of me aching to touch him protests. "What? That's all?"

He pauses and leans down to touch his lips to mine. Despite my firm resolutions to keep my distance, my body melts into his, my hands going up to his chest. He deepens the kiss enough to make me breathless, then pulls away, leaving me wanting. "It's a start."

The couple with the beagle opens the gate, and in his excitement, Rocky bounds out of the opening and down the sidewalk to water the bushes and sniff all the new scents. Logan starts to go after him, but I wave him off. "I'll get him and be right back."

Logan is right, the park has been severely neglected. Rocky disappears behind the bushes and down an overgrown sidewalk. I groan and quicken my pace. The shadows lengthen the deeper I go, and I don't realize until I'm swallowed up by the brush how dark it's gotten.

"Rocky? C'mere boy!"

Twigs snap, and I hear the soft chuff of his heavy pants. I follow the sound around a bend and find him investigating a tree.

"Rocky, Logan's waiting for us. Let's go and we'll get you a treat."

A chill skitters over my spine. One so familiar it steals the breath straight from my lungs. I spin around, but the path behind me is empty. I'm probably being overly paranoid. A year on the run will do that to you. Even if it's only from your own demons.

Rocky finally abandons the bush and trots to my side. I clip the leash onto his collar. "Silly boy. You shouldn't go wandering off like that."

We start to head back down the path. I can see the dog park and Logan's truck through the trees, but we don't make it that far.

Rocky freezes next to me, and I can almost see his muscles

rippling underneath his fur, which is standing straight up. He bunches close to my side, and his body vibrates with a growl.

"Rocky?"

I automatically reach behind my back and then curse underneath my breath. This. This is exactly why I carry a gun and why I don't get involved. I've known Logan for a short time, and he's already distracting me. It could be nothing—probably just a kid—but I'd feel better with the weight of my gun in my hand.

A shadow steps out onto the path, and at first I think it's Logan coming to look for us, but the proportions are all wrong.

Icy fingers dance along my nerves, and this time I pay attention. The figure moves closer, and I curse every single muscle in my body for being frozen in fear. All those hours of self-defense classes are proving completely useless. I try to calm myself—this is a public park . . . not every single person I walk by wants to hurt me . . . I don't have a reason to be afraid.

I'm being paranoid. The incident Logan was called out on stirred up old memories, that's all. This guy seems friendly enough. I'm just overreacting. Rocky's still quivering by my side, but I urge him forward with a sharp tug on his leash.

Just as we pass the man, who's still steeped in shadows, he lunges and light explodes across my vision.

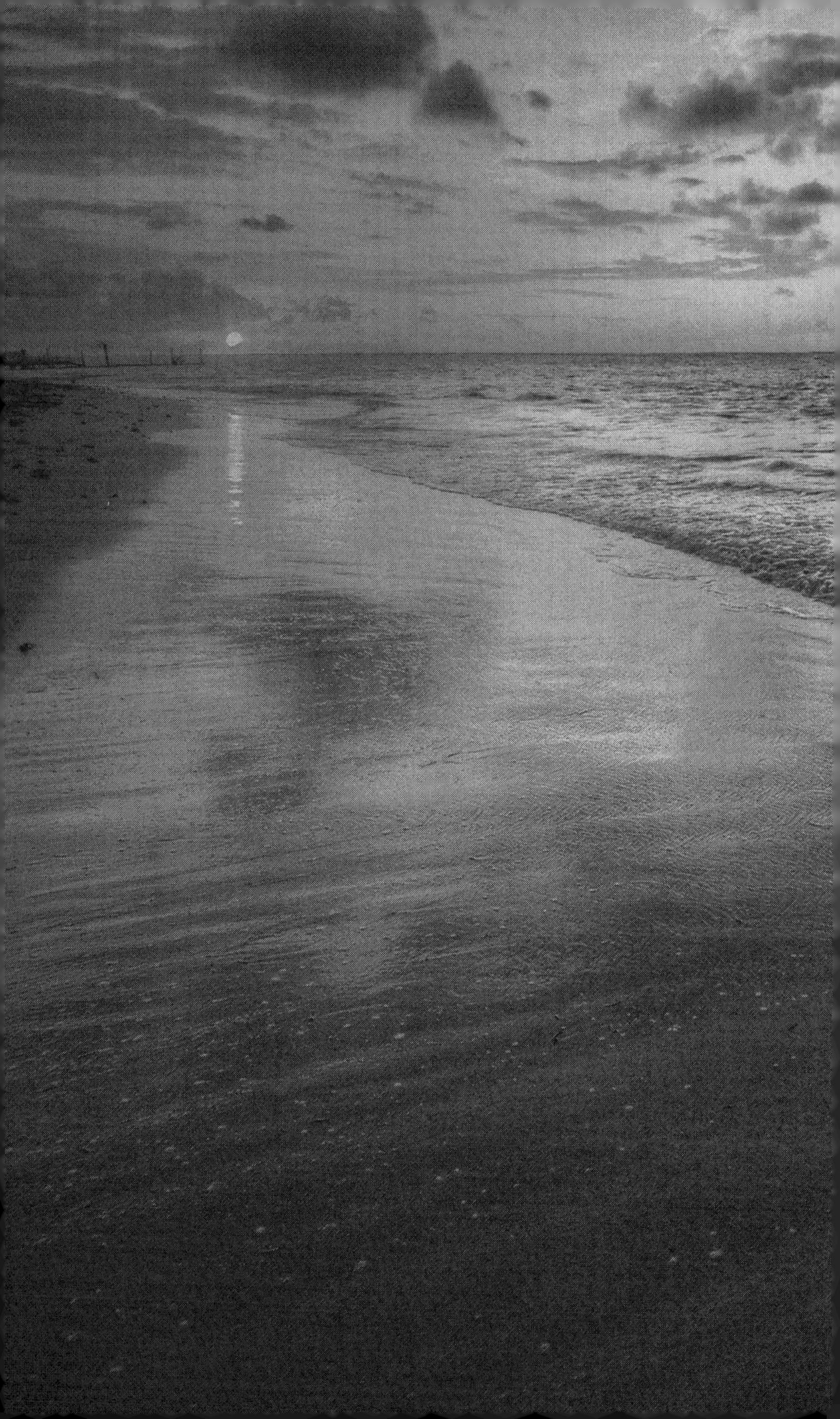

CHAPTER FOURTEEN

LOGAN

AS SIENNA GOES to retrieve Rocky, I start the truck and wait for her. Maybe I'll bring her back to my place, put in a movie, eat the leftovers from the B&B. I've learned the only thing I need to do to get her to agree is distract her, which I'm looking forward to.

A few minutes pass, and I spend it imagining getting my hands on her again and listening to music. A few songs play, and I start to watch the woods a bit closer. She should have been back by now. I pull out my shoulder holster and slip it on out of habit. Her constant vigilance and the attack on Elizabeth Gallagher have my instincts on high alert.

There's a chance I'm overreacting—and I hope to Christ I am—but I've learned to trust my gut. Right now it's telling me there's a reason why she hasn't come out of those woods.

The other family with the small dog have already left, and I'm alone in the lengthening shadows of the decrepit park. Elizabeth Gallagher was attacked under these same conditions: at night, in a park, and with people nearby.

I'd call out, but if there is someone nearby, I don't want to spook them. If there's not, I don't want to frighten her.

I keep my hand at the ready as I move down the same sidewalk that Sienna took. I walk slowly, scanning the dark woods around me and listening for any sign of her or Rocky. Nails click against the concrete sound seconds before Rocky appears around the bend in front of me.

A low whine comes from his throat, and when I put a reassuring hand to his neck, I find him trembling. "Where is she?" I steady him with a couple long swipes down his back. "Find Sienna."

Rocky nudges my leg with his shoulder and then starts off in a steady trot, looking back at me every few seconds to make sure I'm still following close behind.

"Good boy." I pull out my gun as I round the bend. She wouldn't have let Rocky go by himself unless something was keeping her. "Good boy," I repeat. "Find Sienna."

The sidewalk is split by roots from the surrounding trees and is littered with leaves and fallen branches, but there's no Sienna.

I take a few more steps into the blackness, and my foot hits what I think is a branch at first. I glance down automatically to move around it and find it's not a branch at all. Obscured by the shadow thrown by the bush she's half under, is an unconscious Sienna.

Dark liquid trails down her temple and into the tumbled mass of her hair. Rocky tucks himself into her legs and eyes the surrounding area like he's on guard. I fall to my knees by her side, almost afraid to touch her.

My cop's eye immediately takes in the scene. Her arms are splayed above her head, and there are very distinct drag marks that trail from her feet and through the debris covering the sidewalk. Someone incapacitated her and then had to flee the scene—probably because they heard me coming.

In quick succession, I pull out my gun and my phone, hitting the speed dial for the station. "This is Blackwell," I say before they even have a chance to answer. "I'm at . . ." I strain to remember the address on the park sign as we were coming in, "The Fowler Street park, and I have an unconscious woman who's been assaulted. We need paramedics and a car sent out. I'm armed and the perpetrator may still be in the vicinity."

I stay on the line and listen to their directions as I pull her gently into my lap. "It'll be okay. I'm here," I whisper. "Sienna? Can you hear me?"

She groans and her knees curl to her chest. She turns her head, tucking her face against my stomach. Her hand goes to her head and she flinches. "What happened?"

"Shh, it's okay. You're okay."

Hearing my voice causes her to open her eyes, and she blinks up at me with tear-filled eyes. "Oh, God. Logan."

My hands feel too big, too rough, but I wipe away the trails from her cheeks anyway and hope she doesn't notice how bad they're trembling. "Police are coming. Are you hurt anywhere else?"

"Police?" Her brows furrow, and she raises a hand to her head, winching as she touches the bruise blooming there. "Oh my god, what happened?"

"You don't remember anything?"

She closes her eyes, and then they pop right back open and the color drains from her face. She shoots up so fast we nearly knock heads. "Where is he?" The desperation in her voice sends a chill straight through me.

"Don't stand, you hit your head. You could have a concussion."

She ignores me and surges to her feet. "I can't stay here. We have to get out of here."

When she sways, I step in front of her to stop her escape. "I checked, there's no one here."

Her head is on a constant swivel as I lead her down the sidewalk. If she weren't already dizzy from the possible concussion, she would be from all the spinning.

"I was coming back." Her voice sounds so small I have to lean down to hear her. "I was coming back with Rocky, and there was someone on the sidewalk in front of me."

Fuck, her skin is clammy, her eyes drawn, and her skin is still pale. Where the hell are the paramedics? "Did you get a look at the person?"

We break the line of the trees and she sags against me. My arms go around her, and I lift her clear off her feet and carry her the rest of the way to my truck. After I set her on the seat, her legs dangling off the edge like a child, I hunt through my center console and come up with a mint. It's not perfect, but the sugar will help.

I discard the wrapper and hold it up to her lips. "Here, this will help."

She sucks it into her mouth and leans against the headrest. It clicks against her teeth as she talks. "I didn't see him. I mean, I couldn't make out his face. By the time we got close enough, he hit me and that's the last thing I remember."

Then, fucking finally, we hear the sirens. I tuck the hair

away from the uninjured side of her face. "You're safe. They're almost here."

She closes her eyes as if it takes too much energy to keep them open. "I'll never be safe," she says.

Two police cars and an ambulance come to a screaming stop behind my truck.

"They're going to need to take your statement, and then the paramedics will look you over."

"I'm fine."

"Honey, you're not fine. You look like you're about to fall over." She starts to protest, so I put a finger over her lips. "Please. For me?"

Her eyes harden. "I'll give a statement, and they can look me over, but I won't go to the station and I'm not going to the hospital for observation."

"You have a concussion—"

Her gaze cuts to the officers and paramedic who come to our side. She answers their questions and refuses to go to the hospital. I stand back, listening to her recount what she told me and watching as each one of her walls gets built back up.

SHE'S WAITING on the porch for me when I get off work the next day.

"I don't think we should do this tonight," she says before I've even gotten out of my truck.

I jump out anyway, because hell if I'm going to let her close up again. "That so?"

She nods emphatically. "Yes."

I brush by her and into her house. "That's too bad."

"Look, Logan. I can appreciate you're wanting to check on me, but I'm fine." She moves around me to perch on the couch with feigned indifference, but with the bandage on her head, she only looks vulnerable.

"You're fine?"

She nods, but it's stiff and jerky.

"You're fine, even though a man attacked you and knocked you unconscious. If I hadn't come, he would have raped you or worse." This time, she can't meet my gaze. "That's what I thought."

"What are you even doing here? I don't need you to take care of me."

My head snaps back. "If nothing else, I consider you a friend, Sienna, and I was responsible for you. I knew there was someone potentially dangerous stalking women in this town, and I should have been there."

"You think a man like this would care if you were there?" she says, eyes flashing. "He'd kill you if it meant he got what he wanted."

I cross the room and crouch in front of her. Even though she tries to pull them back, I take her hands in mine. "Tell me."

She shakes her head. "I can't."

"You can. I'm here. I'm not going anywhere. Tell me what happened to you, baby."

"Stop."

"No, I won't."

A tear spills over her cheek and she bites her lip.

"I want to be here for you. Let me be here for you, Sienna."

She barks out a laugh. "I don't know how to start."

I sit next to her on the couch, close enough to remind her I'm there, but far enough away that I don't crowd her.

"When I was in college in Miami, there was a man there targeting women, too. He'd attack them when they were outside, alone. At the park, jogging, or walking home from a late night. He'd find them when they were vulnerable, hurt them, rape them, then murder them. He killed three before he was caught. Before I caught him." She looks up then and the pain in her eyes makes me want to hurt someone. "He was my boyfriend, and I never suspected a thing. If I had, maybe I could have saved those women."

"That isn't your fault."

"It is. You don't know—"

"I will if you tell me."

"I slept with a killer. Trusted him. How could I be so *blind*?"

"You'd be surprised how many evil people can keep a perfectly normal life while they commit these crimes."

"Still, I should have known. A part of me should have known. He wasn't a bad person." Her voice cracks on the word. "He wasn't. He wasn't a good one, I can't say he didn't have his faults, but he was normal."

"Did he hurt you?"

She looks away. "He tried to." There's a long pause and then she lifts a shoulder. "After the trial, where I had to testify against the man I thought I loved, I left Miami, changed my name. For the last year I drifted until I came back to Florida. To Jacksonville. I wanted to be back home and I thought it was as close as I could get. That's where I met Chloe." A ghost of a smile drifts across her lips. "She worked in the travel agency I owned for a little while, and it was the best I'd felt in a really long time."

"What made you come here?"

"He won an appeal and I couldn't . . . I just couldn't stay. The reporters found me and it was only a matter of time before he did, too. It was too close. I moved around again until Chloe convinced me to come here." Her shoulders lift. "Guess it wasn't far enough, but I'm pretty sure he could find me, no matter where I went."

Awareness snaps my spine straight. "Are you saying the man who attacked you last night was your ex?"

"I can't be certain. I didn't see his face."

"What's his name? Why didn't you tell the police when they interviewed you?"

"His name is Gavin. Gavin Lance. I think I was in shock at the time." The shadows under her eyes are darker than ever, and she looks like she's about to drop. "I thought I was doing the right thing when I ran. I thought if he couldn't find me, then I could live out my life. I didn't know he'd do this again."

I pull her into my arms. "It could be a coincidence, but I'll check on it, Sienna. I'll find out where he is." Two men committing the same crime hundreds of miles apart isn't likely. I'll go over the reports from the other homicides to be sure and to help ease her mind.

"God, Logan. This is why I didn't want to drag you into this. This is why I didn't want to get you involved. How can you want to be with me when you don't even know me?"

She looks down, unable to meet my eyes. I run a hand over her hair. "I can take anything you have to tell me. I'm here for you. I'm not going anywhere. "

Her gaze still on her feet, her voice barely a whisper, she says, "My name isn't even Sienna."

This time, I make her look up at me. I remember the night I met her, when her eyes were spitting fire as she confronted me in her little robe. How she refused to give me her name. A part of me feels like we've finally come full circle. When I speak, my voice is low, needy and somehow I know her next admission is just as real as her giving me a piece of her own heart. "What's your name, honey?"

She licks her lips, then gnaws on them when they start to tremble. "Piper. My name is Piper Davenport."

When I say, "It's nice to meet you, Piper," her smile nearly washes away the ache in my chest.

"Guess you finally got me to give you my name."

"I knew I'd get it out of you at some point."

Her smile doesn't last and she slumps a little. "I can't stay here," she says into my shirt. "If he's found me, there are people in danger. I can't be responsible for it again."

"You aren't." She tucks her legs up into her chest as if she can minimize the hurt by holding it close. I smooth a hand down her back. "You aren't. He is. And if you keep running, you're only going to change the location, not the events. Men like that don't stop because you change the setting. It's a compulsion."

"I'm just so tired of living my life this way," she says.

"I know you are. But you don't have to anymore. We'll figure out what's happening, I promise."

"What's the point?"

"The point of life is to live it. You'll get through this and you'll see." I pull her closer. "You sleep here," I tell her. "I have you."

THE NEXT MORNING, I leave her curled up on her bed and let Rocky out the back door to do his business as I make a pot of coffee. After she fell asleep in my arms, I put her in her room and slept on the couch. There was no way in hell I was leaving her alone.

I'm not close with many people in the department. After I beat a suspect involved in the kidnapping of Ben's son, Cole, most of the other officers like to keep their distance. As a sniper, I got used to spending most of my time alone. The only person who really doesn't give a shit about any of the interdepartmental politics is a wiry old bastard named Eli Colson. He's older than dirt but moves like lightning. He reminds me of a leathery rattlesnake waiting to strike.

With my phone pressed to my ear, I unwind the hose to water her budding garden. His gruff voice answers after a couple rings. "Colson."

"Hey, it's Blackwell."

"Guessing you have a good reason for calling at the crack of dawn," he says after a yawn.

"I wouldn't say it's a good one. It's about the Gallagher case."

"Might as well get up and get some coffee in me," he mumbles, and I hear the loud squeak of bedsprings in the background. "Lay it on me."

"I need any information you can get on a serial murder investigation that took place in Miami involving a Gavin Lance."

"What does this have to do with the Gallagher case?"

I scrub a hand over my face. "The woman I'm seeing? She was attacked yesterday in a similar fashion. Blitz attack in the park. She gave a statement at the time of the attack, but she'll need to give another. When we got back to her place she explained it could be Lance."

"Why in the sam hell does she think that?"

"She was involved in the Lance case. Her ex-boyfriend was convicted in the deaths of three women with a similar MO."

"Well, shit," Colson says.

"Can you do it for me?"

"I'm surprised you think you have to ask."

"I'm going to stay with her today. She's still a little shaken up."

"You take care of your lady. I'll handle this. Keep an eye out, you hear?"

"I will."

After he clicks off, I wind up the hose and whistle for Rocky, who comes running back up to the door. Sienna is waiting for me in the kitchen.

"Good morning," she says. She's changed into shorts that barely skim the tops of her thighs and a tank top with a rip at the hem. The short robe I like so much is belted at her waist and her hair is piled into a messy knot on top of her head.

"Mornin'."

She pours a cup of coffee and leans against the counter as Rocky winds himself around her legs and butts his head against her thigh. "You didn't have to stay."

I haven't moved from the doorway, but I do at her words, crossing my arms over my chest and giving her a hard look.

"You must not have a high opinion of me if you think I'd leave you after what happened."

"I'm fine."

Nodding to her head, I say, "You've got a goose egg the size of a golf ball on your head that disagrees with you."

Her fingers touch the spot absentmindedly. "It doesn't even hurt anymore."

"Right."

Haunted eyes meet mine. "I just want to forget about this today. I don't want to think about any of it. I know you probably have to work, so I don't want you to feel obligated to stay."

"I took the day off. I'm not letting you stay here by yourself."

She bites her lip, considering me. "Are you ever going to leave?"

"You can try to make me, but I'm bigger and meaner than you." When she doesn't stop shaking her head, I cross the room and cup her cheeks to steady her. "There's something here, Piper." I nearly growl her name because I'm so pleased to have that piece of her. Her own eyes widen as she remembers the admission and then they go soft with vulnerability. "Something you can try all you want to ignore, but I'm not gonna let you."

"I can't—"

I cut off her words with a kiss. I'm done trying to negotiate. Obviously words aren't getting through the walls she's built around herself. Her hands come up like she wants to take mine off her face, but she ends up covering them instead.

"Tell me," I say against her lips. "If you're going to say no, tell me why."

"You don't want to be involved with me." She pulls away and rests her forehead on my chest. "There are plenty of women who'd love to sleep with you."

"If sex was all I wanted, I'd find one of them. I want more from you than fucking."

She shoves me back, but I still have my arms around her waist so she doesn't go far. "I can give you sex. That I can do. I can't give you a relationship right now. I just . . . can't."

"Then, we don't have to talk."

I kiss her again, this time demanding she part her lips, and she does without much convincing. Her arms wrap around my shoulders, and she sighs into me again. I could get used to hearing that little noise, and I make it my personal mission to make her do it as many times as possible. I bend just a little so I can pick her up. She reads my movements and wraps her legs around my waist at the same time as my hands cup her ass to hold her against me.

She lets me carry her from the kitchen and into the living room, where I lay her down on the couch, making sure to brace myself with one arm so I don't crush her. She breaks the kiss and blinks up at me, her eyes wide with confusion when she realizes we've gone horizontal.

"You mean right now?" she asks breathlessly.

"Right now."

Single-mindedly, I slip a hand under her shirt, needing to feel the softness of her skin instead of just imagining it. Her breath catches in her throat when my fingers skim up her ribs.

"I don't think—"

"Good." My hand moves up to cup her breast over the material of her bra. "Don't think."

"Don't you think you should run my credit before we get

to second base?" she asks breathlessly. Did she just make a joke? She grins up at me and adds, "Do a background check?"

I smile down at her flushed face, then she vibrates against me and all blood drains from my head. "After."

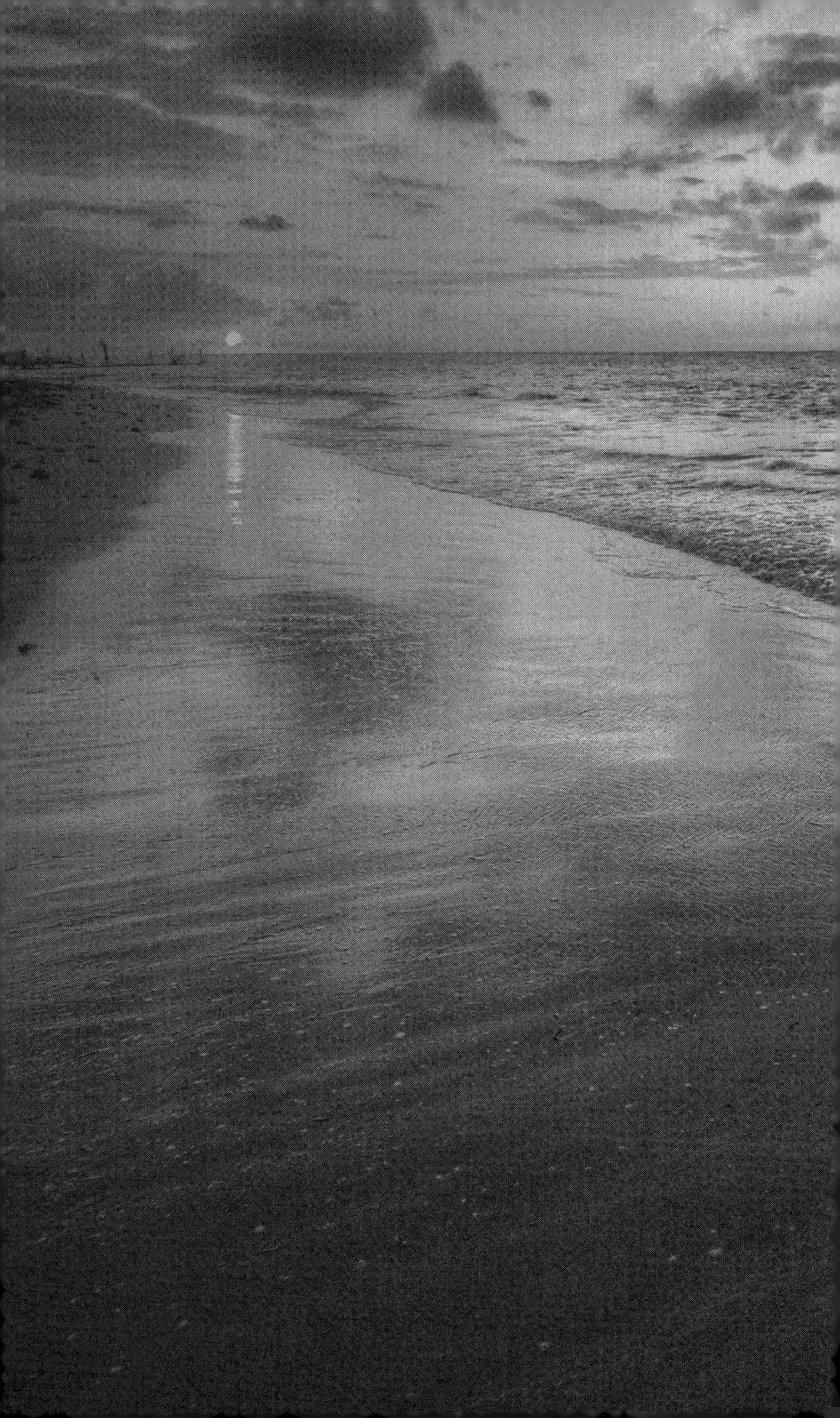

CHAPTER FIFTEEN

SIENNA

I LOSE TRACK OF TIME, track of myself. The only thing I can see, taste, hear, smell, or feel is Logan. I was right, he's dangerous. His drugging touch and intoxicating kiss does exactly what I want. It wipes away everything but him.

He tastes of coffee and cloves from the gourmet mixture I buy because there are some things from my old life I couldn't leave behind. His hands are strong and they span my waist as he scoots me up so he can nuzzle my stomach.

It's been a couple of days since he last shaved, and his stubble stokes all my nerve endings to life. With slow movements, he pushes my shirt up my torso and bares my chest to his gaze. Pinned between him and the couch, I can't do anything but wait for him, which is agony and ecstasy entertained in all the best ways.

With his eyes locked on mine, he lowers his lips to my skin, dragging them back and forth. The soft touch is a direct contrast to the abrasion from his scruff. He kisses up my ribs and down to my navel. With a wicked glance up at me, he nips my hip.

For a second, I think he's going to keep going down, and I want nothing more in the world than for him to slip under the waistband of my shorts. I even move to shimmy them down my hips myself, but his hands stop me. I look back at him in confusion.

"Not yet," he says, his voice rough.

"Logan, don't mess around. If we're going to do this, let's do it."

"So you can get it over with?"

Well, shit, the way he makes it sound is way worse than how it sounded in my head. "No, but I want you. I don't want to wait."

He shifts, presses his lean hips between my thighs and settles, his weight a glorious sensation on top of me. I'd forgotten what it feels like to have the full weight of a man pressing against me.

"The wait is the best part."

I frown up at him and shake my head, pulling my hair out of its band. "No, no you're wrong. The wait is definitely the worst part."

Then he grins, and I shiver at it's ferocity. "Not the way I do it."

Oh, God.

He presses deeper into me, and I only have a fleeting moment of panic. I don't even get to finish the half-formed thoughts of doubt before his lips close over mine and sear them away. He's one hell of a kisser, and there's nothing like a man who knows how to kiss. They should give him awards for the things he can do with his lips.

My arms twine around his neck, forcing his body closer. My breasts ache. My nipples pebbling into the material of my bra is so maddening that I can barely think as I yank and pull his shirt up. I groan into his mouth when my fingers come into contact with the tight, sculpted ridges of his abdomen.

I skim up, exploring almost mindlessly, delirious with the sensations. I delve into the defined muscles, scraping lightly with my nails until his fingers snare in my hair and jerk my head back so he can take the kiss deeper. Moving up, I find the crisp hair of his chest and the softness of his nipples. Curious to his reaction, needing to make him as mindless as I am, I trace its shape with the pad of my thumb, and his breath catches in his throat.

One hand gently tangled in my hair, he uses the other to reach underneath my back and undo the snap of my bra, which gives with a slight twist of his fingers. He releases my lips, and his head moves to drag the edge of my bra up with his teeth, causing the underwire to draw along my nipples, teasing them and leaving them aching for his attention.

I try to do the same and tease his other nipple, but he ensnares my wrists and brings them up over my head. He arranges them over the armrest of the couch and then guides my fingers so they grip the end table.

Then he ducks his head, and I learn his mouth is as talented there as he is when he kisses. "You may wanna hold on."

Then his lips close over me, and I cry out. My fingers tighten on the edge of the table until I'm sure I'm going to break the wood in half. When he's finished with the first, I've changed my mind about having to wait. The way he does it, I can wait forever.

I let go of the table only so I can wriggle out of my shirt. It and my bra go flying over my shoulder. Vaguely, I hear Rocky scrambling out of the way. I'm too busy drawing Logan's shirt up and off to pay attention, and then he's kissing me again. It's hot and wet with tongues and lips going wild. He doesn't just kiss, he dominates, possesses, and I learn for the first time what it could mean to be his.

My feet hook over his legs, pulling his hips as close to me as I can, but it isn't close enough. My hands roam over his bared skin, touching every available place I can, but it doesn't seem to be enough. I explore the brutal strength of his arms and the width of his shoulders.

I learn he has a weakness for my nails on his back when he grinds against me and I forget myself and drag them down from his shoulders to his jeans on a long moan. Eyes wild, lips red, he peels my hands from around his shoulders and places them back on the table.

"Didn't I tell you to hold on?"

"Logan, I can't wait. Please." Breathing ragged, I try to move them, but he holds my wrists with one hand and snakes his free hand down to my waist. Then I give up on breathing altogether, because he masterfully peels down my terry cloth shorts with one hand and then kicks them away with his foot.

"Yes, you can."

He nudges my legs open and settles back between them, then his eyes go to the juncture of my thighs and I fidget, rational thought suddenly flooding back as he studies the most intimate part of me with his heated gaze. I want to move, to use my hands to pull him back to me, but I'm worried he'll stop altogether if I take them away from the table again.

"You're driving me crazy," I say through gritted teeth.

He flashes a wicked grin. "That's kinda the point, sugar."

His lips paint a hot descent down my stomach. "Now hush, I'm tryin' to concentrate."

I squeeze my eyes shut, trying to block out the sensory overload. If he concentrates any harder, my panties are going to wave a white flag and spontaneously combust. When I open them again, a flash of heat so intense washes over me and for a moment, I think maybe they did. Then I realize, it's just the intensity of his gaze on me causing me to burn up from the inside out.

He pulls his lip between his teeth and laves it with his tongue. If I weren't already soaking wet, just watching his obvious enjoyment would have me drenched. His eyes flick to mine and then he rests his weight on one arm. A tentative finger traces the line of lace at my waistband, then down and around the curve of my leg, coming so close to the place that's aching for him. His hand moves down my leg, then back up, across my waistband and to the other side where his fingers dip beneath the cloth.

With a deft movement, he lifts my hips enough to slide the material to the side. Any opening for embarrassment disappears as his fingers trace lightly over me. His head angles and he nibbles on the inside of my thigh, his breath fanning over my leg.

When his attention returns, he moves, shifting even farther down. He glances up at me, his eyes wild and stormy. "Keep ahold of that table," he says. "I'm gonna eat you till you come, but you don't let go. Understand?"

My lips are dry and I'm afraid if I speak, my voice will quake, so I just nod. I'm caught in a whirlwind, and he's at the eye of the storm. All I can do is ride it out.

His shoulders settle between my legs, and I only have a

second to prepare before his tongue is on me. I arch, trying to get away from the tumultuous sensations rocketing through me, but there's nowhere for me to go. He pins my hips to the couch with one arm as his tongue assaults me with lethal precision.

Sounds come from deep within my chest, sounds I don't recognize and have no control over. Wood scrapes across the floor and I realize faintly I'm pulling the table in an effort to strain toward the ecstasy I know is inevitable.

I glance down and find him watching me. There is something so erotic about him between my legs, seeing him, feeling him, is almost more than I can handle. Then he sucks two fingers into his mouth and with my eyes on him, he slides them into me on one long, wet stroke that has me seeing white.

Then his lips and tongue are on me again and the combination of the insistent flicks of his tongue and the wet drag of his fingers inches me up the arduous climb toward nirvana.

My hips roll up to meet him and meet the resistance of his arm. Frustrated, I buck and he lifts his head, lips gleaming and twisted into a satisfied grin.

"Piper," he chastises and licks his lips.

"What are you doing? Don't stop!"

"I thought you said you didn't like the wait?"

I twist my head from side to side and reach for him, but he bats my hands away. "I love the wait. Love it. Please don't stop."

He shifts and hovers over me, his fingers going back to the spot and rolling until I'm writhing once more underneath him. "Don't stop this?" he growls in my ear, then takes my mouth, his kiss a hot temptation that tastes of me. "God, you're so wet," he says against my lips.

I can't resist touching him anymore and my arms go around his shoulders. His fingers abandon my clit and slide inside me, working me in a frenetic pace. Unable to focus on anything else, my head falls back to the couch and I tense in anticipation.

He leans back enough so he can see me, his face still inches from mine. Close enough for me to watch the naked hunger sharpening his gaze. Hunger for me. His fingers slow, sensing that I've reached the edge and he brings his lips back to mine for an endless open-mouthed kiss. I'm arching up to meet him, thrusting my hips up to his hand, clutching at his wrist and going absolutely wild when his phone starts vibrating in the pocket next to my thigh.

He curses, his body one long live wire of tense muscle alongside and above me.

I throw myself backward, the illusive climax draining away, leaving me bereft, wanting, and exhausted. He moves back and his hand regrettably moves away. We both take a mental step back and I scoot up into a sitting position. The call is only an all too vivid reminder of all the things I am trying to escape.

Logan yanks the phone out of his pocket and swipes, pressing it to his ear. He pulls a throw off the back of the couch and covers me with it, sending me a look full of remorse that I'm sure my own face mirrors.

"Blackwell," he says into the phone as he gets to his feet.

My eyes are drawn to his pants, where a thick bulge presses against the material, which only intensifies the disappointment.

Since my ears are still buzzing from the missed orgasm, I don't hear the conversation, but the look on Logan's face says it all.

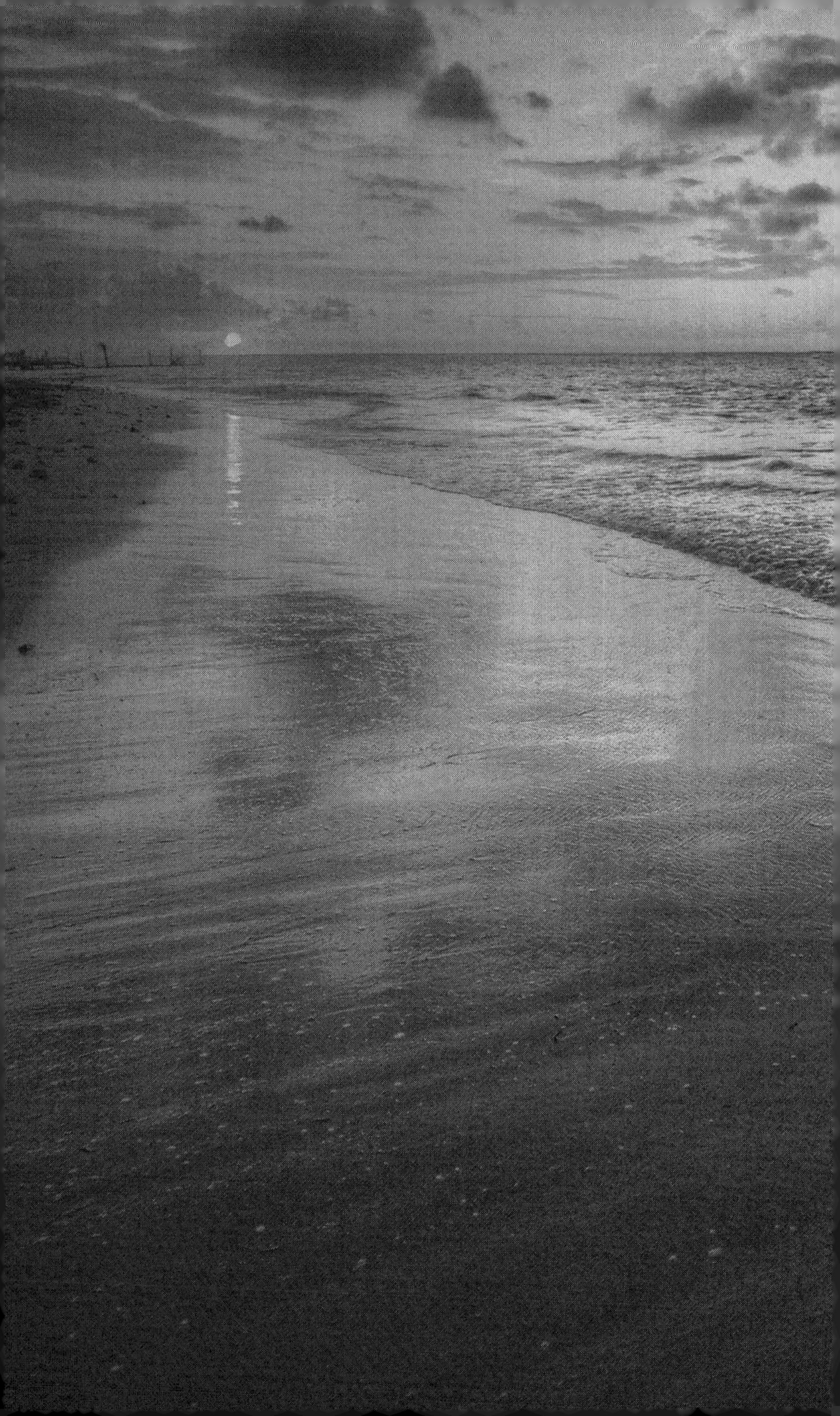

CHAPTER SIXTEEN

LOGAN

A COLD FURY FILLS ME. Not only for the interruption, the senseless violence of the crime I now have to investigate, but also for the haunted look that returns to Piper's eyes the moment I hang up the phone.

Before I can say anything, she gets to her feet and wraps the blanket around her body like another shield. "Go," she says, her hands gripping the blanket between her breasts. "It's okay."

I cross the distance and crowd her. "No, it's not." I kiss her firmly until the tension melts from her shoulders. "I'll be back in a couple hours."

She presses her hands to my chest so she can put some distance between us and shakes her head. "What? Why?"

"I'm not going to leave you alone here until we find out what's going on with your ex. I wouldn't leave you right now if I didn't have to."

"I can take care of myself."

Ignoring her, I pocket my phone. "I'm also going to have a

couple uniforms drive by every half hour just to check on things, make sure you're okay."

"Logan, you don't have to do that. I'm fine."

I trace the angry red mark on her forehead with a finger. "You're tough as nails, I don't doubt that, but I'm not doing this for you. I'm doing it for me. I have to go and do my job, and I won't be able to do that if I'm worrying about you. Please. For my peace of mind. I'll go crazy worrying about you."

Her internal battle is written across her face. Finally, she sighs. "Fine."

"Don't answer the door for anyone you don't know and don't let your gun out of your sight. Stay here until I get back. Promise me."

"Logan."

I kiss her softly. "When I get back, we'll finish what we started here."

She softens underneath my hold. "You don't have to—"

"I want to."

"I'll wait up for you tonight."

I let her go and holster my gun. Keys in hand, I turn back. "Keep Rocky with you."

"I will."

I hesitate and then say, "We're going to have to do some digging into what happened in Miami. I want to find out if this is your ex one way or another. You mean something to me, so I don't want to do it behind your back."

Her arms go around her waist. "I understand."

"I'll bring something to eat on the way back."

She starts to protest but then swallows it back. When she speaks, her voice sounds small. "Thank you."

"Lock the door behind me."

On the drive to the crime scene, I can barely manage to get my anger under control. I drive too fast, brake too hard, and nearly miss the exit for the local state park.

Three times.

Three women who were assaulted.

Three is three too many.

And based on the current victim, the offender is either escalating or exacting revenge for being interrupted with Piper.

I meet Colson at the entrance. A couple black and whites are parked behind him with their lights still flashing. It feels like a carnival in the middle of the woods, lending an otherworldly quality to the scene. Colson is a sight of his own in beat-up, ancient jeans and an oversized cowboy hat. Since he's as skinny as a pole, he cuts an off-balanced figure.

"What happened?" I ask as I cross the parking lot.

His lips twist, as if the words themselves have a bad taste. "Same MO as the last attack and the one with your girl. Public park, but an otherwise secluded area of the trail. Single woman who is approached by a man and then attacked. This one was different, though."

"In what way?"

He jerks his head toward the sidewalk, and I follow him down a ways. There are techs and other officers processing the scene, but I don't need their evidence markers to know what happened.

For one, there is blood everywhere. On the ground, on the trees, in the bushes. It's as if he tried to imitate a morbid Jackson Pollock painting.

Thinking of Piper and how close she came to this conclusion, I hiss, "Jesus *Christ*. How is she?"

Colson sighs. "Not good. She's in surgery now. We won't know anything for a few more hours at least."

"Was she able to identify her attacker?"

"She was unconscious when another jogger found her and scared him off."

"There is a witness?"

Colson nods to a pair of officers interviewing a young woman. "The victim didn't see much and the jogger got there after he lit out. They're hoping she saw enough to provide a sketch to help identify the sick bastard."

I can tell by the drawn look on his face there's something more. "What?"

"By any chance did this creep from Miami have a thing for cutting off his victim's hair?"

Piper's long blonde hair flashes like a beacon through my mind. "I haven't looked at the files yet, they should be waiting for me at the station, but I'll be able to let you know for sure once I get back."

"The bastard cut off her hair. Took it as a souvenir."

I curse under my breath. "Any trace?"

All we need is one piece of physical evidence to link the guy conclusively, either to Piper's ex or otherwise, but Colson shakes his head.

"This guy isn't an idiot. He's smart. Very smart. Based on that and the fact that he's been able to successfully target these women in such a short time frame tells me this isn't his first rodeo. But sooner or later, he'll make a mistake."

I don't say it aloud, but he already has. The moment he came back to target Piper, he signed his own death warrant.

HOURS LATER, the results from the Miami investigation land in the empty tray of the printer. I snatch them up in my spare hand as I pound back a cup of old coffee, and I pull a face at the tar-like taste. It's a sludge-or-nothing night as the part-time communications officer / receptionist went home a couple hours back, leaving the on-duty patrolman and me to fend for ourselves.

Colson gave me the go-ahead to take the rest of the night off after a long evening of interrogating possible witnesses in the investigation, but I brushed him off. After working as a sniper in the Marines, I've learned to pay attention when something makes me twitchy. And there's something off about this one. Something that's making me real fucking twitchy.

As I cross the small bull pen filled with cluttered desks crammed together, my phone begins to ring across the room. I choke back the rest of the stale coffee as I weave though the heavy scents of burnt food, antiseptic cleanser, and the lemon air freshener the lieutenant prefers. Tossing the background check info onto the desk, I snatch up the landline and bark, "Blackwell," into the mouthpiece.

"You gonna come in the morning? Momma's making her famous ham and cheese omelets for breakfast. Bring Sienna, if you like. That girl could use a good meal."

At the sound of Diane's voice, I relax into my rickety old office chair with its customary beleaguered groan. "Only if I can see your pretty face," I reply.

"I'd be just brokenhearted if I didn't get to see your ugly mug first thing."

"Then I'd hate to disappoint you. Make sure to have a cup of coffee ready for me, pretty please. The shit I've been drinking for the past couple hours will more than likely kill me."

"Would serve you right," Diane says, and I can hear the teasing in her voice over the line.

I lean back in the chair, rubbing a hand over the scruff on my cheeks. "Oh, no. What'd I do now?" I ask.

"You know I don't like to meddle," she says, and I respond with a snort. She ignores me and continues, "It's not my business how you run your life or do your job."

"Then why do I have the feeling you're about to stick your nose in it?"

"Logan Elias Blackwell, I'll not have you mistreating that girl."

Her fierce tone makes me scowl and I sit up straight and hang my head in defeat automatically. "Aunt Diane, I've been grown for over a decade. Way past time for you to meddle in my love life."

She snorts. "I'll interfere any time I damn well please, and I won't hear a word from you until I've said my peace." I know better than to argue with a riled woman, so I hold my tongue. "It doesn't take a rocket scientist to realize that girl's been through hell, and now with this on top. It's enough to test even the strongest person."

"That may be true," I say when she takes a breath, "but it's not my intention to hurt her. Now, I love you, Aunt Diane, but it's none of your business."

"I'm not interfering, but you listen to me when I say you

take it easy on her. That girl wouldn't hurt a fly, if you've been paying any attention." There's a pause of the line, and I can hear the familiar sounds of the household coming to life and my Grandma Rosie chatting up a storm as she cooks in the background. "And don't tell me you haven't."

Realizing she's about to go off on a tangent about me remarrying, I start to tune out the conversation and glance over my desk for a distraction. My eyes land on the reports from the Miami-Dade Sheriff's Office, and I pin the phone between my ear and my shoulder to reach for them. While Aunt Diane chatters on in the background, I begin to read.

Piper Sienna Davenport, 26, formerly a resident of Miami, Florida, originally from Alabama, attended Southern University until she was attacked by a Gavin Lance who'd raped and murdered two co-eds before his last victim, a Paige Davenport.

"Are you listening to me, boy?" Aunt Diane demands.

"Yes, ma'am," I say without a pause.

"You better be," she warns. "Sienna is a sweet girl. In fact, you'd do well to have a woman like her."

"She likes to be called Piper," I say absently.

"Piper? Now that's a pretty name. Spunky as she is."

Normally, I'd be the first to remind her that I'm not looking to remarry, but my train of thought derails as my eyes snag on a line of the report. I read it three times over before my brain processes the words. When I do, my fingers clench over the paper and it crumples.

"Hey, Aunt Diane, I have to go, but I'll see you for breakfast later."

I don't wait for her response, which will surely earn me another lecture, but the note on the file has all of my attention.

The investigation included a woman murdered inside

Piper's bedroom. The victim in question, a twenty-five-year-old female, had been viciously beaten and assaulted. Piper found her after she returned home from a bar where they'd both had a couple drinks a few hours before. All of that, I was expecting.

The papers flutter to the top of the desk with Piper's license photo staring up at me as I dial Piper's cell for her to meet me at the station. I try to still my trembling fingers, knowing I won't be able to relax until she's with me. The twitchiness intensifies as all the details snap into place.

All the women attacked in Miami also had their hair shorn off.

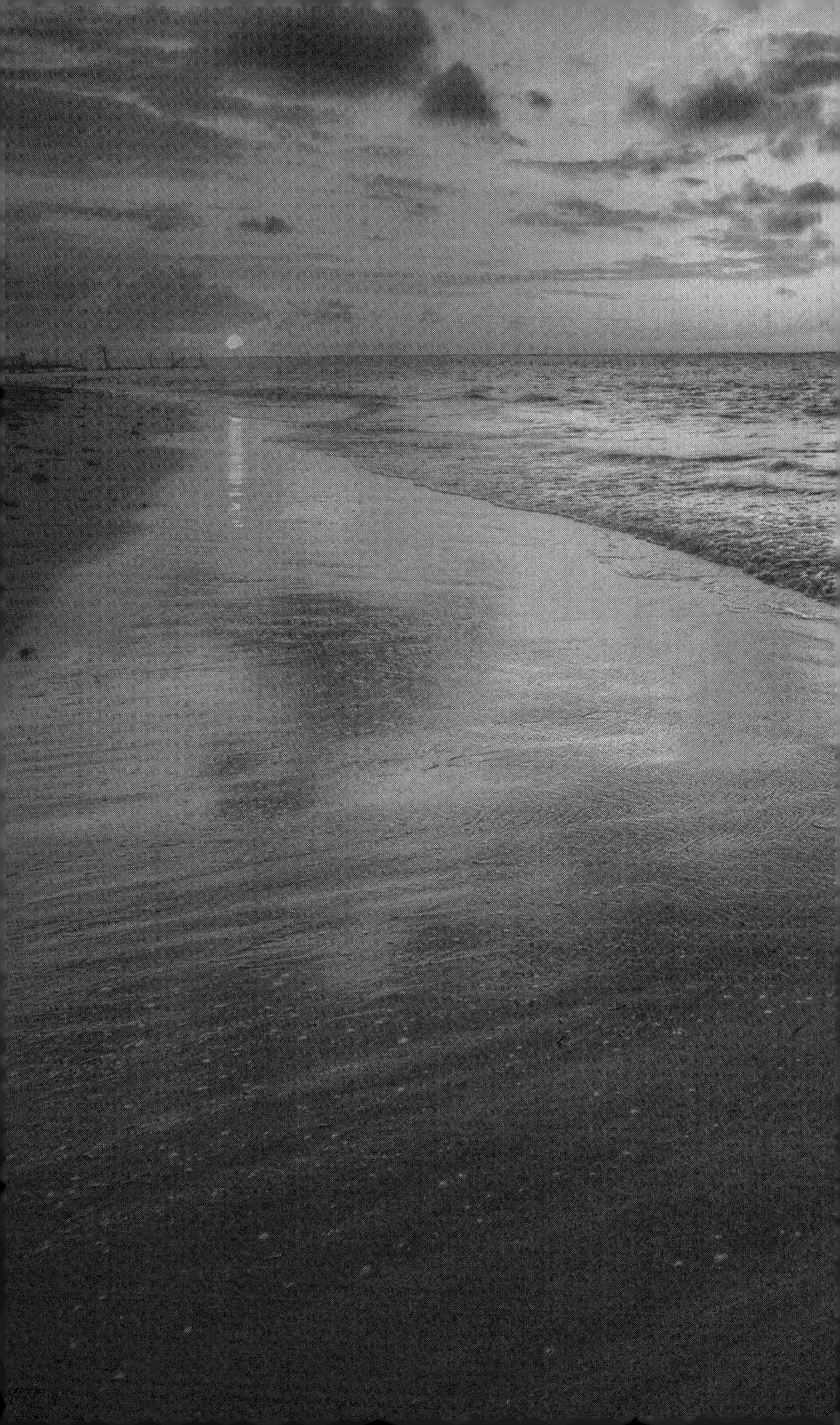

CHAPTER SEVENTEEN

PIPER

I'M unsurprised by Logan's summons to meet him at work later that afternoon. It's the call I've been dreading since we started getting closer. I face it like I've faced every other hard decision since I was ripped from my home: with detached determination.

The sheriff's office isn't what I expect. The plain white stucco stained with years of dirt and grime is underwhelming. The big box stores and discount foods across the parking lot seem out of place. For a man like Logan Blackwell, I expect . . . more. Something as sleek and devilish as the image he inspires whenever I think about our interrupted morning. Or maybe a grimy old Western style jailhouse just as dangerous as the man himself.

Apprehension rolls through me, thick and hot, turning the chicken salad sandwich I'd snagged from the gas station to fill my stomach into a greasy ball. I suck deep breaths in through my nose and exhale through my mouth.

It doesn't help. There aren't enough calming techniques in this world to quiet my growing panic.

Fall is technically upon us, but Florida hasn't quite gotten the memo as a few days of Indian summer have ratcheted up the temperature. The stale air inside the tight cab of my 1998 Ford is about ten degrees over roasting, and the ancient air conditioner does little more than puff out even more hot air. Sweat is already clinging to my hairline, melting off what little makeup I cared to put on this morning.

I thought I'd be more prepared for this, having done it once before, but I guess I can't prepare for giving statements to the police. It's one of those things that doesn't get easier with repetition. Like major surgery or going to a funeral. No matter how much I prepare, it's just going to suck all around.

I wipe my upper lip and forehead and then turn off the car, tossing my keys into my small handbag.

Based on his reputation alone, I'd imagine a huge office with expensive furniture, a lethally sexy blonde secretary, and three piece suits. Not peeling paint and parking spots with faded yellow lines.

Brushing off the sense of foreboding that coats my skin like a sticky layer of sweat, I pull the handle to the front door and simultaneously take a deep breath to settle my nerves. In spite of the lackluster exterior, the inside of the office is pleasantly clean and modern. I wince when my clearance rack sandals squeak against the pristine polished white floors.

The person manning the front greets me and motions me back to Logan's desk in the middle of an empty room full of them. She offers to call him in, but I tell her no. I'd rather wait and allow myself one moment of reprieve. It's not cowardice. It's . . . preparation. Confronting my past should be like dipping into a pool when I'm unsure of the temperature. One step at a time.

As I wait, I study the news clippings lining the walls of his cubicle. In addition to his certificates, I find a prestigious college degree. A ton of commendations. My stomach muscles are finally starting to unclench in small degrees when two burly men burst through the side door, scaring me so bad, I jump to my feet and put my back to the cubicle wall.

"Goddammit. I told you to stop resisting, cupcake," comes a low, gravelly voice that strokes all of my girly parts to life in spite of my apprehension. In contrast to his words, his voice is altogether too delicious, like smooth hot chocolate. "It's your own fucking fault if you break your arm." The 'your' is more like 'yo', and I have to press a hand to my stomach.

Stop it, Piper.

The jangle of nerves multiplies, and I glance at the door over their shoulders. Maybe I can make a run for it before either of them notice me. This was a bad idea. A very, very bad idea. Running is preferable to baring myself to him this way. Physical intimacy is one thing. Emotional intimacy is another altogether.

"Then uncuff me, and we'll make this a fair fight," growls the man Logan's pushing toward booking.

Logan grunts when the smaller man, though only marginally smaller, elbows him in the gut. Then Logan simply body slams his attacker right at my feet, as though it's an everyday occurrence. Based on the easy rise and fall of his massive shoulders, it very well may be an everyday occurrence.

His hooded, jewel-blue eyes spare me the briefest of glances, and I do my best to ignore the fact that he doesn't even blink twice before he hauls the now moaning and handcuffed man to his feet and tosses him into the chair next to me. "You wait right fucking there, cupcake, or we'll move on to round two."

Not wanting to draw his intense stare my way again—at least not for a few more minutes—I very carefully and very quietly take my seat again, even if it's next to a criminal. I'd almost prefer the criminal's presence. Logan didn't look too happy to see me, which doesn't bode well for me and kind of makes me mad since he is the one who called me down here.

The man lifts up the receiver for the landline and angrily punches in numbers. He pauses, keeping those hard-as-granite eyes on my companion. "Hey," he says into the phone. "It's Blackwell. I have a skipper here just waiting to be taken home."

He flashes another cool glance at me and blood rushes to my head, drowning out the rest of his words to whomever is on the other end of the line.

The tips of my fingers and my lips go numb and I have to blink heavily to make sure I'm not staring. He's . . . not like the other police officer's I've had to work with. But at the same time, he fits the role of cop and all around badass about as well as his jeans hug his enormous thighs and firm backside.

"Dude, let me the fuck out of here and we'll work something out," says the man next to me, desperation seeping into his voice.

Logan ignores him, instead reading out something from a piece of paper. Then he says, "Thanks, gorgeous," and sets the receiver back down on its cradle.

The man next to me squirms in his seat, the chain on the handcuffs clanking discordantly against the lacquered chair. "Come on, man. I can't go back to jail," he whines.

I very nearly roll my eyes. When I do manage to look up, I find the man himself staring straight at me.

Now, I'm no wimp, I've dealt with my fair share of intimidating individuals, my ex-fiancé and father included, but no one—and I mean no one—has ever made me freeze like Logan does when he directs that stare my way. My lungs seize and my shoulders lock. Just about the only part of my body that doesn't come to a stop or jump ship, is my heart, which is trying its damnedest to beat itself straight out of my chest.

When he turns away a few seconds later, I suck in air in deep gulps while turning my head to face the parking lot. Anything to keep my eyes off his intimidating form. The energy that surrounds him is palpable and all the sensible parts of my brain are screaming, "RUN!"

If my experiences have taught me nothing else, it's to listen to my instincts.

I force myself to swallow down the panic that threatens to claw its way up and resume deep breathing like I had in the car. At least this time, the air is fresh, clean, and slightly scented from the air freshener plugged into the outlet next to the reception area. When I'm reasonably calm, I manage to glance back, curious in spite of my trepidation.

Logan is bent over the desk, his thick brows furrowed in dark lines as he scribbles something down on a piece of paper. If he weren't so intimidating, I'd think the way his lips twist slightly to the side as he fills out his paperwork was adorable.

But I'm not sure a man his size can actually be classified as adorable.

The gray T-shirt leaves little to the imagination and based on a cursory—okay maybe a thorough—inspection from the other night, he's *all* man underneath those unassuming garments. I give myself a little shake and pull my eyes away from his hunched form. Shit, but *shit*, I promised myself he wouldn't be a distraction.

Focus, Piper. Don't be an idiot.

I don't have much time to consider the curls of ink I'd seen snaking over his biceps from underneath his shirt, because the bulky man beside me decides to lurch to his feet and dive toward the door.

I'm no ninja superstar, but I did take several self-defense lessons. I haven't had much need to use the techniques, but it's like muscle memory. So, when the idiot beside me attempts to make a run for it, I stick out one sandal-clad foot directly in his path and catch his shins just as he's crossing in front of me.

He lets out a girlish squeal as he falls face first against the floor. Logan rounds the desk with a scowl on his face and jerks the lump to his feet. The guy lets out a groan, but Logan shows no mercy when he yanks a side door open and thrusts the guy down a hallway. I use the time to run a trembling hand through my hair to calm my frazzled nerves.

I barely manage to pull myself together by the time he strides back through the door. With my eyes on my pearly pink toes, I'm in the perfect position to see his booted feet stop right in front of me.

Managing to control my racing thoughts, I look up and subtly suck in a breath.

"Why the hell did you do that?" he asks, his face hard and direct.

Um... "I'm sorry?"

"That man is twice your size when he's not a goddamn fool from throwing back gin like it's water. If he would have gotten pissed instead of stupid, he could have hurt you."

My neck snaps back so fast the back of my head bumps into the plaster wall behind me. I'm so shocked, I can't even wince in pain. "Excuse me?" I manage to squeak out.

"Did I stutter?" He runs an impatient hand over his close-cropped hair and scrubs back and forth impatiently. "I'm sorry," he says before I can object. "I'm sorry. I'm just . . . I'm not handling this as well as I thought I would."

Ignoring the tell-tale burn in my throat, I press my lips into a line before saying, "I can speak with another officer if you prefer." When he just gives me a blank look, I add, "I don't mean to drag you into all of this. I didn't want you to be involved."

His expression darkens, and he rounds the desk to put his hands on the chair where I'm sitting. He hunches that powerful torso over, his face stormy with concentration. I can almost feel the electric sizzle of lightning on my bare skin.

"Let me put this to you straight. I am involved and there's no amount of back-peddling that will change that fact."

Indignation, that has nothing to do with his attitude or the anger I know he must be feeling, balloons in my chest. "This isn't like any other statement I've given. Can we just do what you called me here to do?"

The fight goes out of him, and he drops to his knees in front of my chair. His head goes into my lap, and I find I don't know what to do with my hands. After a moment's hesitation, they come to land on his powerful shoulders. His voice is muffled when he begins to speak. "I'm so damn sorry this happened to you, honey," he whispers.

He clamps down around my thighs when I try to heave him upward. Mindless with panic, I don't realize he's pulling me into his arms until we're both standing, and I'm pressed against his broad chest.

"I changed my mind," I say, voice obscured by the cloth. "I can't do this. I can't go through this again." I look up at him, eyes beginning to burn with tears. "I'm not strong enough for this."

His head is already shaking before I even finish my pathetic pleas, and I want to curse myself for ever even considering the thought that he was attractive. For ever allowing him to see all these vulnerable parts of me.

"I think you do want this," he says. "I think you need to get it out. To face it."

"What has that done for me?" I hiss fiercely. "I did what I was supposed to do. I wrote the statements. I testified in court. I relived the worst day of my life for public consumption, and they still released him on a technicality."

Logan takes my hand and helps me down the hall to a secluded interview room. He pauses by the table to look down into my eyes. "I'm doing this because I'm, at the bottom of it all, your friend and I care about you. I want to help you."

"That's interesting considering you were basically biting my head off when I walked in." I whirl away, anger clipping my voice and causing my hands to tremble. I tuck them under my arms so he can't see. "What? Did you think I owed it to you to bare all my wounds?"

I hear his steps come closer and my spine stiffens. "Of course not," he says. He doesn't touch me, but I can sense his presence behind me. I have to snap straight to keep from leaning into his heat. "Of course not," he repeats.

Scoffing, I spin around. "Really? So the intimidating

conversations about my past were . . . what? Occupational hazard?"

He rolls his shoulders, his resolve finally cracking. "At first it was that; I guess you could call it. You were a new woman working with my family. Then, it became something more. I started to care about you." My eyes immediately fall to the floor to avoid this line of the conversation, but he tips it back up. "I could tell something was haunting you, and all I wanted was to take that away. Then you got hurt, and I realized how much it'd fucking bother me if something happened to you."

"I don't want you to care about me," I say vehemently. "Don't you see that?"

His hand drops from my chin and his lips firm. "I wondered why that was. I wondered why you'd guard yourself so much. Why you kept running from what happened to you."

I turn again, eyes roving from corner to corner looking for an escape, but I find nothing but walls. "What? Having a murdering psychopath for an ex wasn't enough?"

"I'm sure that was nothing compared to the fact that he murdered your twin sister." His words are muted, but they may as well be a gunshot.

There's a stunned silence as his voice trails off, and I'm catapulted back to the moments when I realized it was Paige lying dead on the floor. I don't realize I'm crying soft, silent tears until he gathers me up into his arms and sits in one of the chairs by the table with me in his lap.

His arms around me are the only things keeping me grounded. I pour out all my fear and despair and loneliness into his chest until there's nothing left but a hollow ache in my chest.

"Can you tell me what happened?" he asks, when there aren't any tears remaining for me to cry.

A long sigh shudders through me. "I thought it was nothing, at the time. I mean, not that missing people are nothing, just it didn't seem like it would touch me in my little bubble. Everyone on campus just assumed they were isolated events . . ." I trail off for a second and then clear my throat. "Our roommate was the second person to go missing. She was the sweetest person. It's funny. I can't even remember the sound of her laugh anymore. I used to be able to remember her laugh, but one day, it was just gone. He took that from me. He took away Lennox.

"It wasn't until Lennox's murder that the police started noticing the pattern, but we still didn't pay it much attention. We were young and stupid, especially me, and I thought we were invincible."

Logan draws soothing patterns on my back, lulling me into a stupor and allowing the memories and words to roll out like they happened to someone else.

"After that, I walked in on my fiancé, Gavin, kissing another woman. I was upset and I went out drinking. He found me there and tried to patch things up but Paige, P-Paige came and talked to me for a while.

"It's funny, the whole time we were dealing with Lennox's death, Paige was the one who couldn't get out of bed, but the moment I needed her, she was there for me. She was the best part of both of us."

"You were identical twins?" Logan asks when my words bubble up and clog my throat.

I nod against his chest. "Y-yes, but our styles couldn't have been more different. She was very much the girly girl. They used to make fun of me in high school, saying that she got all the female genes, but it didn't bother me because no matter what they said, I still had my best friend as a sister, and not many people get to say that."

"What was she like?"

"I used to say she could have been a pop princess if she'd been a tween in the 90s. She was bright and bubbly. The kind of person who puts a smile on your face by just talking to her."

I pause and realize I'm smiling, which only makes the tears well up again. I haven't remembered Paige and smiled in so long, and I know how wrong that is. Memories of her should bring me happiness, but all I feel when I think of her is the profound loss.

Logan wipes away my tears, his big hands reassuringly gentle, and I lean into him like a cat seeking affection. "You sound like you were very close."

"The closest. We were the kind of twins who finished each other's sentences, had the sixth sense type of connection."

"Did you notice something off the night she was killed?"

Unable to look him in the face, I study his shirt instead as a miserable sucking blackness inside of me clouds out everything else. "That's the thing, I didn't. I didn't, and I should have known. The one time it should have mattered for me to pay attention, I didn't. I was so upset about stupid things that I didn't even consider being more careful. I never should have let her go home alone."

"She came to the bar to cheer me up, like I said, but she had a project due, and I didn't want to distract her." I choke back another sob. "I didn't even think about having someone go with her to make sure she got home safe, even after what happened to Lennox."

"You said your ex was with you at the bar. Did you see him leave after you two spoke? Did he follow her out?"

"The cops asked me all these questions, Logan," I say wearily.

"Humor me," he says.

I think back to that night like I have so many times before. "The last time I saw him was after I walked out of the bathroom. I didn't see him after Paige showed up. Then he showed up at our house after . . . after."

"After Paige left, what happened?"

"Logan," I plead. "I don't—"

"I'm right here," he says. "I'm not going anywhere. You don't have to face this alone anymore, honey."

"After Paige left, I stayed at the bar for a while. She told me to drink and dance and let off some steam—so that's what I did. Then I went home."

"Did you notice anyone around you? Anyone who had been particularly interested in you or Paige?"

I shake my head mournfully. "No one. No one that I can remember. I was so focused on me that I didn't pay attention to anyone else." I look up at him. "If I could go back, I'd do things so much differently."

"I can't compare my experiences to you losing your sister, but I know well enough what it's like to relive memories you'd rather forget. Wish you could change decisions that resulted in a loss of life. You may think I'm a fucking jerk for making you open these wounds, but I do it not only because it can help save other lives, but because you can't let things like this fester. It eats you up."

"I don't think I'll ever get over what happened to Paige. I've tried."

"Let me help you." He tucks the curve of my hair around one ear. "Let me help you put this to rest. You don't have to fight alone anymore."

"I don't want to fight at all."

"I know you don't." He kisses my temple. "After this, I'll take you home, and we'll get a shower and you can sleep for a week."

The tension melts out of me because a shower sounds amazing. "What else do you want to know?"

"I'm going to be straight with you. The most recent attack leads us to believe it's the same person who committed the crimes in Miami, but I want you to know before we get into anything else, that we're already in touch with them and we've even put in a call to the F.B.I. as a precaution."

All the good vibes from the promise of the shower fade away. "What do you mean? What happened?"

"The files on the Miami cases mentioned he had a unique signature."

Bile rises and sticks in my throat. "You mean—the hair," I choke out, "He cut her hair."

"We have officers checking on Gavin's last known address and a detail tracking his movements since he was released from jail. If he jaywalks, we'll know it."

With a thick swallow, I try to stem my rising panic. "I wish there was something else I could do to help."

"You're talking to me, you're dealing. We can't ask for more than that."

We spend the next hour going over my memory of the walk home, then the attack. I tell him everything I remember, even the things I'd rather forget. He doesn't push or prod. He just lets me tell the story at my own pace. I break down again when

I tell him about finding Paige and he holds me through all of it.

"What now?" I ask, when he's done.

"Now, we go home," he says as he puts an arm around my shoulders. "And we take that shower. I'll make you dinner for a change. Then we'll have a beer and watch television until our brains are numb. After that, I think we both need some sleep."

We walk out of the police station together and for the first time in over a year, I don't feel the empty loneliness that had once been such a constant companion. I hold the feeling close and press myself more securely against his side.

I'm not sure what tomorrow holds, but for today, I'll take the comforts he's offering.

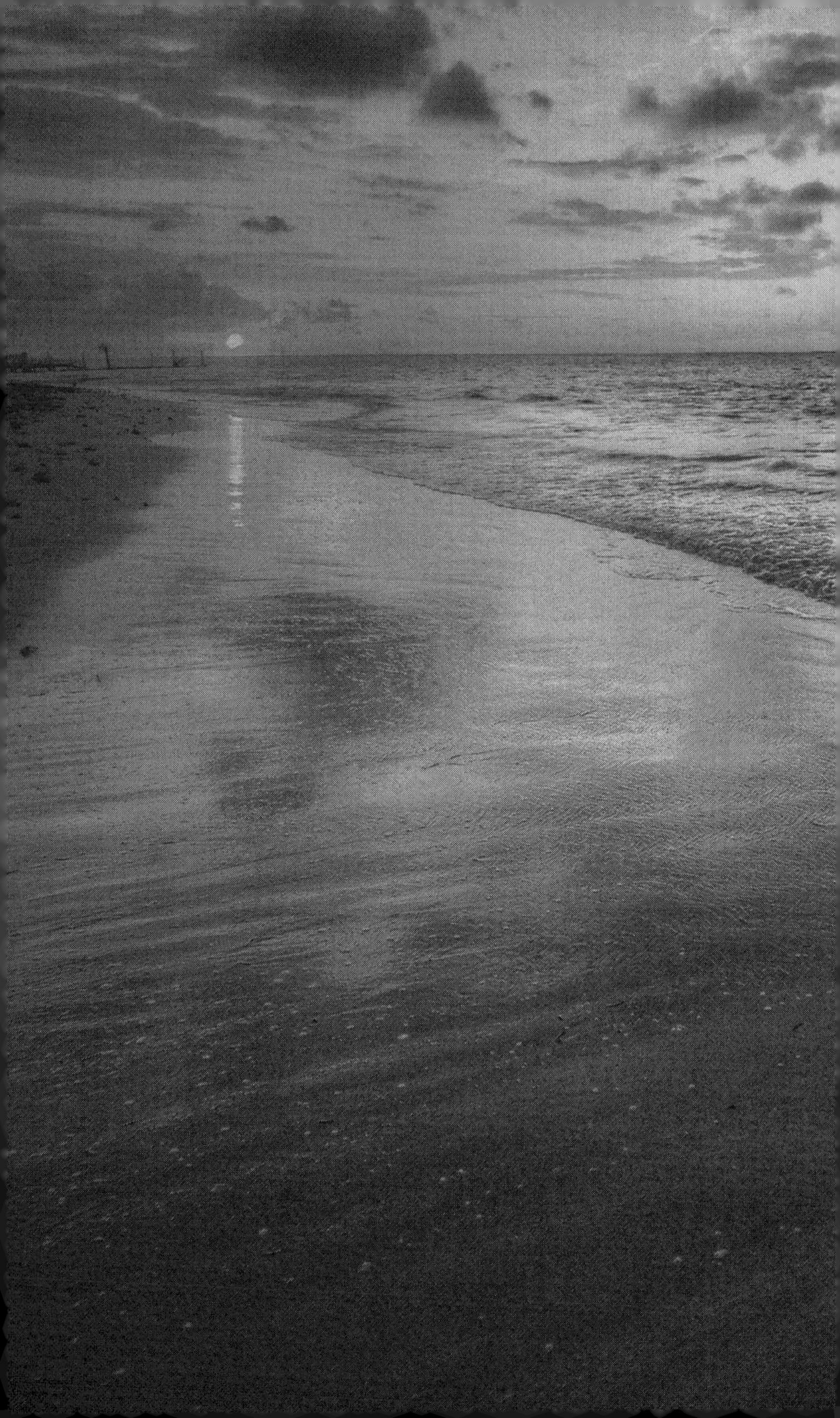

CHAPTER EIGHTEEN

LOGAN

AFTER AN EXHAUSTING DAY for the both of us, I almost sleep through my alarms the next morning. My back creaks when I sit up, and I glare down at Rocky who's curled up between my legs. The bed is barely big enough for Piper and me as it is, but Rocky's decided he sleeps with me or doesn't sleep at all. At three a.m. I caved and let him hop up and curl up next to me. Curling up next to me turned into snuggling. Finally, I just let him and dozed off.

I let Rocky out for his morning business as I down a cup of coffee, then brush my teeth. When he's done, we both check on Piper, who is still sleeping. Even though he whines, I shut the bedroom door and cross to the bed where she's curled up around a pillow, her gold hair fanned out around her.

She simply looks too good for me to ignore. I dive back in to bed and wrap an arm around her from behind. She automatically arches back into me, searching for warmth and mumbling. She's just as soft and warm as I imagined and I couldn't dream up a better way to get up in the morning.

Well, I could, but she deserves what I have in mind instead.

With my body bracketed behind hers, I use the hand wrapped around her waist to dive under her little sleep shirt. She makes a purring sound in the back of her throat and stretches, her body rubbing against me in a way that makes me hiss out a breath. My hands meet bare, soft skin and then it's my turn to make a sound in the back of my throat. She fills my hand perfectly and I knead her breast until the purrs become low moans. When I take her nipple between my fingers the way I remember she likes, her moans intensify.

"Logan, what—" her voice breaks as my hand abandons her breasts and glides down her stomach. "Oh my god."

"Good morning."

Her response is lost on a moan as my hand dips under her shorts. One of her hands grips my wrist, her nails digging into the skin, but I take my time tracing a leisurely path around her abdomen. I mark her hip bones from one side to the other, then feel her thighs quake under my hands. When her shorts become too restrictive, I deftly maneuver them down, but leave them imprisoning her thighs.

"Off," she whispers impatiently.

I nip at her ear. "No way in hell. I don't want to give you any chance to escape."

She chuckles, but it's breathless. "I'm not going anywhere."

"Not taking that chance. You're gonna stay here. I'm gonna finish what we started the other day, then it'll be your turn to have breakfast in bed."

Her breath catches. "I'm not going to argue. I promise there won't be much of a wait this time."

I leverage up so I can see her face. "Wanna bet?" The tortured grimace makes me grin and I use the distraction to slip my fingers between her softness. Whatever objection she was going to make dissolves and her eyes drift closed.

I arrange her underneath me so I can reach her nipples with my mouth as my fingers start to make her writhe beneath me. She clutches me to her chest and the sexy as hell look on her face alone would have me hard as a rock if I weren't already. I'm teasing her to the edge with flicks of my tongue on her rosy nipples when her own hands find my hardness underneath the sweats I forced myself to wear to bed.

I look at her and find a misleadingly innocent look on her face. "Piper," I growl. "The hell are you doing?"

"It'll be worth the wait," she says with a grin that lights up her blue eyes. "I promise."

She pulls down the waistband of my sweats and delves under my briefs to palm me. I hiss out my own breath as her fingers ring my cock with one confident, devastating hand causing me to lose rhythm with my own attention.

"This is why you need a headboard."

"Why?"

"So I can make you hold onto it until I'm done."

She bites her lip, releases. "But I like touching you." To emphasize her point, her hand tightens and explores my length. "I like touching you very much."

All ability for conversation fails me, so I decide to put my mouth to better use. I rip off her shorts and panties in one swift movement, then stretch out alongside her. She sits up at my abrupt movement, but her eyes are on my cock where her hands are working me up and down. Before I can make another move, she leans forward and wraps her lips around me. I look up at the ceiling and my whole body tenses as the pleasure of her mouth on me washes through me.

For a few long minutes, I revel in the suction of her mouth and the grip of her hands. When she uses one to cradle the weight of my balls, I reach over and arrange her naked thighs on either side of my head. The action is so quick she can only shiver and then my mouth is on her. The sensation is double-fold because the second my tongue comes in contact with her clit, she sucks in a sharp breath around my cock.

I'm surrounded by the scent and taste of her and I feast like a starving man. With my hands clamped around her thighs, there's no way for her to escape, and based on the moans she's making against me it won't take long for her to come against my tongue.

Normally, this position doesn't do it for me. I'm either too focused on my own pleasure to attend to the woman's or so focused on her to come myself. That's not the case with Piper. Each of her movements, her sounds of pleasure, only fuels my own. The closer she gets to orgasm, the wilder she gets as she sucks me deep into her throat.

I circle her waist with my arms to hold her still as I intensify my own attention on her clit, sucking it between my lips and laving it with my tongue. She screeches against me and her thighs begin to tighten rhythmically on either side of my head. I have to ignore everything she's doing while I follow the line of her to the source of her desire.

After only a few strokes she tightens against me, then takes me deep into her throat. Her hands constrict around me and the combination of her orgasm and the head of my cock bumping the back of her throat rips my own orgasm straight through me. I try to pull away, but she locks herself around me until I see white.

When I come down, I pull her trembling body back up mine and fit her warmth against me. "So," she says after a deep, satisfied sigh, "you said something about breakfast in bed?"

A few minutes later while Piper's in the shower, I leave her a note, letting her know I took Rocky with me and that I'll be right back, and then I gather up his leash and lead him out to the truck.

We stop at the Sunshine Cafe where Sofie and Livvie like to get breakfast, and I order us a couple breakfast platters and some to-go coffees while Rocky waits outside.

The server is handing me the to-go containers when the two women come in through the doors, their various kids in tow.

Livvie brightens when she sees me, tugging her son Cole along behind her. "Logan! Good morning."

"Hey, ladies," I say and kiss her cheek, then lean down to ruffle Cole's hair.

Sofie gives me a hug. "What are you doing here?"

"Yeah," Livvie adds. "We don't normally see you up this early. Or this happy. What have you been doing?"

I tug on her ponytail and ignore her question. "Just picking up breakfast."

Sofie eyes the containers. "That looks like food for more than one person," she comments knowingly.

"You should have been a cop," I tease.

Sofie smiles and as she places her order, Livvie turns to me, her face serious. "I heard about what happened. Is there anything we can do?"

"No, the only thing I need you two to do is stay safe. The

cops are doing everything they can." They both nod, and then Livvie gives me a half hug around my waist.

"Promise me you'll be careful."

"I promise."

"Hey!" Sofie says as she turns and leans her back on the counter. "You should bring your friend over this afternoon. We're going to carve pumpkins with all the kids at Ben and Livvie's. It'll be fun."

"I think you've forgotten that I don't have kids," I say dryly.

She smacks my arm, then says, "Don't be a smartass. I want to meet her."

The both of them turn and face me with identical looks and I groan. "Look, I'll bring it up to Piper, but yesterday was an emotional day, and she may not be up for all of you in her face."

"If it makes you feel any better," Livvie says, "we'll go easy on her. We both know what it's like to go through horrible ordeals. We just want to help her deal, is all. And part of that is taking her out of her own head for a while."

I hesitate and then cave. "I'll see what I can do."

They both grin and kiss me on opposite cheeks.

I pick up my food and drinks and shake my head as I start for the exit.

"Don't forget to get a pumpkin for each of you!" Livvie shouts behind me.

Their snickers follow me out the door, but the joke's on me, because I stop and pick up two pumpkins from a fruit stand on the way back to the lake.

Piper's on the porch waiting for me when I pull into the

drive. Her curious expression morphs into amusement as I struggle to get out of the cab with two large pumpkins.

"What did you go do?" she asks.

"We've been invited to go carve pumpkins with Ben and Jack's families. I thought we could both use the distraction." I heft the pumpkins up when they start to slip. "I also got you breakfast. It's in the front seat if you want to grab it for me." Leaning down, I kiss her before she can argue and then climb the stairs to put the pumpkins on the table.

With a mystified laugh, Piper bounds down to the truck to retrieve the food and I know I've made the right decision. I'll keep her so busy today she doesn't have time to worry about anything else. We both deserve a step back because I know the worst is probably yet to come.

"ARE you sure you don't mind? They'd understand if you weren't up to hanging out."

Piper's expression is carefully blank. "I'd never insult your friends like that. Just don't leave me alone with them."

"Despite what I may say about them sometimes, they're still a great group of people."

Her hands twist in her lap. "Remind me of their names again? I don't want to get them confused. I never really got the whole list from Chloe."

As I drive down the road toward Ben's, I use one hand to steer and the other rests on Piper's thigh. I consider it progress. "Well, we're going to Ben and Livvie's house. They live on the other side of the lake. Ben is Chloe's cousin, which you already know."

"That one I have, at least."

"Jack is Livvie's brother and he's married to Livvie's best friend Sofie."

"Small world," she murmurs.

"Small town," I correct with a laugh.

"Ben and Livvie have a son named Cole, who's the spitting image of Ben. You won't be able to miss him. And Sofie adopted her two younger brothers, Rafe and Donnie, after her parents passed away." I glance over. "Got it?"

She bites her lip. "I think so. Is it crazy that I'm nervous?"

"Not at all, but you don't need to be. They promise not to pester you with questions."

"And you're sure they won't mind that we brought Rocky?"

I pet the big guy behind the ears. "Not at all. They have a big yard and they both have dogs he can play with. They'll be fine. Plus, if he can handle this brood, then you know he can handle pretty much anything."

"It's very nice of you to invite me to spend time with your friends," she says.

I kiss her knuckles. "It's important to me that you meet them."

"Admit it, you want to get me out of the house."

Grinning, I say, "I never said I didn't."

She leans over and kisses me. "Thank you."

"What's this?" I joke. "You mean you want to get to know them, too?"

"Well, if they're important to you, they're important to me, too, right?" I look over, surprise stealing my words. "I mean, if I haven't scared you away yet, then I must be stuck with you."

"Damn right you are," I say as we pull into the driveway.

She opens the door, and Rocky bounds out with loud barks to join the two little yapping Boston Terriers who spring from the front porch. Livvie and Sofie are already sitting on the steps with their bright orange pumpkins in mid-massacre.

Donnie and Rafe explode from behind them with handfuls of the orange guts and start tossing great globs of it at each other while shouting and laughing. Donnie scrambles around Livvie and Sofie with Rafe following close behind, and little Cole scurries to keep up.

Livvie spots us and her face splits into a huge smile. She and Sofie get to their feet and Livvie comes to Piper.

"We're so glad you came!"

Piper smiles hesitantly. "Thank you for inviting me."

"Why don't you bring your pumpkin to the porch? Now that the boys are gone, the fun can really begin."

Sofie pops up from behind the railing with a handful of ale and a soda for me. "I have refreshments!" she shouts.

"So this is what you mean by carving pumpkins," I say as I take the soda from her and hand Piper the ale.

"Oh we're still going to carve them," Ben says as he comes out of the house. "It's just a whole hell of a lot more fun to do when you're drinking."

Piper glances at me, and I give her a reassuring smile.

"Don't worry," Sofie says. "We won't corrupt him."

"Trust me," Jack adds as he pops the top on his own. "He gets his payback."

"Yeah," Sofie chimes in, "you think the cop would be the

cool one, but no. If you get drunk around him, just make sure there aren't any working cameras."

Livvie cackles and Piper sends me a confused look. "It wasn't my fault they got drunk and passed out." I tell her.

"He likes to draw on unsuspecting people," Ben says, without an ounce of shame.

"You mean passed out people," Livvie says.

"Shouldn't be the first to give it up," I tell them.

"Fuck you," Ben says, losing his reserve. "I couldn't get that permanent marker off for a week."

Piper laughs around a swallow of her beer, and I relax a little.

"Just for that, I'm going to carve a pumpkin that will kick your pumpkin's ass," Ben says to Piper.

She just smiles. "You're on."

The adults whip into a fury of insults and taunts as they gather reams of newspaper and open their carving tools. Sofie and Livvie have already finished theirs with the kids, so they're elected as judges.

"The boys are all set up out back," Jack says as he hunkers down with his pumpkin. "You guys are going down."

"You wish," Piper retorts, causing me to grin. She chugs down the rest of her ale and sets it aside. With her tongue between her teeth, she sorts through the stencil book and selects her pumpkin face. I'm so busy watching her, I get stuck with the shittiest stencil, but it's okay. I'm just enjoying the hell out of watching her.

Sofie and Livvie are overcome by laughter and they sputter out a "Ready, Set, Go!" in between giggles.

"When did you get back from leave?" I ask Jack as he carves out the top of his pumpkin.

"Coupla days ago." He jerks a hand toward Sofie. "This one kept me tied up until now."

Piper's eyes round and Livvie spits out her beer.

Sofie just rolls her eyes. "He enjoyed every second of it."

"Guyyyys," Livvie groans, "how many times do I have to say I don't want to hear that stuff. He's my brother."

"What about girl talk?" Sofie demands.

"Yeah," Livvie says and tosses a pile of pumpkin guts on a piece of newspaper, "you forfeited girl talk when you started sleeping with my brother."

I glance over to see how Piper's handling their craziness and find her laughing along with them. I thought she was gorgeous the first night I met her when she came out of her house wearing little more than her robe and barely-there pajamas, but I was wrong. Dead wrong. Then I only thought of her as a vaguely interesting woman with a hot body and an attitude. Now I know her, and I am completely awestruck by how amazing the woman is.

She must feel me staring, because she looks up at me, her face split wide in a grin and the world slows to a stop as our gazes meet. In the end, no one wins the pumpkin contest. Sofie and Livvie voted for their significant others, and I threatened to arrest them. We settled on tie between us all.

"That was amazing. I can't remember when I last had that much fun." Rocky jumps from the truck and tangles around our legs as we head back to her house. "Thank you so much for inviting me."

"Anytime."

She looks back at me as she unlocks her door. "You seem quiet," she says, but her voice is light and her limbs are loose as she toes off her shoes and throws herself onto the side chair.

I make sure to do up the locks for the front door and follow after her. When I don't answer right away, her smile fades and she sits up. "You okay?"

"Yeah." I tug her to her feet and then arrange her in my lap after I sit on the chair. "I couldn't be better."

"I can't believe you cheated," she says, giggling. "Mine was clearly a lost cause."

"Best pumpkin there," I insist.

She turns in my lap so her mouth is nearly touching mine, and I capture her lips for a kiss. "I had a good day," she says after she leans back.

I toe off my shoes and gather her against my chest. Rocky finds a spot on the floor and settles in to sleep. "Good, I'm glad you enjoyed yourself."

"Your friends are nice."

"They're your friends now, too."

"Thank you, Logan."

I press my lips into her hair. "For what?"

"Everything. Being here. For this morning. For pumpkins."

"Honey, you don't need to thank me. It's worth it just to wake up to you like I did."

She grins up at me. "Oh, really?"

My thumb traces her lower lip. "That, too, but I just meant you. I like being with you."

She kisses my thumb. "I didn't mean for this to happen, but I'm happy it did. I like being with you, too."

"Took you long enough."

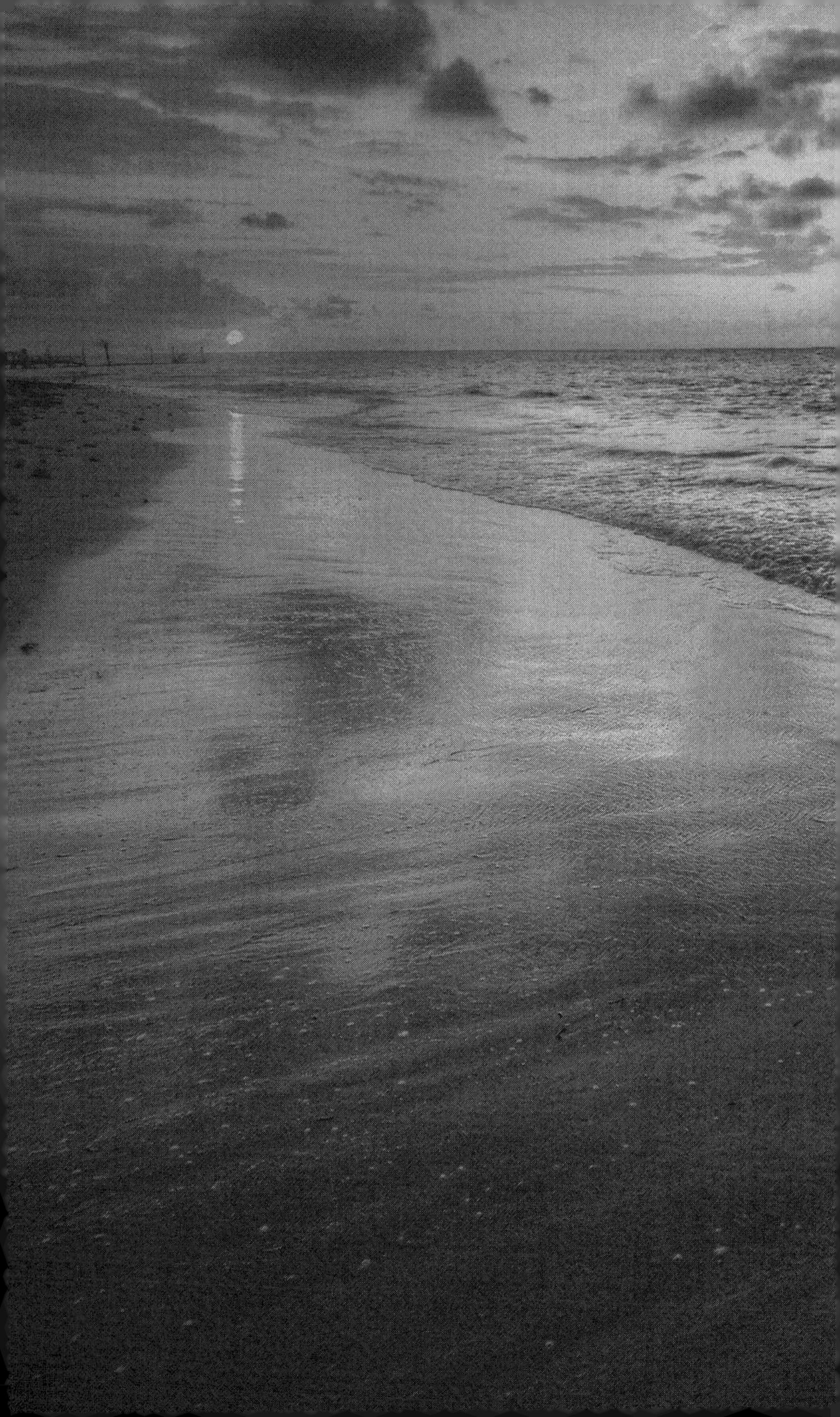

CHAPTER NINETEEN

PIPER

IT'S a beautiful day and I should be enjoying it. There's no reason for me not to. And yet here I am, wracked with indecision as I stare out at freedom on the other side of my screen door.

The influx of last-minute vacationers determined to wring the final remnants of summer before the coming of fall have kept me busy for the last two weeks. So busy, I told Diane not to worry about giving me any time off. I could use the money and the work as well as the distraction. She didn't like it, but she agreed because the inn had been packed without fail, the whole time. As September started to draw to a close, guests gradually began to trickle down to a more manageable number until I couldn't keep putting her offer of downtime off.

When I'm not working, I'm at the little bungalow with it's cheerful paint job and quaint furniture dusting, refinishing, or relaxing with Logan, who's essentially moved into mine since his is still filled with unpacked boxes. Once she saw the many improvements I made on the bungalow, I convinced Diane to let me help with the renovations on the other rentals, too.

But now there are no chores for me to do. There are no guests with urgent demands, and Diane put off my last plea with a stern shake of her head and a pointed look. For weeks, I'd been dreading this moment. It's all too easy to think about the things I've left behind when I pause long enough for them to catch up with me.

As I'm turning away with a promise to myself to try again on my next day off, a loud knock comes at the door. In the following silence, it echoes through the empty hall. Logan's asleep, and I don't want to wake him, but I pause anyway. We haven't actually *slept* together, but he sleeps in my bed every night, anyway, and we spend those nights doing things that make me blush just thinking about them.

The knock comes again, and in the deep porch shadows, a shape shifts. Panic flares molten hot, and instinct tells me to escape into the recesses of the house.

I whirl around, heart in my throat, blood rushing in my ears. How could I be so stupid? I've only been here a short while, and I'm already letting myself get too comfortable. The first thing I should have done when I heard the knock was plan a quick exit. It's what I've always done when I get a bad vibe. Instead I stood there like a damn scared little bunny. I pivot, heading for either the bedroom to wake Logan or to the backdoor to book it.

"Shit." The familiar voice stops me in my tracks, and I feel like an idiot as I press myself against the wall.

"Chloe?" I cross the short distance to the door and swing it open. "What are you doing here?"

Chloe tugs me into her arms, and I wrap mine around her

shoulders. I pull back after a few seconds and look her over. She hasn't changed in the months since I've seen her, aside from the protruding and heavily pregnant belly.

I stare, eyes rounded. "When did this happen?"

She places a protective hand on her stomach and laughs. "Why don't you invite me in, and I'll give you all the dirty details."

Gesturing with one hand and pushing the door open with another, I grin, chastised. "Of course, of course. Guess I've forgotten my manners."

Chloe stands in the hall, her summer dress swishing around her legs in the gentle breeze from the open door. "This is a cute place you've got here."

"Thank you. Why don't you come sit on the couch?"

Chloe flicks me a look. "You sound just like Gabe."

"How is the father-to-be?" I take a seat opposite her on the couch.

Her husband Gabe is as amazing as they come. Not only did the guy face down an armed man to save her from a hostage situation, but he's an awesome father to his little girl and he treats Chloe like a queen. I can only imagine how he's handling the thought of becoming a father again. If I know him, he's waiting on her hand and foot.

She laughs. "You'd think it's his first time being a father. He's so excited he doesn't know what to do with himself." She pauses, her face growing serious. "But that's not why I'm here."

My good mood at seeing her sours. "Chloe," I warn.

She holds up her hands. "I come in peace! It's just you've had a couple months, and I couldn't wait any longer. Ben said you've even been to his house!"

My stern expression softens, and I put my hand over hers. "I'm sorry. I've just been so busy here with work."

Her eyes sparkle. "And? I hear you and Logan hit it off after all."

"Yes, and if you don't keep your mouth closed, you're going to wake him up." She glances around and notes some of his things around the living room. Before she can squeal in excitement, I cut her off. "Don't freak out about it yet, but yes, he's been staying here."

She raises her eyebrows. "Is that so? As in he's been staying here as a round the clock guard / police protection or he's been 'staying here'?" She wiggles her eyebrows on the last two words. "When you mentioned on the phone last week that you'd been hurt I almost drove down here myself, but Gabe wanted to wait until after the twenty-week appointment."

"You're terrible." I shake my head.

"Well, I'm happy for you, Sienna—I mean Piper. It's going to take me a while to get used to that."

To escape her knowing gaze, I get to my feet. "We should feed you. Why don't I go get my purse and we can spend my first day off from work with lunch? My treat."

Chloe gets to her feet, which turns out to be a laborious process. "These days, I don't ever turn down food."

Logan ambles in then clad only in boxer briefs and a cup of coffee. Momentarily stricken by all the glorious skin put on display, I can't seem to form words. It's been a long couple of weeks settling into the new closeness, but the sight of his magnificent body still has the ability to leave me breathless.

I manage to tear my eyes away from his abs, all three hundred and twenty-nine of them, and cross the room to give him a kiss. "Chloe and I are going to go out to eat," I say, when he finally releases me and I hope I'm not blushing.

Logan glances over my shoulder and gives Chloe an easy smile. "Hey, Chloe. Nice to see you again. Make sure you take care of her."

Chloe fans herself with one hand and grins. "You bet."

With one last kiss from Logan, I follow her out of the front door. "You know the area better than I do," I say once we're in Chloe's car. "Why don't you give me a tour and then we can find somewhere for lunch?"

"If I weren't about to pop, I'd beat you for not telling me about this sooner."

"Yeah, let's not. I'd hate to be responsible for sending you into labor."

She backs out of the drive, and I almost laugh at how comical it is for her to maneuver around her belly. "Oh my God," she exclaims. The car comes to an abrupt stop at the end of the drive.

I follow her gaze to Logan who's on the porch now, though he pulled on shorts, and is tossing a ball to Rocky. "What is it?"

"I'm happily married, but damn, that's one sexy ass man."

My neck swivels to keep him in my line of sight as she finishes backing out of the driveway. He's got his shirt off, baring his deep tan to the sunlight.

When I turn back around as the trees along the roadside block him from sight, I find Chloe studying me.

"What?"

"I've just never seen you like this. You were literally staring at him with a smile on your face."

"Then let's not jinx it, okay?"

She turns onto the main road and risks a glance back at me. "Fine, but I want all the dirty details over lunch."

"I don't think so," I say with a laugh.

"I told you everything when I started dating Gabe!" Chloe shoots me a meaningful look.

I swallow back a laugh. "One thing at a time, okay?"

For the next few hours, Chloe directs the car through the winding streets of Nassau. It's a small town, so it shouldn't take long, but Chloe ends up chatting about her family, who've always lived here. Then she moves on to her husband Gabe and her step-daughter Emily.

As she talks, I relax into the cool leather seats and let her voice wash over me. Much as I try to admit otherwise, I've missed talking to her, and am a little sad when we pull into a small restaurant's parking lot.

"I didn't realize how much I missed this place," she says as she tilts her face to the blue sky and takes a deep breath.

"You don't come back here often?" I follow her into the restaurant.

"Not as much as I'd like. Ever since this little guy made his presence known, I haven't had much energy. A large table, please," she says to the hostess behind a stand. "We have some friends joining us."

"We do?" I say with raised brows.

"Well, I haven't seen Livvie or Sofie in a while and since you're all friends now, I thought we could have a girls' day. That's okay with you, right?"

We follow the hostess back to a lengthy table with a beautiful view of the clear sky and bustling city center. I help Chloe into a chair and take one next to her.

We both order drinks from the waiter who appears and disappears a few seconds later.

I sip my ice water as Chloe peruses the menu. "How is the business going?"

Chloe pauses her search, nibbling on her bottom lip. "The business? Oh, it's going great." She hesitates and then comes to a decision. "I never thanked you properly for what you did for me."

"You don't have to thank me." I wave away her comment.

Her dark curls swing around her face as she shakes her head. "No, I really do. The travel agency was your baby."

"Then, I left my baby in very capable hands."

"You know you can always come back." Chloe sets her menu to the side and gives me her full attention. "Since you're back in Florida and everything. I don't want you to think I'm trying to keep you away from it."

The waiter comes back and takes our order. Chloe gets two appetizers, an entrée, and orders the dessert ahead of time without batting an eye.

When she catches my amused look she smiles, unrepentant. "Eating for two."

I shake my head, biting back a laugh. "Convenient. I don't seem to remember any excuses when you ate like this in Jacksonville."

"I have a great metabolism."

As the light mood fades I clear my throat. "I know you aren't keeping the business from me. I don't want it, honestly, and I know you're the only one who will love it as much as I do, but I'm happy here."

Chloe nods and nibbles a piece of fresh bread from a basket on the center of the table. "I understand. I don't know if I told you how much I appreciate it, especially when you let me uproot it to live near Gabe."

"That's what friends are for." I try to keep my tone light.

"Are you ever going to tell me what made you leave Jacksonville? I don't mean to butt in, but I've wondered."

"Well, I told you about my sister." Chloe puts her hand on mine and I continue, "Well afterwards, there was a reporter who liked to find me once I settled in one place for an extended period of time. For a while, I thought I lost him, but after my ex won his appeal, he found me in Jacksonville. I just couldn't stay and risk my ex finding me again."

"God, Piper, if I would have known we could have done something to help you. You could have stayed with Gabe and me."

I shake my head. "No, I couldn't put the two of you out like that. Besides, you helped me out by smoothing the way with Diane and letting me start over here. I can't thank you enough for all you've done."

"I'm glad you're settling in here. You seem happier than I've seen you in a long time."

When I smile again, it's sincere. "I am. This place is exactly what I needed. It's beautiful here. I don't know how you left."

Before she can respond, there's a flurry of activity at the front door and two beautiful women enter. One with deep auburn hair holds the hand of a little boy. The other, a sloe-eyed brunette, is flanked by two teenage boys with identical coloring and wide, toothy smiles. Beside me, Chloe raises a hand and waves them over. Sofie and Livvie wave back and start to head our way. Chloe pushes back her chair to greet the two women.

Two waiters appear out of nowhere to push another table

against ours and rearrange the chairs to make room for the new additions. I take a deep gulp of my water, wishing I was something stronger. It was easier making friends when Logan was by my side.

The women take seats, one on either side of Chloe, and their children next to them leaving me between one of the teenagers and the younger boy.

"I'm Donnie," the teenager says as he gets to his seat. "We didn't get to meet since these two," he jerks his thumb at the older boy who must be Rafe, and the younger who must be Cole, "kept me running around when we did pumpkins."

"Piper."

Both teenagers give me identical smiles and this time my own smile is genuine.

"Nice to meet you all."

Livvie drops her purse next to her chair and fluffs her hair. "I'm so glad you called. I needed to get out of the house."

Chloe laughs, one hand on her belly. "My cousin driving you crazy?"

"Always," Livvie says, but she's grinning good-naturedly. "Logan got a new motorcycle a couple months ago, so naturally he and Ben have been mooning over it. Ben's trying to convince me he needs a new one."

"Really?" The other teenager sits up a little straighter in his seat.

Sofie shoots him a stern look. "Don't even think about it, Rafe."

Rafe slumps back in his seat with a commiserating look from his brother.

Chloe grins at the pair of them, then says to Livvie, "Piper had Logan over this morning. *Early* this morning."

I groan inwardly as all eyes at the table shift to me, pinning me to my chair. All I can think to do is nod because my throat closes up.

"I'm so glad," Sofie says with a rush of enthusiasm.

My mouth drops open. "I'm sorry, what?"

Sofie shares a significant look with Livvie as Chloe's eyes brighten, and she nibbles on another piece of bread. "I've been telling Livvie for forever we should fix Logan up with someone, but he beat us to it."

"Because you're so nosey." Rafe elbows Sofie.

Sofie simply shrugs. "Hey, they were the ones talking loud enough for the rest of the world to overhear. Plus, it's not often Logan of all people talks about a woman." She looks across the table to Livvie. "I don't think he's even dated since he and his wife split years ago."

As the conversation shifts to trash talking his ex-wife, I turn my eyes to my lap. Try as I might, I can't direct my attention anywhere else and my ears strain to listen as they continue.

"Yeah, Piper has been working at the bed and breakfast," Chloe says, once they finish raking Logan's ex over the coals.

"Ohhhh," Livvie sends a longing glance toward me. "I love that place. Ben took me there for our anniversary. The views are spectacular. I'll have to come for lunch sometime. I remember the food is amazing."

There is a pause where all eyes turn to me. For a second, the words stick in my throat. Then I swallow and push through. "I'd like that."

The three women beam at me, and I relax into my seat.

"Do you ever get to eat there?" Sofie asks as she sips from a glass of wine.

I nod. "Diane practically forces me to take leftovers after dinner."

Livvie groans. "Now she's just being mean."

I surprise myself by laughing. Chloe glances over and beams at me, and I have to admit . . . I needed this more than I realized.

THE NEXT MORNING, I wake up before my four thirty alarm, and I'm still smiling as I wake Logan up so he can go to his place to get ready for work. It doesn't even damage my good mood when I find out I've run out of coffee.

The sun is just brightening the sky as I lock and re-lock my front door. Dew sparkles on the patch of grass between my house and Logan's. The sound of a door opening draws my eyes up as Logan exits his own front door. He gives me a grin that warms me from the inside out as he climbs in his truck.

I tear myself away from watching him and keep my gaze on my feet as I go down the steps and cross the front yard to the sidewalk leading to the B&B.

Even though I tell myself not to do it, I glance back before crossing the street, and I find Logan watching me. Surprise and then heat, flares and I duck my head back down as I cross the street with a hidden smile. His eyes follow me until I open the kitchen door and close it behind me.

Leaning heavily against the wood, I focus on catching my breath and calming my racing heart. Once blood isn't thundering in my ears, I push off the door and hang up my purse in the closet just off the kitchen. Work will help me push him from my mind. After the whirlwind lunch with the girls, I could use the monotony of cleaning the now empty guest rooms in preparation for the next occupants.

Before I get started with the cleaning, I make a pot of coffee for Rose and Diane, who normally rise mid-morning to start the light brunch for the early rising guests. Once it's ready, I fill a cup for myself and sip it while I greet the morning sun through the kitchen window as it rises over the deep, calming blue of the lake. Once finished, I rinse out my cup and set it on the drain by the sink. Rocky waits patiently by the back door for his walk. I decide I'd better take him before I get distracted by work. Rose and Diane have taken to Rocky like he's their own child and don't mind if he spends his days being lazy on the porch.

Tonight's the night, I decide as Rocky winds around me on our normal route through the trees to the rocky edge of the water. I'll make him a romantic dinner, and we'll see what happens.

Because he's right. What's the point of being alive if you don't *live*?

Lightness suffuses my being, and I whistle to Rocky, who has disappeared over a small hill leading to the lake. It's too early for the straggling vacationers who like to fish or dip their toes in the cooling water, but it's become my favorite time of day.

"Rocky, you silly boy, c'mon. We've got work to do." His urgent barks answer me, and I speed up.

When I crest the hill, I wish I hadn't. The smell hits me first, and then I recognize the bloody heap below me. Initially, all I can see is Paige. A few panic-stricken seconds pass before I can blink away her face. I can't be sure as she's been badly beaten, but I'm almost positive the dead woman in front of me is the sweet baker I met a few nights ago.

Lena.

My legs threaten to give out, and I stumble back against a tree for balance. As my brain trips over itself to understand the sight in front of me, I put a hand to my mouth to keep from vomiting my breakfast.

When I manage to still my roiling stomach, I run back to the B&B and grab my phone. As I wait for Logan to answer, I press my fingers to my eyes, trying to separate my memories of the past from the terrifying reality of the present.

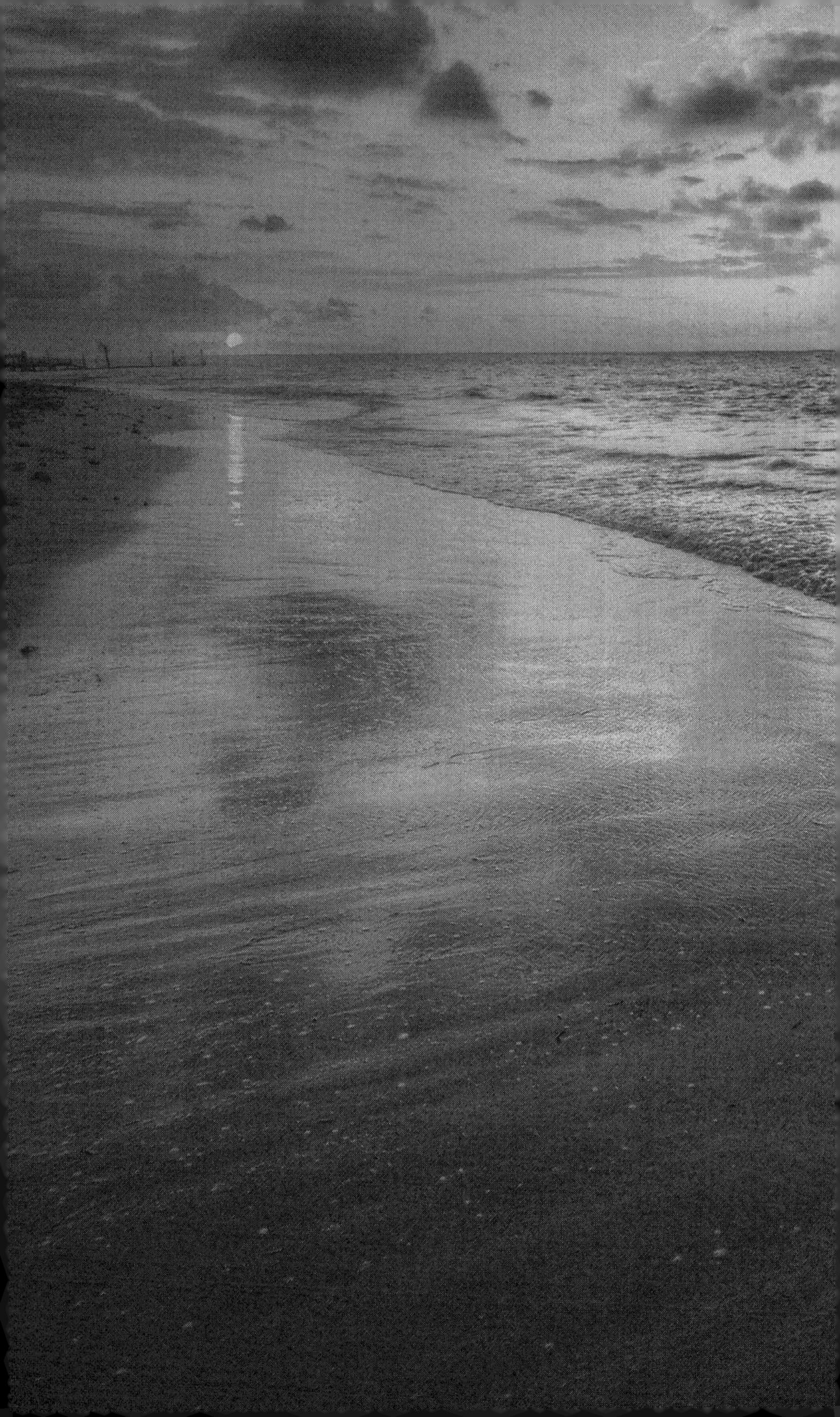

CHAPTER TWENTY

LOGAN

I DON'T MAKE it five miles down the road before my cell phone buzzes in the cup holder next to me. Glancing down, I find Piper's name on the caller I.D. and automatically smile. Replacing the thermos of coffee she fixed special for me before we both went to work with the phone, I answer, "Mornin', honey. Miss me already?"

When she doesn't answer right away the warmth from the coffee cools into lead in my stomach. "Baby, are you there?"

Her sob sounds over the line and I'd rather face a dozen armed men than ever hear the heart-wrenching sound again.

"Piper? Honey, answer me. Are you hurt? Where are you?"

"This can't be happening again," she whispers. "I can't—I don't think I can do this again."

I swerve through lanes of traffic at the first intersection, the blare of horns following me as I make an illegal U-turn. "I'm coming back. I'm on my way. Are you at work? Is it Grandma Rose, is she okay?"

Piper sucks in a long breath over the line and it whooshes through the connection. "No they—they're fine." Then her voice gets more urgent. "Don't let them come outside, Logan. They shouldn't see this. They shouldn't see her like this."

I've been in terrible, fucked up situations before, but I've never felt fear like this. A terror so consuming I find my hands trembling as they grip the phone. "Who, baby? Who is it?"

"Lena Thompson," she says, "she was a baker. God, she's dead."

"Can you walk back to the B&B for me? I don't want you out there alone. Is the dog with you? Keep him with you." I hear him bark as she calls softly to him. "Go back up there and get inside and stay there."

"I am, I'm going now."

"Good, that's good. I'm on my way now. I'll be there in a few minutes, but I need to call this in. Can you tell me what happened?"

She sniffles. "I took Rocky for a walk by the lake before work and found her. God, Logan, she was such a sweet woman and she's dead. For a second . . . for a second I thought she was P-Paige and I blacked out. I couldn't think. When I realized who it was, I called you. I just—I need you here."

The sirens I flipped on nearly drown out my words, but I know she needs to hear them. "I'm comin', baby. I'll be there in a few minutes. Stay here with me on the line while I call this in."

My fingers slip on the radio as I press the button. "187 at the Nassau Bed & Breakfast on McCormick Lake. Officer Blackwell responding and requesting backup." I have to wipe at the sudden cold sweat that breaks out on my forehead.

"10-4, Officer Blackwell. Backup en route," is the immediate response.

To my phone, I say, "Piper, you there, baby? I'm pulling in the drive now. I'm here." But I don't need to because the second I put the truck in park, she's throwing the front doors open and rushing down the steps. She hits my chest like a bullet and I wrap my arms around her shaking form. I tuck her under my chin and lean back against the grill of the truck, needing to provide the comfort as much as she needs to receive it.

"I didn't know what else to do," she says against my shirt.

"You did the right thing. There are more officers coming. We're going to figure out what's going on."

She nods against me, but her arms don't release.

When her shivering subsides somewhat, I glance up and find Aunt Diane and Grandma Rose hovering on the porch, identical looks of worry on their face. Aunt Diane comes down the porch steps first, still wearing the apron she dons on occasion to make breakfast.

"What on earth is going on?" Aunt Diane says as she lays a hand on Piper's back. "She ran through the house like the devil himself was on her tail. Scared the life out of me."

Piper manages to pull away, her face unnaturally white. Concerned, I say, "Why don't you go wait in the truck. As soon as the others get here, I can take you home."

She shakes her head. "No, I'll stay." With a deep breath, she turns to Aunt Diane. "Ms. Lena, the woman in the Lily Suite? I was walking Rocky down by the lake and I—I found her."

Aunt Diane looks to me for confirmation as words fail Piper.

"We've had a rash of assaults here lately," I start, but the rest of my explanation is drowned out as the emergency responders arrive in a blaze of sirens. "Why don't the three of you go back inside while I deal with this." I catch Aunt Diane's eye and flick my eyes to Piper.

Aunt Diane nods her understanding. "C'mon, Piper. I could use your help reassuring the guests if you're sure you don't want to go on home."

Piper moves to follow my aunt and grandma inside, but I find myself reluctant to let her go. She glances back at me and her eyes flick over my face. "Logan?"

Shaking off the sense of foreboding, I force my hands to release their hold. As I watch her walk up the steps, Colson arrives in his customary cowboy hat, his expression grim.

"Well, shit," he says.

As we walk around the B&B to the crime scene already swarming with officers and crime scene techs, I fill him in on the call from Piper, the interview she gave the day before, and my suspicions.

"Elizabeth Gallagher and the assault victim before Ms. Thompson got lucky. A man like this doesn't go from murdering multiple women to assault. He must have been interrupted with them. According to the Miami file, he liked to take his time. Draw it out." With a cool focus borne of years of training, I study the scene, trying and failing, for the first time to separate my own anger from my observations. All I see is Piper running toward me, the fear of God in her eyes.

Colson crouches by the victim's body and tips his hat up. As he studies her, I take in the scene. The chill in the air kept most of the tourists from any early morning walks, but there are lake houses and business all along the lake. Anyone could have seen him.

I glance back at the body, frowning. "Where's the blood?" I ask Colson, who stops speaking to a tech.

"What's that?"

"The blood. He likes to take his time with his victims. He can't very well do that in the open. If we're dealing with the same man, he likes to blitz attack women in a place where he has cover to play out his fantasy. His attacks are often violent, messy." I point to the sand and grass underneath and around the body. "There's no blood."

Colson leans back on his haunches, his shrewd eyes assessing. "He moved the body. Was that part of his MO before?"

"His first kills were somewhat impulsive. He'd come across a woman in an isolated locale and either convince her to go with him or blitz attack her, then he'd beat and rape her and leave her body or dispose of it afterward. They never found the first victim. Miami-Dade thinks he took her off to a spot in the woods. Probably to revisit her. Relive the memory. Why would he change here?"

"Could have been necessity. Someone interrupted him again." Colson takes out a cigarette, lights it. "He would have had to move her if he wanted more time with her."

I shake my head. "That doesn't make sense. Why move her out in the open like this? Anyone could have come—" My gaze whips around to the house. "Anyone could have come across her."

I hear Colson's long inhale, smell the smoke on his exhale. "He wanted her found." He pauses, considering, before continuing, "Does your girl walk this way every morning?"

My gut clenches. "She likes to walk the dog before she starts work."

"Regularly?"

"Pretty much, yeah."

"We'll put the dogs out, see if we can find the primary scene. We won't know more here until they finish processing and conduct the autopsy. I'll take care of the rest. You go see to your family."

I give him a nod because I don't trust myself to speak.

A pair of techs in white lab coats emerge from the sidewalk by the bed and breakfast with a gurney and a large black body bag. They chat idly as they pass and give me a nod. With one last glance at Colson and the remains of Lena Thompson, I turn away and head up the walk.

As many times as I've seen death, it never gets any easier.

Behind me a tech greets Colson. "Helluva Saturday morning, sir," he says.

I pass more of them on the way up the stairs and jerk my head in greeting. Hushed conversation carries through the door, and by the time the screen door clangs shut behind me, I've already forgotten what the tech looks like. All I can think about is getting to my family, to Piper.

Aunt Diane and Grandma Rose huddle together on the couch. Two uniformed officers stand close by. Piper is at the window behind the couch, her face leached of all color and her eyes glazed over. I curse beneath my breath when I realize she's been watching the whole circus.

Aunt Diane glances up as soon as I enter, her shoulders sagging with relief. "Logan." She gets to her feet and crosses the room to my side. "It's so awful. So awful. She was such a nice woman."

"We'll take care of it, Aunt Diane." I tuck her under my chin and realize, not for the first time, how small she seems.

"I know you will."

With a pat on her shoulder, I stride to the window and carefully close the blinds. Piper doesn't turn, doesn't acknowledge me, but she does close her eyes. I know it won't erase the things she's seen today, the memories it's likely evoking, but that doesn't mean she has to torture herself with it.

With the room to ourselves, I bring Aunt Diane back to the couch. "Have the officers taken your statements?"

Aunt Diane takes Grandma Rose's hands between her own. "Yes, they've taken ours. Piper hasn't given hers yet; she was next before you came."

Piper doesn't look when Aunt Diane says her name. "I'm going to call my friend Ben and have his mom take you to her house until we can get everything taken care of here, okay?"

"Oh, dear," Grandma Rose mutters. "What about the other guests? This is just so awful."

"I'll let you know as soon as we've finished up here, and we'll direct the guests to another location for the time being. Why don't you get what you need for the night, and I'll give Ben's mom a call, okay?"

Aunt Diane puts a hand to my arm and squeezes. "Thank you, sweetheart."

After I kiss her forehead, they head down the hallway to the first floor bedrooms, leaving me alone with Piper, who blinks a few times and then visibly trembles as she realizes everyone else has gone. Her throat bobs with a swallow, and she wraps her arms around herself. Her wariness is understandable, but the fear in her eyes when she looks at me is not.

"Do you want to sit?"

Her throat convulses again and her eyes flit around the room before coming back to me. "No, I'm fine."

"Honey, you look like you're about to drop. Sit before you fall down."

She nods but doesn't move, and that's when I know she's definitely in shock. I end up guiding her by the elbow and then leaving her for only a minute to grab her some water.

"Why don't you tell me what happened?" I ask after she takes a couple sips. Then, without looking at me a single time, she tells me about her morning and how she came to find Lena.

"She was a baker," she says absently. "Did they tell you that?" I don't speak because I know the question was rhetorical. "She told me all about how she started her own bakery after this horrible apprenticeship under the most awful man. They got engaged recently." Her voice breaks. "She was going to marry him. Someone needs to call him," she says faintly. "He needs to know."

"We'll find him," I tell her, pulling her close so she can rest her head on my shoulder.

"I thought it was over," she says, her voice watery. "I really did. I was so happy."

"I know you were," I say into her hair. "I know."

Her spine stiffens, and she jerks up. "We have to find him. We have to stop him." Her eyes widen and she brings a hand to her lips. "What if he goes after Livvie next. Or Sofie. God, Logan, this is all my fault."

I turn her head so she's looking at me. When her eyes clear and she focuses in on me, I say, "This is not your fault."

"When my sister—"

"That wasn't your fault either. You didn't do anything wrong. If you'd gone with her, you'd be dead, too. If he'd taken you at the park, you'd be dead."

"Maybe I should be," she says furiously. "Why do I deserve to live and they don't?"

"There is no deserving about it. Everyone deserves to live. Just because you did when they didn't doesn't mean you deserve to die, too."

She buries her face in my chest. "Can you take me home? I need to see to Rocky, and I don't want to be here anymore. I thought I could—I thought I could handle it, but I just want to be home now."

"Of course, honey."

She doesn't say a word as I bundle them up into the truck and back through the gathering crowd to the little road that leads to our houses. When I glance over to check on her, I find her forehead pressed against the glass, eyes closed. Every line of her body looks pulled taut and ready to snap.

She shuffles out of the truck like she has two cement blocks attached to her feet. Even Rocky can sense something is wrong because he keeps butting his head against her legs when she doesn't give him any attention.

When she goes to unlock the door, I put a hand on her arm and motion for her to wait. I'm probably just being cautious, but I don't want to take any chances. "Stay here," I tell her. Her reaction speaks to her shock because Piper doesn't just let me order her around. Gritting my teeth, one hand on my hip in case I need to access my gun, I take a cautious step inside.

The hall and living room don't show anything out of the ordinary. I peer behind doors and curtains, checking locks and closets as I work my way back. The living room is empty, everything just as we left it. The throw blanket is tossed haphazardly over the back of the couch, pillows heaped and smooshed where Rocky made himself a bed. My coffee cup sits on the side table where I left it—had it only been a few short hours ago? It seems like a lifetime. Through the living room, I clear the kitchen and check the back door, finding it locked.

A creak in the floor has me whirling around, my fingers automatically unclasping the catch on my holster. Piper shuffles down the hallway, the shadows accentuating the black smudges I'd never noticed before underneath her eyes.

"I'm going to take a shower, I think," she says without looking at me. She pauses before turning to leave. "Will you stay?"

My irritation at the situation softens. "I'm not going anywhere. I'll be right here."

She pads out of the room, her normally strong shoulders slumped. I hear the water turn on in the background and the sound of her undressing travels through the small confines of the house. The shower curtain screeches as she steps in and then the water cascades over her.

I let out a long breath I didn't know I was holding and lean against the kitchen counter. I have to grip the edge of the counter hard to stop my hands from shaking. The thing about being a sniper is you need those steady hands to make the shot when you're under pressure. *She's* going to need me to have steady hands, to be there for her. But while she's tucked away in the shower, I give myself a second to come to terms with the fact that a homicidal sociopath is after her.

And if I'm not careful, if I can't protect her, find the bastard responsible for putting the shine of fear in her eyes, the relationship I've been trying to build with her will be over before it's even started.

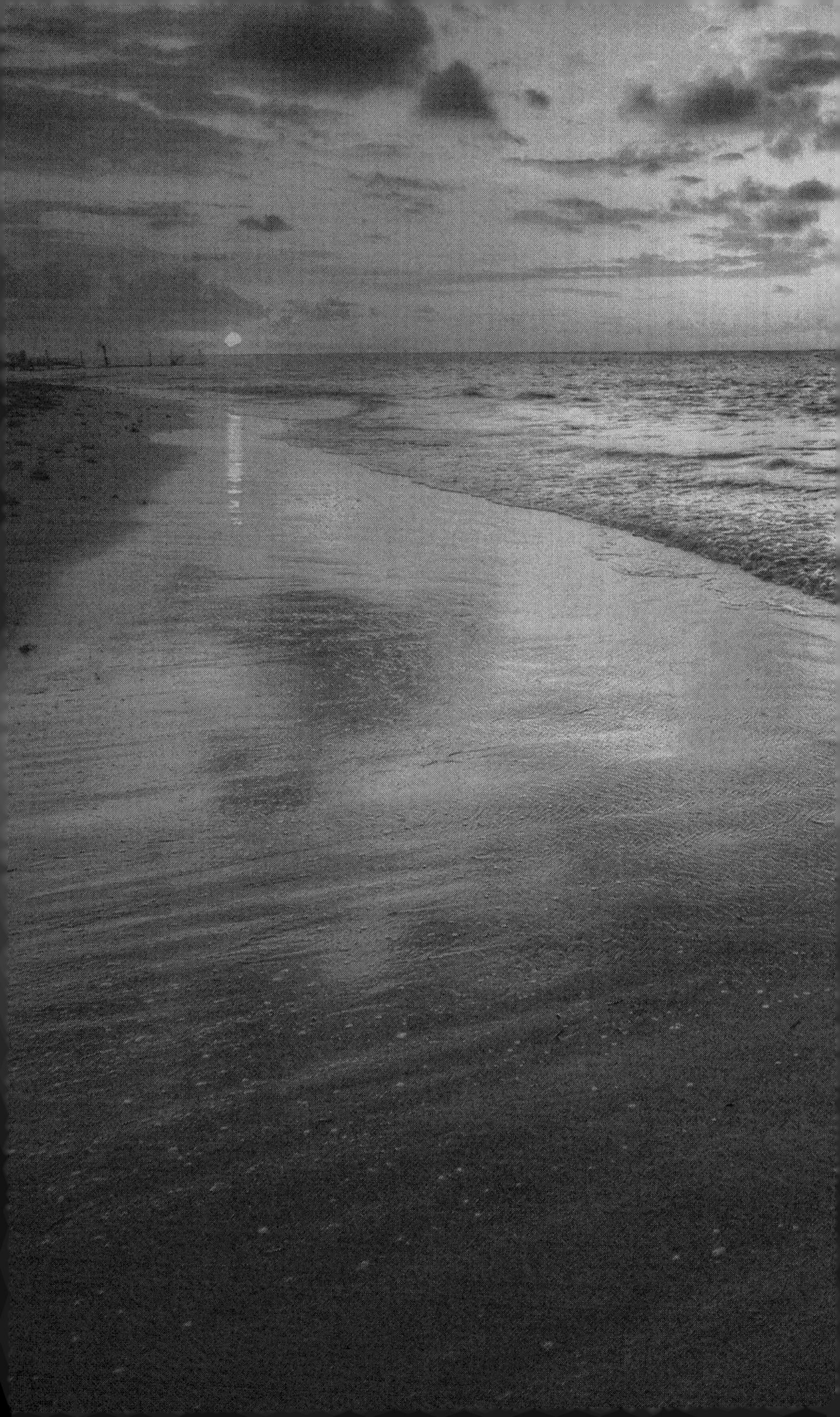

CHAPTER TWENTY ONE

PIPER

THE SHOWER HELPS, but no matter how hot I set the water, it can't erase the oily, sick feeling taking up residence in my chest. I rest my forehead against the cool tiles underneath the showerhead and let the water stream down my back. It pounds against the ceramic in a soothing pattern, lulling me into a sort of half-sleep.

Thoughts tumble one over the other, like a kitten chasing a ball of yarn until it's so tangled there's no hope of unraveling the mess. The urge to cry is there, a knot of tension in my chest, a hot pressure behind my eyes, but I squeeze my eyes shut. Tears won't help me. I learned a long time ago they can't bring people back from the dead. They're as useless as I feel and as unproductive. Feeling bad for myself won't change Lena's fate, but it doesn't erase the misery.

Movements sluggish, I straighten and reach for the bottle of shampoo out of habit. I don't need to wash my hair, but I don't know what to do with myself, so I give into the simple routine of it all. I turn my back to the spray and I'm scrubbing the coconut scented soap into my hair when I hear the sound of the bathroom door opening.

"It's me," Logan says followed by the sound of the door shutting behind him.

"Any news?" I ask automatically. Part of me wants to know the answer, but another is terrified and I hold my breath until he responds.

"Nothing yet," he says.

"I'll be okay if you need to go back to work. I have my gun and Rocky is here. You can even have them come check on me if you want." My fingers are numb as they work the soap out of my hair and they're so clumsy they keep getting tangled in the strands.

"I thought we were past all that."

I peer out from behind the shower curtain and find Logan leaning against the sink, his expression unreadable. His shoulders alone are too big for the cramped bathroom. The sight causes my lips to bow up and a giggle bubbles out.

He quirks a brow. "Something funny Ms. Davenport?"

"Just imagining you in the shower. Do you even fit?"

His eyes flick down to my bared shoulder and then trace my shadowed form behind the curtain, stealing the remnants of laughter straight from my chest. Then his eyes come back to mine and it doesn't take long for me to read the desperate hunger there. My smile fades and the aching emptiness I'd been lamenting is swallowed by a much more visceral yearning. Reflexively, I tighten all over. My fingers clamp down around the shower curtain, lungs strain against the dense steam, and my pussy throbs.

I should tell him I'll be out in a few minutes. If I had any sense of self-preservation left where he was concerned, I'd press him to go back to work, to leave me be, but I can't seem to force the words around the lump in my throat. And if I'm being honest with myself, I don't really want him to go. I want those big arms wrapped tight around me like they can protect me from everything. I know the second he walks out the door I'd be waiting for him to return. Somehow, he's become as essential to me as my own breath.

He steps close enough for me to reach out for him. I shove the curtain aside, heedless of the spray that soaks him, and my own nakedness. My hand fists his collar and pulls him closer and I gasp at the sensation of the rough material against my sensitive nipples. His hands go to my waist, his grip cautious.

"So I'm too big for my shower, but you think the both of us can fit in there?"

My fingers tighten, I nod, unable to speak. One touch and he lights me on fire.

He cocks his head. "Why don't you finish up here and we'll order some pizza, watch a movie."

When he moves to step away, I move my hands to his shoulders. "You don't have to baby me. I'm not going to break."

"I didn't say you were."

"Then don't treat me like I am."

"I'm not."

My hands slide down his chest to his abdomen. I take his shirt into my hands and start easing it up. "Then trust me when I say this is what I want. What I need. Please, Logan."

I pull his shirt the rest of the way up and it stops under his arms. I meet his eyes and plead wordlessly. The moment he gives in to his internal struggle, he rips the shirt from my hands, over his head, and then tosses it to the floor, baring the wide expanse of his chest and my mouth waters. He is a veritable feast and all I want to do is eat him up. I want to drown myself in him, in how he makes me feel.

Free.

The realization strikes me as his hands slide from my waist, up my ribs and skirt the sides of my breasts to frame my face.

He makes me free.

When he doesn't make the move to kiss me himself, I surge upward and drag his lips down to mine. Even with the lip of the tub between us, Logan towers over me, surrounds me, overwhelms me. He blots out the light from the dim overhead bulb like an eclipse. I cling to him, loving the way he makes me feel comfortable in my own skin for the first time in years. Needing it, and him, I take the kiss deeper.

Logan groans against my lips and pulls away. I follow him with a sound of protest and he says, "We're getting water everywhere."

I look down and find the shower curtain splayed wide and water cascading to the linoleum floor in torrents. The clink of metal draws my attention upward and my breath strangles in my throat as I find Logan undoing the buckle of his pants and sliding them down his thickly muscled thighs. I grip the shower curtain, more to keep myself from melting into a puddle of need right there in front of him than anything else.

Try as I might to get a handle on my staring, I can't tear my eyes away from his body. Muscles ripple beneath caramel skin as he toes out of his boots and then pushes his pants the rest of the way off. He moves with subtle male grace and a confidence that can only come with the knowledge of just how good he looks. Abs ripple and I don't need the Adonis belt leading down to find his cock, though both are mouth-watering.

With hungry eyes Logan steps into the shower and I back away to make room. He yanks the shower curtain closed with one deft flick of his wrist, trapping me between him and the wall. His body blocks the spray, but I don't need its warmth. Desire unfurling in my belly heats me from the inside out and he's barely even touched me yet.

"I didn't come here for this," he says, even as his hands come to skim my back.

Needing him, I press forward and gasp without sound as his hands press down my back, pushing me closer against his hard chest. The head of his cock presses against my stomach and everything south of my navel clenches in delicious anticipation. His mouth the other morning blew my mind. Based on the long, thick length of him, sex will obliterate me.

True to form, instead of diving right in, Logan reaches by me and I give up on breathing at the way the soft hair on his chest scrapes along my already sensitized nipples. Then I hear the popping sound of a bottle cap and his hands are in my hair massaging conditioner through from scalp to tip. I forget my protests as his fingers knead at the tension in my scalp and then work the knots out of my shoulders as the conditioner soaks. When my body turns to mush, he somehow manages to maneuver us around and tips my head back to rinse it out.

My knees liquefy and I have to press my hands to his chest to keep myself upright. As he works the conditioner out of my hair, I begin to tremble with anticipation. Having him so close and not devouring him is torture.

"Is this the part where you make me wait again?" I manage

to ask. I'm pleased when my voice doesn't betray how much the thought of his brand of foreplay is going to kill me.

He gives a dark, self-satisfied chuckle, then leans forward and his lips skim my ear. "This is the part where I make you want."

If my knees weren't already precariously loose, he would have made them weak. "I'm pretty sure I already do."

Logan brushes back my clean hair, then leans back to study my face. He must find whatever he sees there to his liking because he gives a low growl and then his lips cover mine and I have no choice but to forget everything that's happened because there's nothing left but the wanting.

When he breaks to heave steamy breaths of air, I'm plastered against his wet body. "You're so very, very good at that."

"Kissing you?" he asks absently, as his hands traverse my back and dip down to cup my butt possessively.

A powerful shock of pure pleasure shoots through me and I have to turn and bite his shoulder to keep from crying out. When I speak, my voice sounds like I've spent the last few hours screaming, "Everything. Just . . . everything."

"Like this?" he asks, and I only have seconds to prepare before he's palming the heavy, yearning weight of my breast in one of his big hands.

My skin is pale against his and I watch, absorbed by the sight of his thumb teasing one nipple to a desperate peak. Then he does the same with the other, then both at the same time, sending my head back and underneath the spray of water. A shiver courses through me and his lips twist with dark satisfaction.

Needing him, his taste and scent, I bring my lips back to his. There's nothing tentative about this kiss. It's wild and all consuming. There's little room in the stall to maneuver so Logan forgoes his studied calm long enough to press the length of my back against the cool tiles. His lips fused to mine, I twine my arms around his neck and wrap a leg around his waist, needing to be closer to him in every way possible.

His hand comes to my thigh, opening me to him. I can't seem to get close enough and I shift against him, needing something I can't quite communicate in words. With a grunt, he shifts his arm beneath one leg, then the other, and hefts me up against the wall. He starts to say something, but when he backs away my lips follow and I swallow his words.

I can tell the moment he breaks.

As his body inches closer the length of his cock brushes against me, the head resting against my clit. Beneath my hands his muscles turn to stone and I revel at how strong it makes me feel to cause a man like Logan to have such a reaction.

His breathing rough in my ears, his body shaking beneath my hands, he hovers on the precipice of indecision. My own body thrums with potential and after a few beats of temptation, I can't resist writhing against his cock, my body searching for the pressure it needs to assuage the ache. If I had the ability to speak coherently, I would have begged. I would have offered him anything.

"Fuck." His breath is harsh against my ear as his body presses even closer against mine and his arms stretching my legs so wide it'd be uncomfortable if I had the presence of mind to give a damn.

"Now, now, now," I pant. Arching against him only causes more frustration. "Please."

My half-lidded eyes catch his and I can't look away. He shifts his stance and then presses the head of his cock to my entrance. I suck in a swift inhale and my hands clamp down on his shoulders. As he presses forward, a long, low groan steals from my throat. The first taste of fullness sends a tidal wave of pleasure through me and I wonder briefly what the hell I was thinking when I wanted to push him away.

Now, all I want to do is get closer.

His head comes to rest on the tiles beside me and his harsh breathing fills my ears. Trembling hands grip the small of my back and the long, slow glide of his cock is seemingly endless. Twisting against his hold is useless as he pins me against the wall with his weight, thwarting my attempts to speed up his claiming.

"Stay fuckin' still," he growls. "I'm trying not to be too rough. You're so . . ." I squirm against him despite his warning and his lips press into a line. "Jesus Christ."

My movements cause him to slide the rest of the way in and we both inhale simultaneously at the fullness. Even if my head weren't spinning from the effort of drawing in the steamy air, the sensation of having Logan inside of me would have sent me on a tailspin. He hasn't even moved and already I'm towering on the edge of completion.

I can't help it, I shift on him, using my hands on his shoulders to grind against him. I'm not able to lift my hips as they're pinned by his hands and weight, but each little movement our position allows is electric.

He hisses out a breath and shifts to pull out in a wickedly slow stroke. My breath catches in my throat and I freeze. It's never felt so good before. It's never felt so *right* before. My eyes flick up and I find him watching me. When he thrusts back in I watch his own pleasure streak across his face.

Emotion rises up inside of me as his slow strokes cause my belly to tighten. His own response is mirrored in his eyes and the moment swells between us, a moment of connection so pure and timeless I don't want to break it by speaking. He must approve because the determined gleam in his eye warms, his lips soften.

"That's it," he says.

"W-what?"

"That's what I was waiting for." He takes my lips for a long, leisurely kiss.

"What were you waiting for?"

"Don't bullshit me."

His thrusts slow, his hips a fluid piston that somehow knows just the right angle to hit just the right places. My mouth falls open and had I the breath, a scream of frustration would have ripped out of me.

"You feel it?"

This time, I can't bullshit him. The rawness inside my chest is tantamount to carving myself wide open and giving my heart to him, but with Logan's strength around me, I know he'll keep it safe. If I run, I know he'll be right there behind me every step of the way.

"Yes," I hiss. "I feel it."

With renewed vigor, his thrusts resume and he invades my mouth, his tongue just as demanding as his cock. He begins fucking me without restraint and with my legs hooked over his arms, there's no escaping it—or him. I can't contain my response and I whimper against his lips as heat blooms.

I can't tell where one kiss ends and the next begins. I wish I could stay in his arms like this forever, the rest of the world and my worries completely obliterated. There is only us, only this.

As I cling to him I realize I won't ever be able to let him go after this.

As the climax rises inside of me with stubborn insistence, I fight against it, not wanting the connection, the moment, to end. But the denial of pleasure only increases it and Logan shudders against me.

"You feel so fuckin' good, honey. You're almost there, I can feel you around me so tight."

"Wait," I manage to say after I tear my lips. "Wait. I don't want it to be over."

"We got plenty of time," he says, then kisses me again.

I sink against him and it forces his cock inside me impossibly deeper, hitting a place that rips a scream from me. He takes it along with my pleasure, drawing each thrust out to maximize the crashing waves of the most intense orgasm of my life.

He shifts again and then the orgasm catches and flings me higher. A strangled sound escapes him and then he's pumping his hips faster and he stiffens, shuddering against me with his own climax chasing mine.

I swim out of the haze of bliss some time later to find Logan turning off the now chilly water. Without speaking, he offers me a hand and helps me out of the tub. My legs shake and nearly give out when I step onto the bath mat, but he catches me and carefully wraps a fluffy towel around me. A matching one is tied around his hips, dipping enticingly low. For a half-second I consider the arrow of that Adonis belt and then he's herding me out of the bathroom and to my bedroom.

I manage to sit on my bed and give half a thought to getting dressed, but my tired muscles give a scream of protest. Dismissing that idea, I crawl right up the bed, remove the towel and toss it on the floor. I grab Logan's hand from where he's standing beside the bed and tug him down. He follows without comment and pulls the sheet and comforter over the pair of us.

"You tired?" he asks as he wraps his arms around me.

"No, not really. I just wanted an excuse to hold onto you a little longer."

He kisses my temple. "You don't ever need an excuse to hold onto me."

Looking up, I blink away the mist of tears. "You're a good man, Logan."

He tucks me closer into his side in response and hits a button to turn on the T.V. to something that will take our minds off everything else outside of our little bubble. As I rest my head against his chest, I'm tempted to stay in it and never leave.

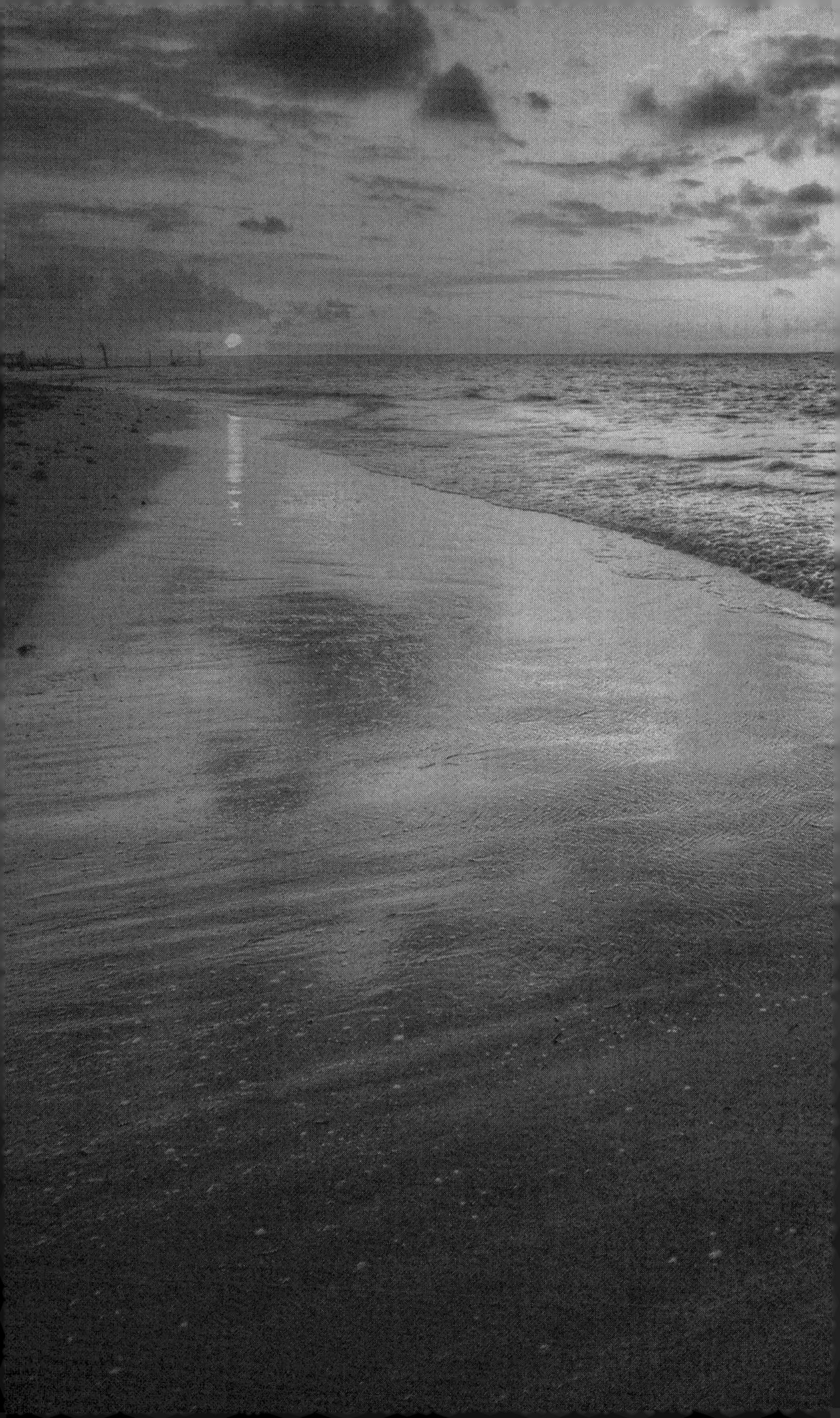

CHAPTER TWENTY TWO

LOGAN

THERE'S a comfortable air between us the next day. Hell, I was there and I can't even explain it. Something changed. When I watched her tip over the edge of orgasm this time, a piece of me went along with her. I've slept with my fair share of women, but sex has never been an emotional act for me. Probably because I never *let* it be one. I wince, considering my ex-wife. I guess she wasn't the only person to blame for our failed marriage, if I'm being honest.

Piper looks up from the pot of chili she's tending at the stove and I want to lick the little smile she sends me straight off her lips. Truth be told, I've had a hell of a time making myself keep my hands off her now that I know what it feels like—really feels like—when she comes. But she needs space, not a big ass guy crawling all over her, no matter how much she insists that she's fine.

"Do you want sour cream with this?" she asks as she ladles up a bowlful of the fragrant mixture.

My mouth watering, both for her and the food, I nod, not trusting myself to speak.

She tops the chili with a generous helping of cheese and sour cream, then brings it to me along with an entire sleeve of crackers. "Sweet tea?"

"Yes, please," I say after a spoonful.

My phone rings as she sets the glass in front of me. I pick it up with a carefully blank expression as I note Colson's name. She gives me a curious glance as she retrieves her own plate and sits down in front of me.

"Blackwell."

"Logan, I have news. Are you with Ms. Davenport?"

I glance up at Piper, who studies me around a sip of tea. "Yes."

"We had the dogs search the area, follow the trail we believe he may have taken." As he speaks, I set down my spoon and carefully lay my hands on my thighs. For a second, I'm concerned I'll snap the utensil in half with all the tension coursing through me. "They led us through the woods and across the street." He pauses, sighs. "Dammit, Logan, he's been camped out at one of your aunt's unoccupied bungalows. We found the victim's hair, a bunk he'd made. Empty food containers."

"Logan?" Piper says at the fierce look on my face. "What's wrong?"

"What about him?" I force out of stiff lips, though a sinking feeling in my gut already knows the answer. If they'd found him, he would have led with that news instead.

"It was empty by the time we got there. We spoke to the lodge across the street and the receptionist there gave us a description, but it's not much to go on. Man in his twenties or early thirties with hair that could have been dark blonde or light brown. Average height and build."

"Vehicle?"

"None that they've seen, but he has to have a way to get around. He didn't wander to Nassau out of thin air."

"What's your plan?" at my low voice Piper places her cup and spoon back on the table, chili forgotten.

"We have officers out now canvassing the area. If I were you I'd recommend taking your lady to a safe place for the night while we look for this guy. Just as a precaution."

I lock eyes with Piper. The fear that had been there this morning returns when I don't respond to her tentative, encouraging smile.

"I'll have her out within the hour. Take her to someplace safe."

"Where?" He cuts me off before I can answer, "Never mind that. Don't tell anyone. If I need you, I have your number."

"If I don't answer, you can call hers." I rattle off her number.

"I'll have an update for you by tomorrow morning if we don't have any results tonight."

"What about Lance?"

Colson's responding sigh is drawn out. "No updates yet on his whereabouts, either. They're still looking."

"Thanks for the update, Colson, I appreciate it."

"Take care now, you hear?"

"Will do. Talk to you tomorrow."

"What happened?" Piper asks before I have the chance to end the call. "Did they find him?"

Heart heavy, I stand and move to her side of the table where I take her hands in mine and crouch by her chair. "They found where the person's been staying. He's been camped out at one of the cabins Aunt Diane hasn't had the chance to renovate and rent out yet."

Her hands jerk underneath mine. "He's right here?"

"He was. They found the place empty when they got to it. They're going over it now."

"And they still haven't tracked down Gavin's whereabouts, have they?" Her words are slow and measured, like she's taking great pains to keep the words even.

"That's right, but he'll call if there's anything new."

She bites her lip, releases it. "And what was that about taking me somewhere?"

"I'm not going to let you stay here knowing he's had eyes on you this whole time. We're going to grab some stuff to go and we'll go to a hotel down the highway a ways where I can make sure you're safe until this mess is resolved."

For the first time, she doesn't fight me. Instead, she removes one hand to run it over my hair. "All right, then. I guess we'd better finish this quickly."

I kiss her hands and we sit to eat the chili, though the comfortable feeling between us has been poisoned with both of our worries. Rocky sits by our feet, his tail wagging every few seconds when we glance down at him throughout the rest of the meal.

After we're done, I gather the dishes to rinse and put in the dishwasher while Piper retreats to her room for suitcases. I let Rocky out to do his business and water the garden one more time. Vaguely, I hope they last through the first chill bound to come, as the flowers have been enjoying the few days of warm weather.

Rocky and I find Piper in her room, her movements

robotic as she folds and stuffs laundry into her suitcases. "I'm going to run to my place to pick up some things, then we're going to head out."

She nods without speaking and, not wanting to betray my own fears, I leave her to her packing and turn silently. I cross the short distance between our places and unlock my front door. The first thing I notice is the stale air—the smell a place gets when it's left empty for too long. Seeing it after hearing Colson's news causes me to imagine what he must have been doing all this time, what he must have been thinking.

Through the far living room window, the one facing Piper's, I can see the repeated flash of police lights. About three doors down, on a curve that follows the road, officers walk in and out of the front door. Others amble about along with the crime scene techs and the bobbing of Colson's signature hat.

With the angle of the road the way that it is, he would have had at least the sliver of a view into her home. Surely the whole porch and space between our houses. If he's been watching, he's definitely seen us both going back and forth over the past few weeks. Seeing me with her may cause him to be even more aggressive.

That in mind, I stride to my bedroom and grab random clothes that smell relatively clean and stuff them into a bag. I don't bother with toiletries; if we're gone longer than a couple of nights I can pick some up at a store nearby. Instead of heading to the bathroom, I detour to the closet, where I keep a Glock 22 .40 caliber pistol. I strap it into a shoulder holster and put a jacket on over it. Colson said to play it safe, so I also take my Smith & Wesson Model 60 Chief's Special 5-shot .38 Special and secure it in an ankle holster.

I don't want to leave Piper alone in the house, even if I'm

next door, for long, so I grab my bag and lock up behind me. Piper is waiting on her porch with a suitcase on one side and Rocky, tail swishing back and forth, on the other.

She starts down the steps with him following close behind and they both meet me at the truck. Without saying a word, we load up our bags in the cargo area behind the front seat of my truck and get in.

I glance over and find her eyes glued to the activity going on at the other cabin. Streams of people flow in and out, everyone with a serious look on their faces. Nassau is a small town and hasn't seen violence like it did today. When things happen here—everybody feels them. As we pull by, Colson nods, then he has to turn his attention back to the scene and the techs clamoring for his attention.

"Where are we going?" she finally asks when we put the scene in the rearview mirror and are out on the main road.

"The interstate is just up here. I'm going to drive a couple exits over and we'll stay there for a few days. At least until they're certain he's out of the area and not watching you."

"They think he's coming for me, don't they?" she asks. I glance at her and find her slumped against the door, her head propped up on her hand. "He's going to come for me to finish what he started in Miami. Because I got away."

If I didn't have bumper to bumper traffic surrounding me, I would have pulled the truck over. Instead, all I can say is, "He's not going to do a damn thing to you."

She shakes her head. "You can't stop him Logan."

I grit my teeth. "Fuckin' watch me try."

Finally, she glances over and for a second, I take my eyes off the road to send her a look. "If he—if he hurt you, I don't know what I'd do, Logan. I can't lose you, too."

My anger fades and I tug her over on the seat to me, nudging Rocky to the other side. "You're not going to lose me."

"Promise?"

I take her hand and press a kiss to her knuckles. "I promise. I told you, I'm not going anywhere."

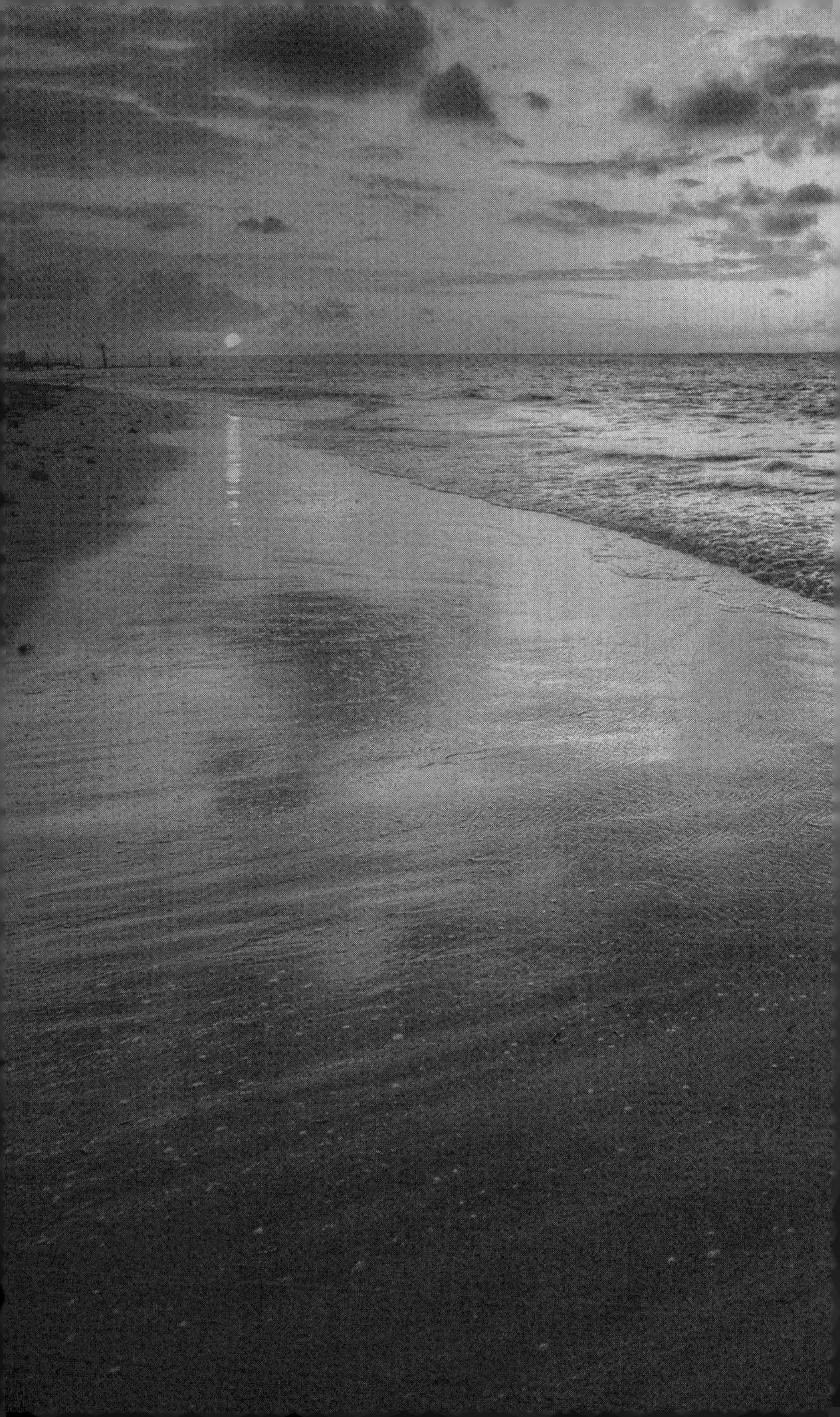

CHAPTER TWENTY THREE

PIPER

I DON'T KNOW what I would have done if I didn't have Logan's hand to hold on to. He is my beacon in the darkness. We drive on the interstate for a while, passing at least four exits on the way. He really wasn't kidding about putting distance between us and him, wherever he may be.

After about an hour, he takes an exit to a nondescript little town. There isn't much by way of accommodation, but there is a squat little hotel. They take cash, don't bat an eye at Rocky, and don't ask many questions. Logan pays for a couple days up front and the manager gives us a key and gestures to the back of the lot.

"Nice place," I comment as his truck jolts through potholes. He spares me a scathing glance, causing me to laugh for the first time in what feels like forever.

The hotel is a dreadful pink monstrosity, but it's cheap and anonymous, so beggars can't be choosers. Logan pulls the truck up in front of our room and we haul Rocky and our bags inside. He'd taken the police decals off and the siren is located beneath the grill so it looks like an ordinary truck. Unless the creep followed us here, we'll be safe.

As I roll up to the door, I start to wonder, when did I start thinking of he and I as a we? I have to admit, I love the concept more than I would have thought. We. Us. A couple. It's funny how the things we fight the hardest against are the things we end up needing the most.

"How long do we have to stay here?" I ask as I place my suitcase on the dresser in front of the bed.

I don't mind the peeling paint, the obnoxiously colored bedding or the faded watercolor artwork. I do mind being forced out of my home—again.

"A couple days at the most. If we're lucky, then just tonight."

Logan shucks his jacket and I note the shoulder holster he's wearing. A gun shouldn't be sexy, but the way he wears it is undeniably attractive. The holster accentuates his shoulders and when he turns I notice it frames his chest. I find myself just watching him as he moves throughout the room until he looks up and catches me.

He notices me looking at the gun. "Just in case," he says and places the holster on the nightstand next to the bed.

"Do you have more guns hiding in other places?"

His grin is quick and lethal. "Just one." He lifts one pant leg and I eye the small silver pistol strapped there.

"Well aren't you handy to have around?"

A quick glance around the room shows a small table and chair situated in front of the big window with the air conditioner underneath. A long dresser fills up the wall opposite the two double beds. The innermost wall is occupied by a long sink and counter with a coffee pot and hair dryer.

As I set out our things to keep my hands busy, Logan settles in at the table with his phone and proceeds to make a series of hushed phone calls. Not wanting to eavesdrop, I motion that I'm going to go outside to talk on my own phone to give him some privacy.

The midday autumn sun does little to warm my chilled insides. I dial Chloe's number and immediately feel lighter as soon as her voice comes over the line. "Hello?"

"Hey, it's me."

"Jesus, I've been so worried about you. I was just telling Gabe I was going to call you to see what was going on. After the story in the news, I about had a heart attack!"

My heart slows to a dull thud and the *womp, womp, womp* of blood rushing in my ears nearly drowns out my response, "Story?"

"They did a story on you today in the *Miami Herald*. It was picked up by the stations in Jacksonville because I own your company. They like to tie any sensationalist news with my name ever since the kidnapping. Honey, if you would have told me what happened, I would have understood. I'm so, so sorry about what happened to you."

I have to lean against the column to keep upright. "Do you have the paper there with you? Could you tell me the byline?"

"Sure, just a second. Umm, it looks like a Phil Exeter? Why? Does that ring a bell?"

I thought after everything that's happened, I'd lost the ability to be surprised. Apparently not. "There's a lot I should catch you up on, but I really can't right now. Logan and I are staying at a hotel while we try to sort this mess out. As soon as the dust settles, we'll make another date, okay? I promise, I'll tell you everything."

"I'm going to hold you to that. Is there anything I can do to help?"

A rush of affection surges through me. "No, but thank you for offering. You're a great friend."

"Of course I am."

"I'll call you as soon as I can."

"Love you. You know that right?"

Tears fill my eyes and make my voice rough. "I know. I love you, too, Chloe."

I stay outside until I can get control of my emotions. Logan is still sitting on the chair when I open the door to the room, except now he has the air conditioning unit running full blast and the television is on a local station, the volume turned down low.

"Everything okay?"

"Yes, I just got off the phone with Chloe."

"Are you sure everything is okay?"

I sigh. "Remember Phil? The reporter? He got wind of Lena's . . . of Lena and finally got his big break. He published a piece with the *Miami Herald* about everything."

Logan comes to me and takes my hands. "I knew I should have arrested him when I had the chance."

"For what?"

He frowns. "I'd figure something out."

I kiss his cheek. "My hero."

"Smartass."

"Did you fill up on chili or do you want to order something for later?" I ask as I move to the dresser to take out pajamas. If we're going to be holed up here, I may as well be comfortable.

"I'm all right. I have a few more calls to make."

"I'll give you some privacy. I wanted to take a shower anyway."

At the mention of a shower and the stirrings of our last, he grins and my cheeks heat. I escape to the bathroom while I still have a chance.

Twenty minutes later, I get dressed in my pajamas and emerge from the bathroom and find him sitting, more like sprawling, on the high-backed desk chair, his legs spread and his dark brows slated over blue eyes gone molten. I lean against the far wall of the hotel room near the rattling air conditioner and watch him.

Then he spreads his legs wider and jerks his chin. Before I make a conscious decision, my body makes one for me and is moving across the room. I don't know if I need his closeness or just need him, but I just . . . need.

It's as simple and as complicated as that. One taste of him apparently wasn't enough. Despite all that's happening, my body craves him.

He grabs my arm as soon as I'm close enough and guides me between his legs until I'm kneeling in front of him, feeling like very much the sacrifice. It's the same position as the last time we were intimate, but this time there's no question about who holds the power. Everything about his posture screams alpha male.

Something swims in the depth of his eyes, but I can't read it. All I can do is grip his muscular thighs through his travel-worn jeans to hold on, because if I don't, I feel like I'll just spin right out of the room and into orbit.

He lifts one of those big, strong hands and threads it through my wet, matted hair. It catches on the tangles and then his gentleness gives way to violence and he jerks my head back with one flex of his powerful fists.

My head now bent backward, my neck at his mercy, he leans toward me, the ancient chair creaking, and fastens his lips to the delicate curve of my bared throat. His hot kiss marks me like a brand.

I inhale swiftly, my insides turning tight and hot, forcing me to go limp against him. My fingers clutch his jeans and slip over the smooth material to his waist. At the first glancing feel of his hot skin against the tips of my fingers, my breath seizes in my throat. I delve under the material of his shirt and whimper, aching desperately for more. More skin—more contact—more *him*.

He groans, and his fist clenches in my hair almost impossibly tight as his tongue samples and his teeth nibble. The leisurely journey he takes from the base of my throat to my lips is agony. By the time he finds my mouth, I no longer have a breath to spare, but it doesn't matter—everything but his kiss simply ceases to matter.

I don't think about what's going to happen tomorrow. About the horrors from the past. I've never felt so completely overtaken. He plunders, his kiss waging a battle. It should go down in history because by the time he lets me up to breathe, I'm waving a white flag, never having experienced tactics quite so masterful.

His other hand comes to my waist and urges me up to his lap so I'm straddling him.

"You want this?" he asks, and nudges his hips upwards in a slow, rhythmic roll. My response lodges somewhere in my throat, and he chuckles darkly. "Oh, yeah," he growls. "You want it."

I suck his lower lip into my mouth and nip it between my teeth as I release. His eyes flash and his hands flex, and I smile just as darkly causing him to grin against my lips.

When I speak, it's guttural and I worry it betrays more of what I'm feeling than I'd like. "Yeah, Logan. I want it."

The closeness is almost too much. All-consuming. Overwhelming.

My legs dangle off either side of his hips as he cradles the rest of my body in his lap. All I can do is clutch his head with my hands as our kiss turns carnal, all teeth and tongues and heat. I lose myself and can't tell where he ends and I begin.

When I'm limp from it, he gets to his feet with me in his arms and crosses the room in two long strides to place me on the bed. He wastes no time ridding himself of his hoodie and shirt, then shucking his jeans, leaving himself completely bare.

Any other time, I'd give in to studying each and every blessed inch of his tawny, inked skin, but I barely have time to take him in before he's ridding me of my own clothes. By the time I catch up, my shoes and socks are gone and his thick fingers are fumbling with my pajama bottoms.

"Here, let me," I say when he growls in frustration and starts to rip them right off me.

His hands frame my hips as I work them down. Our eyes lock, and he dips his head, capturing my lips again. I keep getting distracted by the sleek, muscular body pinning me to the bed. There are acres upon acres of gorgeous skin for me to explore, and I can't wait to trace every inch of it with my lips and tongue and teeth.

I start to do just that, scooting my body under his to trace his sternum and abdomen with my tongue, but he captures me under my arms and hauls me right back up. My shirt disappears next and then we are naked and bare against each other, and I don't think I've ever felt anything so exquisite in my life.

In a few quick, efficient motions he pulls a condom practically out of thin air and opens it with his teeth. When he positions his hips between my legs, my eyes are drawn down to his hands as they sheath his cock with the layer of latex.

Then his eyes meet mine and he nudges me backward, crawling up my body until his weight rests above me. He bumps my thighs open wider, deliciously, uncomfortably so, and then he thrusts, and I see white. His own hoarse growl of satisfaction is low and sends warmth radiating through me. There's no seduction this time, but I don't need it. It's all heat and need, mindless want.

Everything I'd been denying, all the feelings I wasn't able to put a name to—or I didn't *want* to put a name to—come rushing to the surface as he thrusts into me, slowly, inexorably, and we lock eyes.

"There it is," he says.

I shake my head against the rise of sensation, the firestorm of emotion.

One hand comes to grip my jaw, and he forces me to look up at him. There's no hiding from the tumult of sensation, no running from the inevitable tumbling over the edge. He has me trapped. As it overwhelms me, I give a cry of surrender, and he swoops down to swallow it with greedy lips. My orgasm sweeps through me, and I clench around him with greedy, wet pulls. It consumes me completely.

CHAPTER TWENTY FOUR

LOGAN

A COUPLE of days locked in a room with a woman might terrify a lesser man. Instead, I picture it as a challenge. Here, I have her all to myself without any interruptions. Hell may be raging outside, but I have my own little slice of heaven within these four walls.

Sure, there were plenty of times during the past three days we've been sequestered in the hotel room when we got mad as hell at each other, but for the most part, the isolation has only brought us closer.

"What does this mean?" I ask, tracing the little tattoo of a moon on her wrist.

She smiles, one I'm coming to learn means she's about to talk of her sister. She hasn't gotten a sad look on her face in a while, I've noticed. Now all she thinks about are the happy memories. "Paige and I both got them when we graduated high school. She had a matching one. A sun."

Piper lifts to an arm, uncaring of her nakedness and traces the ink on my back. "What about yours? Must have taken forever."

I peer over my own shoulder, loving the way her pale fingers look against my dark skin, my darker ink. "It's a work in progress."

Her eyes widen. "You mean it's not even done yet?"

"Nah, I add something to it to mark important moments in my life."

"Really?"

"Mmhmm."

"What are these names?" she asks, tracing the lettering scrawled over my shoulder.

"Brothers I served with who died."

Her finger stills for a second, then she resumes her exploration. "It's kind of like a patchwork quilt," she murmurs.

I bury my face in the pillow, my shoulders shaking with laughter. "God, don't tell Grandma Rose that. She'll be wanting a tattoo next."

Laughing, Piper throws herself back down against the pillows and I lift my head to watch her perfectly round breasts bounce. We just got done having sex and already I want her again. One hand goes to cup the weight of her and she sighs into it with a soft smile on her face.

She turns to me and moves close underneath the blankets. I shift so she can fit herself against my chest, resting her head on my bicep. My arm will probably go to sleep, but it's worth it just to have her close.

Her left hand comes to my chest and slides up to cradle my cheek. "Logan, I—"

My phone vibrates on the nightstand. Knowing Colson is the only person it can be is the sole reason why I reach across her to answer it. She goes quiet as our little bubble bursts. He'd called regularly with updates, what little there was to update us on, anyway. No leads. No news. Stay gone. Even though I know it's probably more of the same, adrenaline surges through me.

"Blackwell."

"We got him," Colson says triumphantly. "Her ex. Jacksonville P.D. caught him with a moving violation of all things. He's in transport now."

I let out my pent up breath in a violent exhale. "Jesus Christ," I whisper. Part of me thought we wouldn't get out of this without a fight.

"They're bringing him in now for questioning, but we got the son-of-a-bitch."

"That's great news," I say.

"What?" Piper asks. "What's great news?"

I cover the microphone with one hand. "They found Gavin in Jacksonville. They're transferring him now for questioning."

Her smile is radiant and even though Colson's started talking again in my ear, I lean forward to press a kiss on her lips. Even Rocky jumps on the bed to join in when we shout out our excitement.

"IT FEELS SO good to be home," Piper says as she wheels her suitcase into her living room.

"What? You didn't like our love shack?"

She snorts. "What I liked was having you naked and to myself the whole time. After the first day, I forgot there were other places on this earth except that bed."

"You shouldn't say things like that. Gonna make . . . ego big."

Piper levels me with a look. "As if your ego needs any encouragement."

"I'm going to go to the station to be in on the interrogation. According to the cops in Jacksonville, he was trying to high tail it out of there. Must have been the news article that spooked him."

"I never thought I'd say this, but thank God for Phil Exeter."

"Remind me to buy him a gift," I say as she lets Rocky out the back door. "What time is Aunt Diane coming to get the B&B ready?"

She checks her phone for the text. "In about an hour? Gives me just enough time to shower and unpack. Do you want me to throw your clothes in to wash, too?"

I cross the room and take her in my arms for a kiss. "That sounds so . . . domestic."

"Least I can do for my big, bad bodyguard."

"Oh, the least, huh?"

When her laughter fills the room, I cover her mouth to savor it on my tongue.

She breaks off, her cheeks pink and eyes dilated. "Don't distract me. We both have things to do."

"What if I changed my mind? We can both go back to the hotel and stay there. Sex and pizza for the rest of our lives."

"Tempting," she says, and squirms out of my hold, "but your aunt will have my hide if I'm not there to help clean up."

"Are you sure you're going to be okay here by yourself?" I ask as she pulls away to sort through our laundry for the first load.

"I'll be *fine*. They caught him. Your aunt will be here in a little while and I have Rocky to keep me safe from bad men like you."

I pin her against the washer from behind as she leans in to fill it. "How about I show you what this bad man can do after I get back?"

She twists around to kiss me. "It's a date."

THE ANTICIPATION I experience on the way to the station causes me to speed all the way there. I roar into the parking lot and take the first available space without even checking to see if it's reserved for a high ranking officer. Colson meets me at the entrance to the station and I clap a hand around his shoulder.

"Thanks for everything you've done for me about all this. I appreciate it."

"Remember that when I decide to run for Sheriff."

I laugh. "You got it."

My long, hurried strides eat up the distance between the foyer and the hall leading to the interrogation rooms. Since I'm personally involved in the case, I'm not allowed in the room, but they do let me watch from behind the two-way mirror as Colson goes in to initiate the questioning.

I wanted to hate the man on sight. I wanted to feel the low hum of twisted expectation I used to get before I went in for a kill, but it doesn't hit me.

"Mr. Lance, my name is Detective Colson. Do you understand why you were brought here today?"

Instead of answering with a sneer like I expect, the man's shoulders round and he looks more exhausted than anything. He shrugs. "I don't know. Whose murder am I being accused of today?"

Instead of answering, Colson offers his own question. "What were you doing in Jacksonville?"

Lance's back stiffens and he glances around the room warily. "What is this about?"

"Were you trying to find your ex-girlfriend?"

Lance grits his teeth. "Look. I did my time. All I wanted to do was start over. My Dad's family is from the area. They were helping me to find a job, a place to live. It's not easy being an ex-con, you know. Ask them! I just moved in with my uncle and his wife. Ask them if you don't believe me."

"Then why did you run when the officers approached you?"

Lance snorts. "I know you probably don't understand what I'm about to say, but I didn't do anything wrong. I didn't do anything wrong then, I didn't now, whatever it is you're trying to accuse me of. I haven't hurt anyone." Pit stains bloom underneath Lance's arms. More than anything I want to bust open the door and haul the guy up. A couple right hooks to his perfect jaw should loosen whatever truth he's got left in his brain. "It's about the woman that was murdered here, right? The one in the paper. The one they linked to Miami. To Paige and Piper. I'll tell you now what I told them that night. I didn't kill anyone. If that's all you have to ask me, we're done here. I'd like a lawyer."

A phone rings next to the door of the interrogation room. Colson picks up the line as he walks out and then he turns to face me. I don't have to listen to his next statement to know deep down in my bones that I just fucked up.

"His alibi checks out. We got the wrong guy."

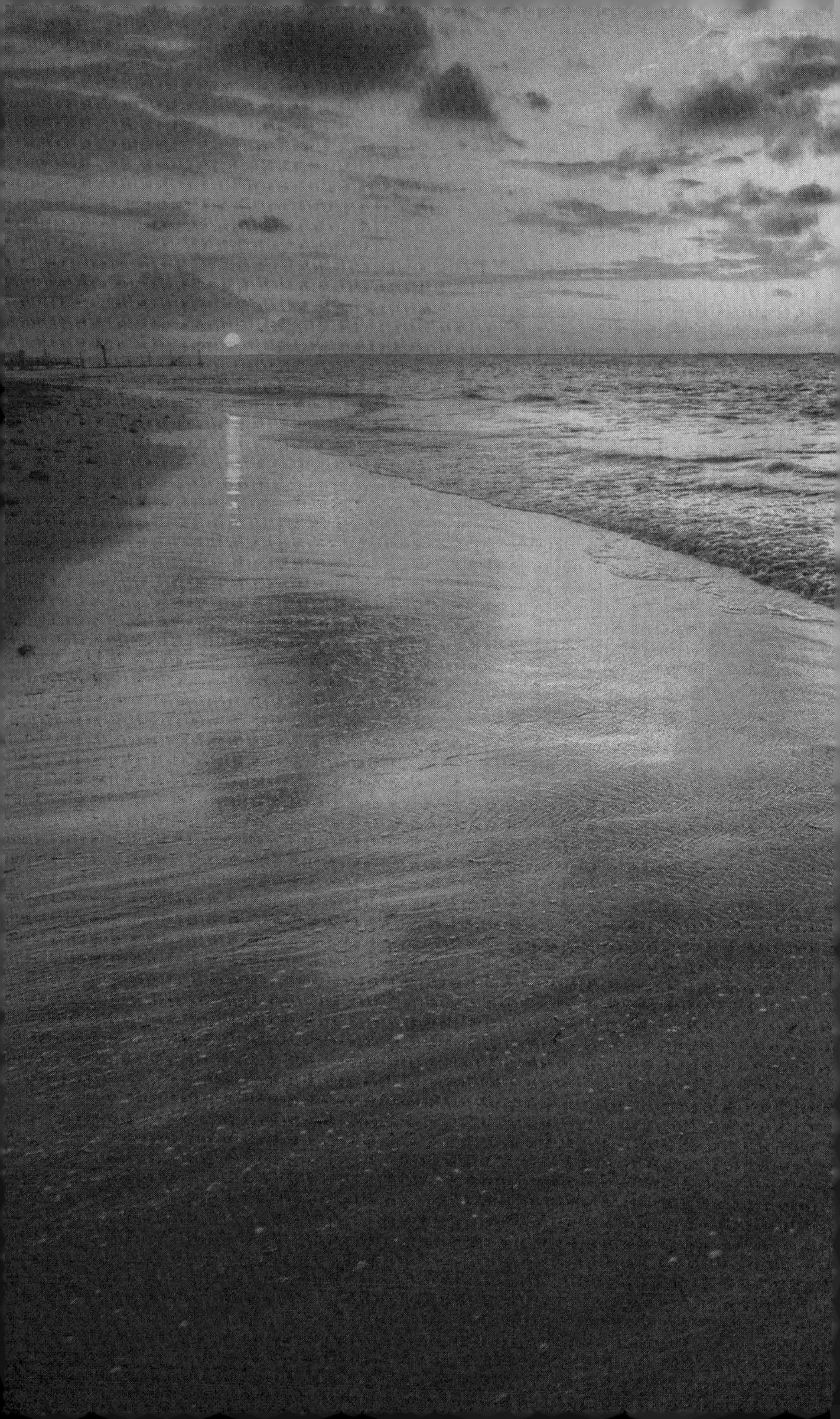

CHAPTER TWENTY FIVE

PIPER

I LET Rocky back inside at the same time as the front screen door opens with its customary *screeeech*. I remind myself to have Logan grease it up the next time he has a chance and pick up the vase of flowers that Diane is coming to pick up.

I open the front door with a smile on my lips. "You're early! I was just about to head—"

"Hello, Piper."

I don't recognize him at first and then he takes a step toward me with a scarred hand lifted and the memory clicks into place with an awful clarity.

"Joseph?"

My whole body turns to ice. I don't even notice the glass I step over as I take automatic steps in retreat.

"Been a long time," he says as he closes the front door behind him. The eerie smile on his face causes me to shiver, and I can't believe I never pieced the two together. I thought I'd never be able to recognize his voice, but I do.

I manage to regain my own. "What are you doing here?" The question is a stupid one, because I piece together the reason for his presence the second he stepped through the doorway. My mouth hasn't quite caught up with my brain.

"Why don't we go to the living room to talk?" he says.

I wish he'd stop smiling. The uptick of his lips makes me want to throw up all over his feet. This was a man I'd considered to be a friend. All this time, I thought Gavin had been the person who killed Paige.

Oh my God.

"You . . ." I have to suck in a deep breath to combat the swift, potent rage that crashes over me like waves of molten lava. "You killed Paige."

He gestures to the living room. "It only took you years to piece it together."

"You shouldn't have come back here."

He cocks his head and sits on the corner of a chair. "And why is that?"

"Because I'm going to kill you."

Eyes twinkling, his eerie smile widens. "Trust me, I doubt you have it in you."

Rocky ambles into the room, but his tail isn't wagging. He can sense the tension thick in the air. Joseph turns his attention to him and I whistle. Rocky comes to lay at my feet, but he keeps a keen eye on Joseph.

"I seriously doubt you know anything about me."

"Sure I do." He gets to his feet and prowls around the room, picking up pictures of me and Chloe, knickknacks I'd gathered from traveling around the U.S. and books I'd meant to read, but haven't yet had the time to. He studies each one calmly, like he has all the time in the world. "I've been watching you for a while, you know."

"I've figured that out," I say through my teeth with forced calm. "We found your little hide out. Your trophies. Did it make you feel powerful to hurt those women?"

He puts down the photo of Chloe and then turns to me. "What do you think?"

"I think you're a sick bastard. What are you waiting for? Why don't you get it over with?"

"Now Piper, we've waited years for this and we've got all the time in the world. I'm not going to rush it."

"If you think I'm going to sit here and let you finish what you started, you're sadly mistaken."

Rocky starts growling and I place a hand on his neck. I wouldn't tempt Joseph to harm him, too.

"Why?" I ask, my voice betraying my amped emotional state with a tremor.

Joseph clucks his teeth. "Really? We're going to devolve into psychology? Is this where you want to know if I hated my mother or if I was abused by my father?"

"Were you?" Part of me wants to know. I need an explanation for the evil that tore my world apart.

"Would it matter? I do it because I like it. Because there's nothing like watching a person die by your own two hands. It's powerful."

Anger causes me to lose control over my tongue. "So that's why you've followed me this long. Did I take your power away? Did that make you feel like less of a man?" I laugh, but it's watery because at some point tears started streaking down my cheeks. "I'm the one who got away." My laughter takes a turn toward hysterical and Rocky gets to his feet to lick my hands.

When my vision clears, the expression on Joseph's face wipes away all traces of humor and my body comes to life with the presence of danger. My throat runs dry and I have a fleeting thought that his face is the last thing Paige saw. This face.

My body reads his movements, the shift of his weight to the balls of his feet, the poise of his arms by his side, so I tense to flee. When he hurls himself across the room in my direction I shoot to my feet. He's inches away from me with hands outspread and I spin, dodging to my left and sending him crashing into the couch.

I sprint for the hallway, Rocky right by my side barking like a hellhound. Joseph's footsteps thunder behind me and I make it to the kitchen. He's mere feet away. I won't have time to fling the lock open and get the door wide enough to go through so I make a split second decision and spin to my right at the last second and dive through the open door to my room. If I can just get to my nightstand, I'll be able to get my gun to defend myself.

Just as I reach the bed his hand snares in my shirt and he jerks me backward against his chest. This time, I don't go quietly. Before he can get his arms around me, my elbow goes up and connects with the corner of his eye. He cries out in pain and I use the distraction to tumble over my bed so that it's between us.

My fingers fumble with the pull on the drawer, but I manage to get it open with a sound of triumph. I jerk the gun out, but my arms connect with his torso as he tackles me to the ground. We land with a thud and his weight knocks the breath straight from my lungs. The gun skids across the ground and over to the wall.

Straining to breathe, I push at his chest and try to wedge

my knees up between us. He manages to straddle my waist and wrap his hands around my throat. My already oxygen deprived brain screams in protest as he applies pressure. Black spots dance in front of my vision.

It'd be so easy, so easy to give in to him, to join Paige, but Logan's face flashes in front of my eyes and I fling my arms wide, my fingers scrabbling at the gun only mere inches away. Garbled sounds come from my throat and the ringing in my ears tells me if I don't get him off me, and soon, it won't matter how much will I have left to fight.

Then, a shadow launches itself off the bed and right onto Joseph's back. With a godawful yell, he releases the hold he has on my neck and tips to the side, catapulting a growling Rocky against the wall. He collapses on the floor in a silent heap.

While Joseph's momentarily distracted by Rocky's lifeless form, I scoot back on my butt to the wall and get my gun. I flick off the safety and point it at him. When Joseph looks back surprise causes his eyes to widen fractionally. He tilts his head and studies me like I'm an insect he doesn't quite understand.

He takes a step forward and I scream. "Don't come any closer!"

"You don't have the stomach for killing," he says with a sneer and he takes a step toward me.

I try to slow my breathing, focus. It's hard to do when everything inside of me is screaming, but I have no other choice.

The next step he takes is his last. I squeeze the trigger and a bloom of red spreads on his shirt. He looks down at it, confused, and then back up at me, in awe. He takes another step and I shoot again, this time I wing his cheek and his eyes grow hard. With a last burst of energy, he crosses the room on unsteady feet and I squeeze off one more shot.

This time I don't miss.

He stops, sways for a few pregnant pauses, and then crumples to the ground at my feet.

I drop the gun as convulsions overtake me.

An indiscernible amount of time passes and I hear Logan shouting my name. He bursts through the living room door and I hear his footsteps pound down the hallway. Outside, the distant wail of sirens grows closer.

Logan appears around the corner and comes up short in my bedroom doorway, surveying the wreckage of my attack. When his eyes get to me, he's pale beneath his tan.

I try to get to my feet, but the shaking is so bad, I stumble twice before he gets to my side and helps me upright.

"Rocky?" I manage to ask.

Logan shifts me to the bed and kneels by Rocky's prone body. He crouches down and when he gets back up, Rocky springs to his feet and comes immediately to my side.

I bury myself in his fur. "Good boy," I tell him. "You're such a good, good boy."

"Police!" I hear from the front door. "Is anyone here?"

"We're back here! One officer. I'm armed. The suspect has been subdued."

More footsteps thunder and Logan urges me to the bedroom door and around the responding officers. He shields me from the already arriving media—include Phil Exeter—and places me in his truck. Rocky jumps up behind me, tail wagging, the trauma already forgotten.

Logan pauses by the door long enough to lay his head on my lap. "I don't think I've ever been so scared in my life."

His warmth washes away the chill and my fingers lift to his neck, then slide to his shoulders. "I'm okay."

He shakes his head against my legs. "I never should have left you."

"You couldn't have known."

"I could have lost you."

I tip his face up to me and lean down to kiss him, my blood sparking back to life at just one touch. "But you didn't. I'm still here."

He kisses me back, this time more deeply. When he finally releases me, he says, "I'm never letting you out of my sight again."

"I'm okay with that." I lean into his arms as he wraps them around my waist.

"You're moving in with me tomorrow."

I brush my hands over his closely cropped hair. "Gonna be pretty cramped."

"Then I'll build you a bigger house."

"No, I don't think that'll work for me."

He glares up at me. "You don't really have a choice in the matter."

I kiss him again. "I'd much rather we get married first."

The hard mask of pain and fear disappears and a big smile breaks through. "I can live with that."

Yeah. I take another mind numbing kiss. *I can live with that.*

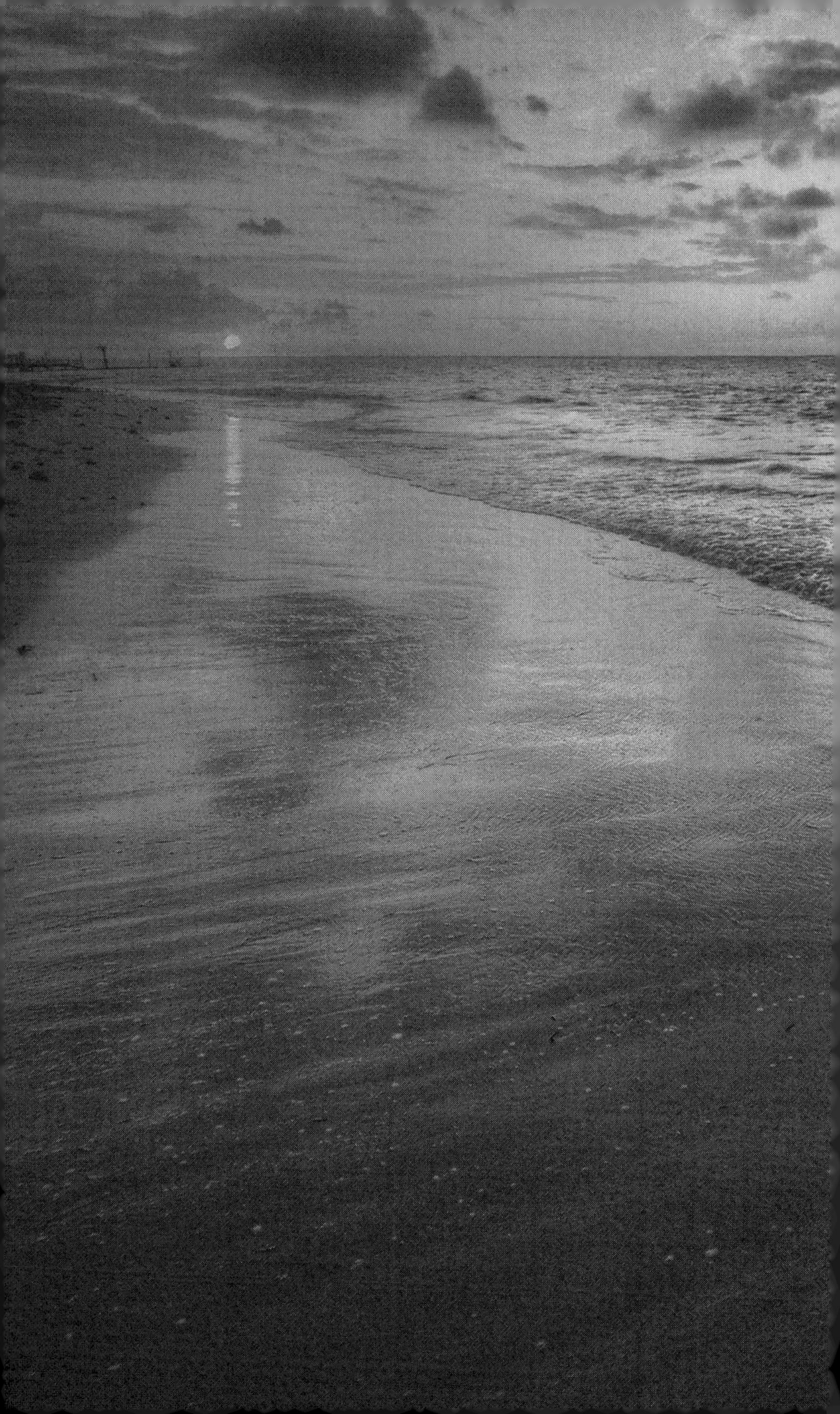

EPILOGUE

LOGAN

"BREATHE, JUST BREATHE," Ben says. His face is annoying the shit out of me, so I punch him in the jaw, and he sprawls backward on the floor.

Jack throws an arm around Sofie and grins at me. "He's taking it worse than I did."

Sofie shakes her head and elbows him in the ribs, causing him to grimace. "You nearly passed out when they told me it was time."

"No," Donnie pipes up from the other side of the room. "That was Rafe. Jack just turned really white and pretended he had to go to the bathroom."

Rafe ambles in with a cup of coffee in one hand. "Let's just say it ensured I'd practice safe sex for the rest of my college career."

Sofie scowls at her two younger brothers. "You're all useless," she says.

"Jesus Christ." Ben groans as he gets back to his feet. "Did you have to hit me so hard?"

"He should have hit you harder," Livvie says.

I slump on a chair and put my head between my knees. "I'm sorry, man. I'm just a little out of it."

Someone claps a hand on my shoulder. I can't be bothered to look up because I'm focusing my energy into not throwing up all over their feet.

"You'd think a cop and a Marine would be used to emergency situations," Jack says.

Sofie snorts. "We've already established you were no better."

"Yeah," Jack says, "but it's so much more fun when it's not happening to me."

The patterns on the floor are starting to give me a headache so I just shut my eyes. "I hate all of you."

"Poor guy," Livvie says. "I always said having kids was worse on the men than the women. And we're the ones who do all the hard work!"

"Why did they send you out of there, anyway?" Ben plops down on the chair next to me.

"Piper told me to go before I punched the doctor."

"So you punched me instead?"

"Seemed like a good idea at the time."

"Shouldn't be long now," Livvie says.

I groan into my hands, then stand, and hope the room doesn't decide to turn on its head. "I'd better get back."

"Don't worry," Sofie says from behind me. "You're going to do great!"

I don't have as much faith, but I shoulder through the door to the hospital room anyway. Much as I'd rather turn and high-tail in the other direction, I can't leave Piper. She's probably terrified.

Instead of finding her wild-eyed and screaming at the nurses, I find her laughing and chatting with them. I rush to her side and take one of her hands in mine. She looks up at me and smiles. "There you are."

"How are you doing? Is everything okay?" I look to the nurse who's standing at the end of the bed, but she just smiles at me.

"Well, things are going good—" she breaks off, and her face crumples. She takes my hand and draws in a deep breath through her nose.

The contraction lasts a hell of a long time, but I focus on brushing her hair back from her face and stroking her arm until it passes. When it does, she blinks up at me. "Hey," she says.

I kiss her brow. "Hey."

"So, I have some news."

"News."

"Yeah. Well remember how you didn't want to know the baby's sex?"

Frowning, I straighten. "Yes?" The word is drawn out. "Where are you going with this?"

"Well, since you wouldn't let me tell you, I couldn't tell you—"

I put my hand over her mouth. "Don't you dare. I don't care what we're having so long as he or she is healthy."

"But—"

I don't have time to cut her off because another contraction hits, and she grits her teeth.

"Shh, it'll be okay," I say. Then I find myself echoing Ben's advice. "Breathe, just breathe."

When it passes, she's panting. "They're coming closer together," she says.

"Almost there." The nurse stands and slips her glove off. "You're right at ten centimeters."

"I'm trying to tell you—"

"No," I say and kiss her. "It doesn't matter. I have everything I've ever wanted right here in this room. I want it to be a surprise."

"Oh, it's definitely going to be a surprise," the nurse murmurs, giving us a small smile as she slips from the room.

"You're so frustrating," Piper says.

"But you love me."

She leans up to kiss me. "I do."

"So let's have a baby," I say.

An eternity later, pandemonium erupts inside the little hospital room as Piper does the impossible and brings our child into this world. I used to be convinced nothing would ever be more beautiful than she was when she walked down the aisle the day we were married, but I was wrong. The most beautiful thing I've ever seen is the moment they place the squirmy, squalling, red-faced baby onto her stomach with her looking down, tears streaming down her face.

I put my hand on the baby's back and lean down to kiss Piper's forehead. She's a wreck, her hair is sticking in a million different directions, and she's sweated off all the makeup she'd applied before she went into labor. She's absolutely stunning. My angel.

There's a flurry of activity, and then the baby is whisked away to be wiped down, measured, weighed, and then wrapped up. I describe all of the actions in Piper's ear as I watch from my place by her side. Finally, they call me over, and I take a sleepy bundle in my arms.

"It's a boy," one of the nurses tells me.

I look down at the new life in my arms in awe. "A boy," I whisper, and then I look at Piper. "We have a son." Her face is brilliant with a huge smile, but then pain flashes in her eyes. "Baby?"

"Here we go," the nurse says as she rushes by me.

"Baby? Are you okay?" With the sleeping boy cradled in my arms, I crouch by her side.

"Yes," she says through panted breaths. "His brother is just impatient."

I stare at her, unable to comprehend simple English. Finally, my brain catches up with her words. "Brother?"

"I tried"—pause—"to tell you"—pause—"but you didn't"—pause—"want to know."

"Are you saying what I think you're saying?"

"If you think I'm saying you're about to be a father again, then you're right."

I'm struck dumb and only manage to hold onto her hands as she works a miracle for the second time in one night.

While they repeat the same procedure for the second baby, I turn to Piper. "Twins?"

She laughs softly and holds out her hands. "I tried to tell you a million times, but you wouldn't let me."

I can't find words.

"Here you are, Daddy," a nurse says and then places another baby in my arms. "Ten fingers and ten toes," she announces happily.

The baby in my arms is identical to his brother. It hits me

like a shockwave, and I look up to my wife, who's smiling softly at the baby in her arms. "Twins?"

"Twins."

"Two boys."

She laughs. "That's right."

"I should have known."

"Well, I was the size of a small country."

With our boys asleep in our arms, I lean over and kiss her. "You were beautiful."

She smiles and gazes at me with tired eyes. "Thank you," she says.

I trace the curve of my son's cheek. "For what?"

"For everything."

This causes me to look up and frown. "What do you mean?"

She cups my cheek with her free hand. "If you weren't so damn persistent, I'd never have this. I'd never have you. So thank you. When I lost my sister, it was as if I lost a part of myself. Finding you, it's almost as if I have it back. You made me whole again, Logan. So *thank you*."

I kiss the baby's forehead. "I'm pretty sure you've just given me the only thank you I'll ever need."

"I've been thinking about names."

"Oh yeah?"

"Preston and Lennox."

She doesn't have to explain. P for her sister and Lennox for the friend she lost. "They're perfect."

Later that night, after the doctors have cleaned up the room and the babies have been fed and are sleeping in their respective bassinets, I climb into the bed with her and hold her close to me.

"What a day," she says and yawns.

"Why don't you get some rest?" I suggest. "You have to be exhausted, and they'll be up soon."

"Just a little nap," she says and snuggles against my chest. "Stay right here?"

I wrap an arm around her waist and rest my chin on her hair. "I'm not going anywhere."

ACKNOWLEDGMENTS

Writing is no solitary endeavor. I've enlisted the help of several people over the years and there's one who deserves a second (and eternal) thanks for his tireless help and friendship. Pierre Rhodes, without your friendship and tireless patience, I'd be lost. You're always there with an open ear for my questions and never fail to respond with irreplaceable knowledge. You are in these pages, my friend, but it will never be thanks enough for all of your help.

Melissa Fisher, you are honestly indispensable. One of my first, and most enthusiastic cheerleaders, you've become a person I turn to when I'm excited about news I can't share with anyone else and you never fail to serve up devotion as keen as mine for these projects so close to my heart. Whenever I need you for an eye or an ear, you're there. Please know I am eternally grateful for your guidance and friendship.

To all of my readers, and most especially to my reader group, the Knockouts, there are never words suitable enough for the depth of my gratitude. It's almost as if you know when I need your encouragement the most because you're always there with a kind word or a morale boost just when I need it. Thank you for going on this journey with me. I couldn't do it without you!

ABOUT THE AUTHOR

Nicole Blanchard is the *New York Times* and *USA Today* bestselling author of gritty romantic suspense and heartwarming new adult romance. She and her family reside in the south along with menagerie of animals. Visit her website www.authornicoleblanchard.com for more information or to subscribe to her newsletter for updates on sales and new releases.

- facebook.com/authornicoleblanchard
- twitter.com/blanchardbooks
- instagram.com/authornicoleblanchard
- amazon.com/Nicole-Blanchard
- bookbub.com/authors/nicole-blanchard
- goodreads.com/nicole_blanchard
- pinterest.com/blanchardbooks
- tiktok.com/@authornicoleblanchard

ALSO BY NICOLE BLANCHARD

First to Fight Series

Anchor

Warrior

Valor

Box Set: Books 1-3

Survivor

Savior

Honor

Box Set: Books 4-6

Traitor

Operator

Aviator

Captor

Protector

Armor

A Salvation Society Crossover: Reckless

Friend Zone Series

Friend Zone

Frenemies

Friends with Benefits

Box Set

The Lost Planet Series

The Forgotten Commander

The Vanished Specialist

The Mad Lieutenant

Journey to the Lost Planet (Books 1-3)

The Uncertain Scientist

The Lonely Orphan

The Rogue Captain

Return to the Lost Planet (Books 4-6)

The Determined Hero

The Arrogant Genius

The Runaway Alien

Saving the Lost Planet (Books 7-9)

Dark Romance

Toxic

An Immortal Fairy Tale Series

Deal with the Dragon

Vow to the Vampire

Kiss from the King

Standalone Novellas

Bear with Me

Darkest Desires

Mechanical Hearts

Made in the USA
Columbia, SC
30 June 2024